3 1994 01557 7908
P9-DUS-903
ARY

saving Jake

SHARON SALA

sourcebooks
casablanca

SANTA ANA PUBLIC LIBRARY

Copyright © 2016 by Sharon Sala
Cover and internal design © 2016 by Sourcebooks, Inc.
Cover art by Tom Hallman

Sourcebooks and the colophon are registered trademarks of
Sourcebooks, Inc.

All rights reserved. No part of this book may be reproduced in any form
or by any electronic or mechanical means including information storage
and retrieval systems—except in the case of brief quotations embodied
in critical articles or reviews—without permission in writing from its
publisher, Sourcebooks, Inc.

The characters and events portrayed in this book are fictitious or are
used fictitiously. Any similarity to real persons, living or dead, is
purely coincidental and not intended by the author.

Published by Sourcebooks Casablanca, an imprint of Sourcebooks, Inc.
P.O. Box 4410, Naperville, Illinois 60567-4410
(630) 961-3900
Fax: (630) 961-2168
www.sourcebooks.com

Printed and bound in the United States of America.
LSC 10 9 8 7 6 5 4 3 2

Dear Reader:

I welcome you to Blessings, Georgia, the best small town in the South.

No, there aren't any secrets kept here, and yes, everybody knows your business, but when bad things happen, good people come to your rescue.

I grew up in a place like that—a place everyone should live in at least once in their lives, but since that's not possible, I'm offering the next best thing: stories about that way of life—touching stories, funny stories, stories that will break your heart on one page and heal it on the next.

"Count Your Blessings" was the novella introducing my readers to the Georgia landscape.

You and Only You was the first full-length novel set in Blessings. It's a story about the faithfulness of friends and family and what it means to be Southern to the core, as well as being a sweet love story to enjoy.

I'll Stand By You was the second full-length novel. It's a story about how people starting life off on the wrong foot can still find a way to live happy ever after.

Saving Jake is the next story, the one you're holding in your hands. It's a story that gets to the heart of what matters in life: redemption, forgiveness, and trust. It's a story of the times, and yet timeless in its simplicity.

Pick up one of my stories and take a visit to Blessings with me.

You just might like it enough to stay.

See you between the pages,
Sharon Sala

Chapter 1

THOMAS WOLFE ONCE WROTE, "YOU CAN NEVER GO HOME again." Jacob Lorde never took the word of a stranger. He was on the way home, marking the passing of every mile with a war-weary soul. He needed a place to heal and Blessings, Georgia, the place where he grew up, was calling him.

He'd come back briefly over a year ago to bury his father, and the calm and peace of the place had stayed with him long after he'd returned to his unit. Only a couple of months later, an IED on one patrol too many earned him a long stint in the hospital and brought his time with the army to an end.

Now he was coming home to try and bury the soldier he'd been.

He wanted to be done with war.

He needed peace.

He needed the emotional security that comes with knowing where he belonged.

He needed that like he needed air to breathe, so when the Greyhound bus in which he was riding came around the curve and he saw the city-limit sign of Blessings gleaming in the early morning sunlight, his eyes blurred with sudden tears. He took the sunglasses from the pocket of his uniform and slipped them on, then held his breath as the bus began to stop.

The brakes squeaked. They needed oil.

Jake stood slowly, easing the stiffness in a still-healing leg, walked down the aisle, and then out into a sweet Georgia morning. He took a deep breath, smelling pine trees on the mountains around him and the scent of smoke from someone's fireplace.

He was home.

The driver pulled his duffel bag from the luggage rack beneath the bus, shook his hand, and got back on board. The rest of the trip home was on Jake.

Ruby Dye had just opened The Curl Up and Dye when the Greyhound bus rolled through Blessings, belching black smoke from the exhaust. Because the bus came through Blessings on a regular basis, she never paid it any attention, but today it began slowing down. When it stopped, she moved closer to the window, waiting to see who got off, but the only person she saw was the driver who circled the bus to remove luggage from the carrier beneath.

A few moments later, the bus drove away in a small cloud of the same black smoke. It was then Ruby saw the man in uniform reaching down to get his duffel bag. From this distance she couldn't tell who it was, but he was limping slightly as he walked away.

"Welcome home, soldier," she said softly, and then went back to work.

Jake paused on the sidewalk and took a deep breath as the early morning air filled his lungs. Enveloped by the silence, he exhaled slowly as the weariness of the bus ride fell away. Shifting the duffel bag to rest easier on his shoulder, he headed south. Unless he caught a ride somewhere between here and home, he had a six-mile hike ahead of him, but after sitting for so long, he didn't care.

As he walked through town, it was somewhat comforting to see everything pretty much looked the same. Granny's Country Kitchen still appeared to be the main place to eat. He thought about stopping there for breakfast, but food wasn't as urgent a need as it was to see home.

He continued south down Main, noticing one thing had changed. The old barbershop was closed. There was a sign in the window that read: Haircuts Available at The Curl Up and Dye. He smiled, remembering Ruby Dye and the girls at her shop.

When he noticed a school bus heading out of town, he guessed the driver was beginning his route and thought of all the boys and girls hurrying around in their homes right now, getting ready for school, still innocent of what life could do to their dreams.

Traffic was picking up by the time he reached Ralph's, the small quick stop at the edge of town. He'd already had the utilities turned on at the house a month earlier, had cable set up so he'd have television service, and had the house cleaned at that time as well. But there wasn't any food, and picking up a few things here would be enough to tide him over while he settled in. The bell over the doorway jingled as he walked in, which made everyone in the store turn and look.

Jake knew the army uniform he was wearing and the military duffel bag marked him as a vet and wondered if there was anyone inside who might give him a ride.

Ralph Sinclair, who had always reminded Jake of Santa Claus because of his white hair and beard, was behind the counter. "Jake! I heard you might be coming home. It's good to see you!"

"Hi, Ralph. It's good to be here," Jake said.

He set his duffel bag against the counter, picked up a small shopping basket, and started moving down the aisles. He was reaching for a squeeze bottle of mustard when he heard someone call out his name. When he turned to look and saw Truman Slade standing at the end of the aisle, the first thought that went through his head was, *Well, hell.* Probably the only enemy he had in the entire state, and he was not only out of prison, but back in Blessings. A muscle jerked in his jaw as he forced himself not to react.

Truman Slade was two hundred and twenty-three pounds of pure mean, exacerbated by the years he'd spent in prison thanks to Jake Lorde's testimony against him. Truman didn't give a damn that all of that had happened when Jake was still in high school. All he knew was the kid's statement at his trial sent him to prison for eight years. The years and Truman's lifestyle had not been kind to him. Even when he was young, his short legs and big, round face, plus a distinct underbite, had given him a bulldog look. Now he had the big belly to go with it.

The moment he'd seen Jake Lorde walk in the door, his first thought had been *time for payback.* He walked up to where Jake was standing, pushed himself into Jake's personal space, and waited for him to react. He so wanted to whip his ass.

To Truman's dismay, Jake didn't acknowledge his presence. Instead, he calmly reached over Truman's head for a loaf of bread, which accentuated how short Truman really was, and how tall Jake had grown. As he did, his elbow grazed the tip of Truman's nose, which made Truman flinch. Jake was acting as if Truman were invisible. When he turned around and moved a few steps down and put a box of granola in the basket with the bread and mustard, Truman followed.

"Still afraid of your own shadow?" Truman whispered, then made a gun with his hand and pointed it at Jake.

Jake stared at Truman until he flushed a dark, angry red and shoved both hands in his pockets. Jake walked back to his duffel bag, pulled a big handgun from a side pocket, gave Truman another look, and then slapped it down on the counter in front of Ralph.

"Hey, Ralph, do you know where I could get ammo for this?"

Truman heard Ralph talking, but he couldn't focus on the words, thinking of that look Jake had given him. It was just beginning to dawn on Truman that war had changed Jake Lorde in a dangerous way. By the time he tuned back in on what was being said, Jake had shoved the handgun back into his bag and was at the deli, waiting to get some lunch meat and cheese sliced to take home.

Truman was leaning against the counter with a smirk on his face, and when Jake approached with his shopping basket to pay, Truman purposefully slid his shoe in front of Jake, intending to force him to step aside. Instead, Jake took the next step right on top of Truman's shoe and then stopped.

Truman inhaled sharply. The bastard was standing on his foot! He started to push Jake off, and then something told him not to lay a hand on the man. By his own actions, he was momentarily pinned to the floor.

Jake paid, picked up the groceries, shouldered his duffel bag, and left the store.

Truman groaned beneath his breath when the pressure on his foot was released and then hobbled out the door and drove toward town. He needed to put distance between him and Jake Lorde to recoup his swagger.

As for Jake, his head was pounding as he walked out of the store. The blood raced through his veins the same way it had done at the end of a deadly exchange of gunfire. Even though the morning air was cool, he could almost feel the desert heat. Despite his inability to focus, instinct kept him moving toward home.

—◆—

Laurel Payne was on her way into Blessings to an early morning cleaning job. She would have to drop her daughter, Bonnie, off at a friend's house in town until it was time for them to walk to school. There were always difficulties arising from being a single parent, and having good friends to help her out like this made her life a little easier.

She was less than a mile from town when she saw the soldier walking on the side of the road. Her heart skipped a beat. The sight of a man in uniform was still a painful reminder of her own husband, Adam, who'd come home from a war without a single wound and then shot and killed himself only a few months later.

As for the traveler, she knew who he was even before

she got close enough to see his face. She knew because she'd been the one who'd cleaned his father's house weeks earlier. He was not a stranger. He was a few years older, but she'd known him all her life.

When she passed him, the first thing she thought was that the neighborly thing to do would be to give him a ride home, but she didn't want to reawaken the sleeping demons in her life by befriending anyone who reminded her of Adam. Then she glanced in the rearview mirror, saw the slight limp in his stride, and her heart sank. Despite her reservations about getting involved, she hit the brakes.

"Mommy, what are we doing?" Bonnie asked, as Laurel made a U-turn in the road.

"I'm going to give Mr. Lorde a ride home," she said.

Bonnie frowned. "But Mr. Lorde went to heaven already. Did he come back?"

Laurel sighed. "No, honey. That man we just passed is his son."

"Oh," Bonnie said, but her curiosity was piqued.

Jake saw the old pickup coming toward him but paid it little mind because it was going the wrong way to do him any good. When it came closer, he noticed a young woman and a child inside, but didn't recognize them. He nodded politely as they passed and kept on walking.

When he was a little farther down the road, he heard the vehicle braking, then turning around, and his first instinct was to brace for another confrontation. When the pickup caught up with him and stopped, he didn't know what to expect.

Laurel rolled down the window and managed a brief smile.

"Jake Lorde?"

"Yeah?"

"I'm Laurel Payne, your neighbor down the road. Get in and I'll take you home."

Jake breathed an easy sigh of relief. "Thanks," he said, and put his things in the truck bed. He saw the little girl in the backseat as he opened the door and winked at her as he got in.

Bonnie was immediately charmed, partly because he reminded her of her father, whom she missed, and partly because he belonged to Mr. Lorde, whom she had adored.

Laurel waited until he settled before she accelerated.

"Welcome home," she said shyly, and kept her eyes on the road.

"Thank you," Jake said, trying to figure out who she was, and then it hit him. "You were Laurel Joyner, right?"

She nodded.

"You said it's Payne now. By any chance did you marry Adam Payne? I knew him in high school."

"Yes, I did," she said.

"My daddy is dead," Bonnie announced.

Laurel sighed. "That's my daughter, Bonnie. She's a first-grader this year."

"Hello, Bonnie. I'm sorry about your daddy, and I'm sorry for your loss," he told Laurel.

"Thank you," Laurel said, but when she wasn't forthcoming with any further information, Jake didn't push the issue.

A few minutes later they drove up on the mailbox at the end of his driveway. Laurel slowed down, and when she turned off the road and headed up the driveway, the ruts were so deep that they bounced in the seats all the way to the house.

"Sorry," she said.

"Looks like you just pointed out the first repair I need to put on my list," Jake said.

She pulled up to the fence surrounding the yard, put the truck in park, and started to get out.

"No, don't get out. I can get it all," Jake said. "I really appreciate the ride and hope I didn't make you late to wherever you were going."

"We're fine with the time," Laurel said. "Have a nice day, and again, welcome home."

"Thank you," Jake said.

Laurel waited while he gathered all of his things from the back of her truck and then headed for the front door. As soon as he was clear of her truck, she began backing up to turn around.

When Jake turned to watch her hasty exit, he saw her little girl on her knees in the backseat watching him. She waved.

He waved back and then they were gone and he had no other excuses to delay the inevitable. He reached above the door for the key, unlocked it, and went inside. He set his duffel bag against the wall and then headed to the kitchen with the groceries.

His footsteps echoed on the old hardwood floors, and despite the cleaning, the rooms smelled musty. He set the groceries on the counter and then opened the two windows in the kitchen to start airing the house. The house might get chilly, but he was choosing fresh air rather than airless, musty rooms.

Opening the cabinet doors as he put up food was like turning back time. His mother's dishes were still stacked in the same places they had been when he was growing up. A couple of coffee cups were missing, probably broken from years of use. When he opened a drawer to the left of the sink and found the notepads and pens they'd used to make lists and saw his father's writing on the top page of one pad, a moment of anger swept over him. His father's grocery list was still here, but he wasn't.

He picked up the one on top to begin a new list of things he was going to need, then took it with him as he walked through the rooms, making notes of what he needed to buy.

He knew for sure he needed toilet paper, bath powder, and toothpaste for the bathroom. Laundry soap, stain remover, and cleaning supplies for the utility room. Light bulbs for the house, and everything it took to restock a kitchen.

He was passing a window when he saw the school bus go by the house. He glanced at the clock and smiled. Fifteen minutes to eight—the same time he'd always caught the bus. He continued through the house, checking off things needing repairs. The showerhead was leaking and he'd noticed loose boards on the front porch when he'd stepped on it.

Several times he thought he heard footsteps in the house and would turn, expecting to see his father walk into the room with a big welcome-home grin on his face, and then remember. He made a note to get a Wi-Fi connection at the house and to set up his email.

It was moving toward noon when he finally closed all of the windows and turned on the central heat to warm up the house, then grabbed the keys to his dad's pickup from a small nail inside one of the upper cabinets and headed toward the barn. It's where he'd left the truck after the funeral.

A trio of pigeons roosting in the rafters flew off when he entered. The red Chevrolet truck was a little dusty but otherwise intact. Jake unlocked it with the remote and then looked inside. It was just as he'd left it. He backtracked to the last granary where he'd hidden the battery and put it back in the vehicle. He checked the oil, the transmission fluid, and the air pressure in the tires before he was satisfied, and then started it up and drove it to the house and parked beneath the carport.

He was back in the kitchen making a sandwich when he thought of Laurel Payne again and wondered where she'd been going so early, then wondered what she did for a living. It had to be tough being a single parent.

He sat down in the living room to eat and turned on the television to catch local news, only to realize he didn't recognize any of the journalists reporting. So some things had changed after all.

The food he'd made was tasteless, but his hunger had been satisfied, and that was all that mattered. He was thinking about going into town and setting up his banking, then checking in with the post office to let them know he was home and to resume delivery.

But then he fell asleep and went back to war.

The explosion from the IED sounded like the end of the world, and when Jake came to, he thought he was dead. The pain from his wounds had yet to register, and

*he was trying desperately to stand. He couldn't hear,
he couldn't see for the smoke and dust, and he couldn't
feel his legs. This was a blistering disappointment. He
thought heaven would be prettier than this.*

*Someone yelled at him. DeSosa! He was telling him
not to die, but the way he felt, he wasn't making any
promises. It wasn't until the ground began vibrating
beneath him and the air was spinning above his head
that he started yelling for help. That was a chopper, and
he didn't want to be left behind.*

Jake woke up in a sweat, his heart pounding and tears
in his eyes.

"Son of a… Ah, God," he muttered, and bolted off
the sofa as if he'd been launched, trying to get as far
away from the dream as possible.

He yanked the front door open and strode onto the
porch, taking in the fresh air in gulps. The sweat on his
forehead began to cool as the tears dried on his cheeks,
and he began to pace. The loose boards squeaked,
reminding him of a job still undone. Furious from the
dream and frustrated because the war still haunted his
life, he went straight to the toolshed for a hammer and
nails, then back to the house.

Every time the hammer made contact with a nail, it
took everything he had not to duck, because it sounded
like gunshots. He was so focused on getting rid of the
nightmare that he didn't see Laurel Payne driving home,
but she saw him.

Laurel was already exhausted and she still had four
loads of laundry to do and supper to cook for her and

Bonnie. She'd actually forgotten about seeing Jacob Lorde this morning until she drove past the house and saw him on his hands and knees on the porch. She saw the hammer in his hand and remembered the loose boards when she'd been there last month to clean the house. It was obvious he wasn't wasting any time putting it to rights.

But when she consciously noticed how broad his shoulders were, she looked away. She didn't care what he looked like. He didn't matter in her world and never would. She had a daughter to raise, and she wanted nothing to do with another war vet.

Her head was hurting by the time she got home, and climbing those steep steps into their double-wide trailer seemed like insult adding to her injury. Once inside, she breathed a sigh of relief at being in her own home, not someone else's, and headed for her bedroom.

The first thing she did was take down her hair. It was thick and a slightly curly auburn that hung well below her shoulders, and sometimes having it up all day gave her a headache. As soon as it was down, the release of tension in her body was palpable. She quickly changed her clothes and got to work.

By the time the school bus stopped to let Bonnie off, Laurel was taking the last batch of cookies from the oven. She had the third load of clothes in the washing machine, a load in the dryer, and vegetable soup simmered on the back burner.

The sound of Bonnie's footsteps coming up the steps of their trailer was Laurel's signal for an emotional shift. Whatever was bothering her did not belong on her little girl's radar. She turned toward the door with a smile. Seconds later, Bonnie came inside in a rush, talking nonstop.

"Mama, I got a happy face on my new words, and Lewis threw up on my shoe at lunch. Mrs. Hamilton washed it off but it still smells funny. I think it got on my sock, too. Milly was mean to me at recess but I told her she was acting like a baby. Then she cried, which proved I was right. Can I have a cookie? How long till supper?"

Laurel grinned. "Come here and give me a kiss. I missed you today."

Bonnie threw her arms around her mother's neck and kissed Laurel's cheek as she reached for a cookie.

Laurel grinned when she saw the second cookie in Laurel's other hand and stopped her long enough to get the stinky tennis shoes and socks off Laurel's feet.

"Change out of your school clothes before you go feed Lavonne, and put on socks with your old shoes. It's chilly out today."

"I will," Bonnie said. "Can Lavonne have a cookie, too?"

"No. Chickens don't need to eat sugar. Just her regular feed, okay?"

"Okay, Mama," Bonnie said, and ran barefoot to her room, her little feet making *splat, splat* sounds as she went.

In minutes she was out the back door and running toward the little chicken coop. Her daddy had built it for Lavonne, and she thought of him every time she went to feed her pet, but it was getting harder to remember what he looked like. That scared her a little, but she was afraid to talk to Mama about it. She heard Mama crying sometimes at night. It was hard being Mama's big girl when she still felt little and scared.

When she unlocked the gate to the fence around the coop and Lavonne came running, it made the sad thoughts go away. Lavonne was her buddy and had the prettiest black feathers ever. Mama said she was from a family of chickens called Australorps, but Bonnie disagreed. Lavonne was from the family of Paynes.

The chicken's constant clucks sounded a lot like Bonnie's chatter as Bonnie scooped up feed and put it in the feeder inside the coop. When she left the chicken yard to get fresh water, Lavonne was right beside her, clucking and occasionally pausing to peck the ground.

"What was that?" Bonnie asked. "Did you get a bug? Good job!" Then she suddenly squatted and pointed her finger in the grass. "Oooh, look, Lavonne, there's another one!"

Lavonne was on it in seconds, then wandered off a few feet while Bonnie carried fresh water back to the coop and filled the watering station. As soon as she was through with all that, she pulled a fresh hunk off the bale of straw and loosened it. She was getting ready to put it in Lavonne's nest when she saw the egg.

She squealed and dropped the straw then came out of the chicken coop on the run, screaming, "Mommy, Mommy."

When Laurel heard Bonnie's scream her heart stopped. She dropped the armload of wet clothes back into the washer and went out the back door on the run.

"What's wrong?" she cried, as Bonnie ran into her arms.

Bonnie held out the egg in two hands as if it were pure gold.

"Look, Mama, look! Lavonne laid an egg. Does that mean she's all grown up now?"

Laurel was so weak with relief it took a moment to answer.

"Well, my goodness, I guess it does. Way to go, Lavonne," Laurel said.

Bonnie giggled.

"We're both growing up, aren't we, Mama? Here, you take the egg. I'm going to play with Lavonne some more."

Laurel sighed as she watched Bonnie running back to the coop. Yes. Her little girl was growing up. She turned around to go back to the house, carrying the proof of Lavonne's launch into hen-hood, and the farther she went, the angrier she became at Adam. By the time she reached the back steps, she was crying.

"Oh, Adam, just look at what you're missing. Why did you have to go and blow your damn head off? We need you. Life wasn't supposed to be like this."

Chapter 2

TRUMAN SLADE DROVE UP TO HIS HOUSE, A PLACE HE'D
been renting for almost a year that was a couple miles
outside of Blessings. He wished he'd had the foresight
to pick up some barbecue before he'd left town. It
was almost sundown, and with no lights burning from
inside the house, it appeared uninhabited, which suited
Truman just fine. He liked flying under the radar.

The night air was cold, making him hurry as he
moved toward the house and unlocked the door. He
locked it behind him and then went through the house
turning on lights, then ignited the fire in the fireplace.
It didn't burn real wood, but the fake logs behind the
propane flames made it look real pretty. The stove
popped as the flame caught, and then he turned on the
TV for company before heading to the kitchen.

A quick search through the cabinets and then the
refrigerator confirmed what he already knew. There
were no leftovers of any kind anywhere. Forced to
make do with what was there, he ate peanut butter and
crackers for supper, washing them down with reheated
coffee, and blamed his forgetfulness on Jacob Lorde's
return to Blessings.

Truman had been back in town for some time now
and deceived himself into believing people had forgotten his past transgressions, but that would no longer be
possible now that the man who'd sent him to prison

would be a physical reminder.

This place wasn't big enough for both of them, but he wasn't sure how he could bring that to a successful resolution without winding up back in jail.

Ruby Dye was carrying trash to the alley behind The Curl Up and Dye while the twins, Vesta and Vera Conklin, were sweeping the floor and folding towels, getting everything ready for the next day.

Mabel Jean, the manicurist, was about to lock the front door when LilyAnn Dalton from Phillips' Pharmacy came hurrying inside with a big smile on her face.

"Oh, you're locking up," she said. "I won't keep you, but I just heard news Ruby will want to know."

"What news?" Ruby asked as she came in from outside.

"Jacob Lorde is home!" LilyAnn said.

Ruby smiled. "So that's who I saw getting off the bus this morning. Is he staying for good?" she asked.

"That's what I heard," LilyAnn said. "Remember he was here for his daddy's funeral, and then he went back to his unit? So, they said he suffered some pretty severe injuries not long after that. Anyway, he's out of the army on an honorable discharge."

Ruby frowned. "He's out there all by himself. We need to get some of the ladies at church to make some food. We can take it to him tomorrow evening. Like a welcome-home visit."

LilyAnn grinned.

"I'm in for macaroni and cheese casserole," she said. "I'll bring it by the shop tomorrow before you close, and I'll volunteer my Ford Explorer to make deliveries if others will go with me."

"That's wonderful," Ruby said. "I'll go, and I'll get at least one more to go with us."

LilyAnn waved good-bye and left as abruptly as she'd appeared.

"Well, now," Vesta said. "I remember him as a really nice-looking young man."

Vera frowned.

"Isn't he the one who testified against Truman Slade while he was still in high school?"

Ruby nodded.

"I'd forgotten about that, but now that you mention it, he sure did."

Vera's frown deepened.

"That no-account Slade lives outside of town. I wonder if he'll try to bother Jake?"

Ruby shrugged.

"Truman Slade went to prison. Jake Lorde went to war. My money is on Jake no matter what occurs. Now, as far as I'm concerned, this day is over. Let's go home."

"I vote for that," Mabel Jean said.

A few minutes later they were gone.

———

Laurel put the last glass in the dishwasher and started the cycle, then went to get the final load of laundry from the dryer. Since it was all towels and washcloths, she carried them to her bedroom to fold later. She could hear Bonnie playing in her room as she passed the door and smiled. It sounded as if she was playing school and using her stuffed toys for students. Bonnie was always the teacher, and Panda Bear was her worst student. He suffered a lot of time-outs.

Laurel tossed the towels on the bed, then went to get Bonnie ready for bed. As she walked in, Bonnie was putting Panda Bear in time-out again.

Laurel grinned.

"It's bedtime, honey," she said lightly.

Bonnie frowned. "Oh, Mommy, not yet. Panda was naughty."

"Well, you go brush your teeth and put on your nightgown. By the time you're finished, his time-out will be over, okay?"

"Okay," Bonnie said, and then shook her finger at the bear as she walked out of the room, as if to say *you better behave*.

Laurel could imagine Bonnie's teacher doing the same thing at school. Teaching was one job she could never do. She wouldn't last a day with a room full of six-year-olds.

Bonnie had squirted a little toothpaste on the end of her finger and was writing on the mirror when Laurel walked in.

"Bonnie Carol! Why on earth are you doing that?"

Bonnie looked startled.

"But, Mommy, when Daddy used to shave it made the mirror get all foggy, and he would write *Hello* to me on the glass. I just wanted to write *Hello* back to Daddy…in case he came to see me while I was asleep."

There was a knot in Laurel's throat, but she made herself smile.

"You are right! I forgot he used to do that. So, finish writing your word and then wash your hands. It's time to get in bed."

"Okay," Bonnie said, and added the last L and O, then washed and dried her hands.

Laurel waited in the doorway, then followed Bonnie across the hall to her room. Bonnie skipped over to where she'd left Panda and tossed him on her pillow.

"I'm gonna sleep with Panda tonight so he won't feel bad for getting in trouble today."

"Good idea," Laurel said, still struggling not to burst into tears. She sat on the side of Bonnie's bed to hear her prayers.

"Okay God, here's the deal," Bonnie said.

Laurel rolled her eyes. Now she didn't know whether to laugh or cry as her daughter continued. "I wrote Daddy a note on the mirror. Tell him it's here so he can some see it. Also, bless Mommy, who works very hard. Bless Daddy, who is in heaven. Bless Lavonne for laying her first egg. And bless Mr. Lorde's son. I think he is lonesome. Amen."

Laurel was so stunned to hear Jake Lorde added to the prayer list that she didn't know what to say, so she said nothing. Instead, she pulled the covers over Bonnie's shoulders, tucked in the naughty Panda, and kissed her good night.

"I love you very much," Laurel whispered.

"I love you, too, Mommy. Don't forget to leave—"

"I know, I know," Laurel said. "I'm leaving the night-light on."

Bonnie sighed. "Thank you, Mommy. You and Lavonne are just about the best friends I have."

Laurel patted her daughter's shoulder.

"Thank you for putting me in such fine company,"

Laurel said, and then reached over and turned on the angel night-light plugged in near the headboard and tip-toed out of the room.

She went into her bedroom with tears rolling down her cheeks, folded the towels on her bed, and put them away, then took a quick shower and put on her pajamas. She paused in the hall outside Bonnie's door, making sure she was asleep, and then walked through the house, making sure both doors were locked.

She didn't have to be at work tomorrow until 10:00 a.m. That meant she could make a decent breakfast for Bonnie before she caught the bus. She closed her eyes, whispered a quick "thank you" prayer for getting through another day, and then thought of what Bonnie said about Jake Lorde being lonely, and impulsively added a quick prayer for him to be well in mind and body. The moment she said it, she felt guilty. It was the same prayer she'd prayed for Adam, and it hadn't worked.

A little uneasy that she'd somehow marked Jake Lorde's future as iffy, she turned over, pulled the covers over her shoulders, and cried herself to sleep.

Jake's rest was never sound, and sleeping in a new place exacerbated the process. He had been gone so long that the sounds of the old farmhouse were unfamiliar again.

The pop at the window behind him was nothing but a limb from the azalea bush blowing in the wind. The creak on the floorboard in the hall was just the house settling, and the drip he kept hearing was the shower-head in the bathroom. He knew the sounds when he was awake, but when they filtered through his sleep into the nightmare he was having, they sounded like an enemy ambush.

He could see them moving through the shadows, heard the clink of metal against metal, and knew he needed to run, but his feet wouldn't move. He tried to shout a warning to the others, but he couldn't make a sound. He could hear someone crying and was afraid to turn around and look, for fear he'd see yet another one of his buddies dying. And then the world exploded.

He woke up to realize he was the one in tears and rolled out of bed, anxious to leave the nightmare behind. He glanced at the clock. It was a little after 6:00 a.m. He hadn't intended to get up so early, but no way in hell was he going back to bed after that dream, so he got dressed and went to the kitchen to make coffee. While it was brewing, he got one of his dad's work coats out of the closet. When the coffee was done, he put on the coat and took a cup of coffee to the back porch swing. He eased down onto the swing and then took a quick sip. It was still too hot to drink, so he pushed off in the swing, while he gazed across the back of the property, waiting for sunrise.

He thought about Laurel Payne and wondered if they were up yet, and if Bonnie was getting ready to catch the bus. If he closed his eyes, he could almost imagine his mother in the kitchen behind him, making biscuits and frying bacon, while making his dad's lunch for the day. He would have been getting dressed and smelling all those wonderful scents drifting down the hall toward his bedroom, secure in the knowledge that all was right with his world.

He wished his parents were still living. He could

use a little pep talk along the theme of "this too shall pass." God, he hoped even a little bit of that could be true. He couldn't imagine living out the rest of his life in this violent state of mind.

And so he sat on the swing until his cup was empty and sunrise was just a breath away. At that point, he stood, walked off the porch and into the middle of the yard.

The sky was already lighter in the east. The moon was still in the same place in the sky, but swiftly fading from sight. While he was waiting for sunrise, a flock of geese took off from the pond, resuming their winter flight south. He watched until they had flown out of sight, thinking how quickly they'd left their past behind. If only it were that easy for him.

He turned toward the east just as Mother Nature swept the horizon with a light brushstroke of gold, followed by a faint overlay of pink. Just after the pink turned to purple and the gold turned orange, a tiny portion of the sun was suddenly visible.

Once again, tears blurred Jake's vision. There were too many days from his past when he had believed he would never see a sunrise from this location again.

"Thank you, God," he said softly, and lifted his head, standing witness to the new day in much the same manner as he'd stood at attention during morning inspection.

When the sun was finally a valid orb too bright for further viewing, Jake went back in the house. He hung the old coat on a hook by the door and refilled his coffee cup before pouring himself a bowl of cereal.

Breakfast was served.

Ruby Dye was at The Curl Up and Dye early, verifying the number of ladies who were making food for Jake Lorde. She needed to make sure they knew to bring it to the shop by four this afternoon.

Rachel Goodhope, who ran the Blessings Bed-and-Breakfast, offered food and a helping hand to Ruby to carry it in, so they were all set. Ruby checked to see if there was a phone number for the Lorde property, but couldn't find one. They would have to hope Jake Lorde was at home when they arrived.

With the extra time to make breakfast this morning, Laurel made pancakes for Bonnie. The treat was unexpected and so exciting that Bonnie almost made herself late because she talked so much through the meal. She was on her way to the bus stop when the big yellow bus came around the bend.

"Don't run!" Laurel shouted as Bonnie started to sprint. "He'll wait on you."

Bonnie slowed down, and sure enough the driver stopped, honked the horn at Laurel, and waved. Laurel waved back and then waited until she saw Bonnie take a seat inside the bus before she relaxed. She'd just put her daughter into the hands of the Blessings school system and wanted her back in the same shape in which she'd sent her. Maybe a little dirtier, and hopefully a bit smarter, but safe. She took her time cleaning the kitchen and then changed her clothes and headed to work.

Today she only had two houses to clean. One

belonged to P. Nutt Butterman, Esquire, and the other was at the Blessings Bed-and-Breakfast. She cleaned rooms while Rachel Goodhope, who owned the B and B, did laundry and all the baking. She only worked at the B and B when Rachel called because they didn't always have overnight guests.

She made herself a sandwich and packed it in her lunch bag with a banana and a cookie and, at nine thirty in the morning, headed out the door.

The radio was on in the truck, and she was humming along with the song when she drove past the Lorde place and saw Jake at the barn. He was working on broken rails in the corral, and once again, she was impressed that he was being productive.

She started to honk and wave and then didn't. No need encouraging him in any way. She was not on the market. But to her disgust, he was still on her mind when she drove past the city-limit sign and into Blessings.

Jake heard the vehicle coming before he saw it and immediately recognized Laurel's old pickup. He kept working as he watched her pass. As soon as he nailed the last loose board on the corral, he put up his tools and headed for the house. He had business in town and wanted it over with.

Truman Slade didn't punch a time card or bother himself with a regular job. He got a disability check from the welfare department for an injury to his back from when he was in prison. Truman considered not having to work was fair compensation for having been beaten within an inch of his life. He had a couple of pins in his spine as a result.

The way he looked at it, if he hadn't been convicted, he wouldn't have been hurt. He blamed the state for his troubles and considered it his due. It was how his daddy had lived, and his mama had never complained.

He and his brother, Hoover, had been named after presidents. It had been his mother's hope that they would therefore aspire to higher goals than the ones their father had never set, but it hadn't worked. Both Truman and Hoover had spent most of their adult lives in and out of prisons. Truman was out. Hoover was still in. Truman thought about doing better, but not hard enough to change his life to make it happen.

~~~

Laurel liked Mr. Butterman's house. She liked cleaning it. She had known him all her life and when she was little thought his name was funny. She used to wonder who would name their child P. Nutt, but his parents had. Now it said something about how he walked through life to have taken a crazy name and turned it into an asset. She also loved the big shade trees at both ends of the house. They reminded her of sentinels guarding the property.

Today Mr. Butterman had left a note asking her to clean out the refrigerator before she left and apologized ahead of time for anything growing its own beard. Laurel giggled when she read the note. She'd seen his leftovers before.

She got to work on the house first, changing sheets

on his bed, cleaning the bathrooms, dusting, and then running the vacuum over the carpets before running a dust mop on the hardwood flooring. She left the kitchen for last.

She began by cleaning the stove and countertops, then opened the refrigerator and began removing all of the covered bowls and carryout containers. Once it was empty, she quickly scrubbed down the shelves and drawers, then closed the door and threw away cartons, emptying the little dabs of leftovers Peanut seemed obligated to keep but never ate.

By the time she was through, it was almost 1:00 p.m. She had to be at Rachel's Bed-and-Breakfast by one thirty. She pocketed the check Butterman had left for her and ate her lunch as she drove to Rachel's. By the time she arrived, she was ready to start all over again.

————

Jake had a grocery list in his pocket and a cashier's check to open an account at the bank as he drove into Blessings. The familiar sights were reassuring. Seeing a farmer's cab-over John Deere tractor rolling down Main was commonplace, but it still made Jake smile, especially when he saw the Great Dane sitting beside the driver, calmly looking out the windows as they passed. Jake laughed. It was obvious it wasn't the big dog's first tractor ride.

He was still smiling when he parked in front of the bank and went inside. He saw the president, Carl Buckley, sitting in his office with a customer. Two of the tellers were with customers, but the lady at the customer service desk recognized Jake and stood up.

"Jake Lorde! It is so good to see you," she said.

Jake smiled. Hattie Morris had been one of his mother's good friends.

"Hello, Mrs. Morris."

"How can I help you?" she asked.

He took the cashier's check from his wallet and handed it to her.

"I want to open a checking account."

"Certainly! Just have a seat here at my desk." Jake sat, stretching his long legs out in front of him and eyeing the autumn decorations as he waited for her to be seated. "So are you home for good?" she asked.

"Yes, ma'am, and glad to be here."

"That's wonderful. I drive by your home every time I go see my grandchildren, and it will be good someone is in residence there again. We all miss your father. He was a good man."

"Yes, ma'am. I miss him, too," Jake said, and then sat quietly as she went to work setting up the new account, ordering checks, explaining their debit card system and the app for online banking features.

Jake left the bank, heading to the post office to reestablish rural mail delivery at the farm, and once again he was on the receiving end of a big welcome home. By the time he headed to the grocery store, he was feeling good about his decision to return to Blessings.

He pulled up in the parking lot and, as he was getting out, saw Lon Pittman leaving in his police cruiser. When he saw the young man sitting in the backseat with an unhappy expression on his face, he guessed someone might be getting a life lesson on the perils of shoplifting, then flashed on witnessing Truman Slade beat up the cashier at a gas station before he robbed it. He frowned, still disgusted this memory had the ability to bother him, and headed for the store.

He paused just inside the Piggly Wiggly to get a basket, pulled out his list, and started down an aisle. It had been a long time since he'd had a chance to enjoy something as mundane as buying groceries, and he went at it with gusto, even adding candy and snacks that weren't on the list. He was shopping through the canned goods aisles when he heard someone say his name. He looked up and saw Lovey Cooper, the owner of Granny's Country Kitchen, coming toward him.

"Jake Lorde! Is that you?" Lovey said.

He smiled. "Yes, ma'am. It's me."

She eyed the groceries and then him. "Looks like you're setting up housekeeping. Are you home for good?"

"Yes, ma'am, and happy to be here."

She beamed. "Well, that's wonderful news. Next time you come into my place, your first meal is on me. I'll make sure all my servers know ahead of time."

"That's really kind of you," Jake said.

"Just thanking you for your service," Lovey said. "Say, are you going to be home this evening?"

"Yes, ma'am. Why?"

"I happen to know there are some ladies making you some welcome-home food. They were worrying about how to notify you they were coming."

"Oh, they don't have to do that," he said.

Lovey rolled her eyes. "Now you know better than to turn down some good, home-cooked food, right?"

He laughed. "Yes, ma'am. I guess I do."

"Then that's that. I'll let them know you'll be home,

and you don't bother cooking any of that food you're buying for a while. Save it all for another day."

"I will do that," he said.

Even after she walked away, the news that he was going to be on the receiving end of more heartfelt wishes and home cooking made him smile.

He was standing at the checkout lane later when he remembered the ruts in his driveway. He'd meant to put the blade on his dad's tractor and grade the road smooth, but he didn't even know if the tractor would start.

After he paid, he hurried to the parking lot to load his purchases and then headed out of town. If the tractor would fire up, he'd smooth the road before company arrived.

Chapter 3

RUBY DYE, RACHEL GOODHOPE, AND LILYANN DALTON
were in high spirits as they drove out of Blessings.
When Ruby got Lovey's phone call and found out Jake
had been notified they were coming, she was relieved.
It would have been a mess trying to deliver all this food
if he'd been gone.

LilyAnn was driving and talking about how excited
her husband, Mike, was about the upcoming arrival of
their baby, chattering on about the colors they'd chosen
for the nursery and what all she'd received at the baby
shower they'd given for her at church.

Rachel was talking about how their business was
growing and the early bookings they already had for the
bed-and-breakfast. She was excited for the fact that there
were only a few nights still open between Thanksgiving
and Christmas. She was bragging about what a smart
move she'd made by hiring Laurel Payne to come twice
a week and do the heavy cleaning in the rooms, so that
Rachel had more time to devote to holiday decorations
and baking for the constant turnover of guests.

Ruby wasn't paying much attention. She'd chosen to
sit in the back and hold the three-layer coconut cake
Rachel made, thinking about Jake Lorde and what it
must have been like for him to come back to that empty
house. Then her attention shifted as LilyAnn turned off
the blacktop to the road leading to the house.

"Oh, look! The driveway looks like it's just been graded," she said.

"Hold on to that cake just in case," Rachel cried.

She glanced back at Ruby and then gave a sigh of relief. She was competently steadying the cake with both hands. When the car finally stopped, they breathed a bit easier.

LilyAnn got out, then opened the back door and took the cake from Ruby so she could exit the vehicle. Rachel went around to the back and opened the hatch to the array of covered dishes. Ruby was on her way to the house with the cake when Jake came out the front door, smiling.

Ruby started talking, even as she was waving a hello.

"Good evening, Jake!" Ruby said. "I'm glad Lovey ran into you to give you a heads up. We brought food—the best kind of welcome-home gifts."

"This is so kind of you," Jake said. "What can I do to help?"

"Come carry this ham," Rachel yelled.

He ran to her aid and the four of them entered his house, loaded down with all they could carry. By the time they finished, there were at least a dozen different dishes on his kitchen counter—from salads to desserts and everything in between.

"This is amazing!" Jake said, as he peeked beneath the lids and foil-covered dishes. "And it all smells wonderful. I can't thank you enough."

Ruby handed him a list.

"These are the names and addresses of the women who donated, and I made a note of what they sent, so you can thank them personally."

"Thanks," Jake said. "I'll get some thank-you cards in the mail soon. I promise."

Rachel was used to being the center of attention around good-looking men. She had an eye for them too, but a recent brush with infidelity had taught her that looking was one thing, but never to take that next step again. And Jake Lorde was obviously not in the market, because the only vibe she was getting from him was related to good manners.

LilyAnn was hovering, pointing out things that would need to be reheated and how to do it, things that would freeze better than others, because her mothering instincts were on constant overload. She was completely comfortable with Jake because they'd grown up together, so they had a history in common. When Jake congratulated her and Mike on the baby on the way, she beamed.

"We own the gym on Main Street. It's the only workout place in town," LilyAnn said. "Mike told me to tell you, if you're interested, that your first visit is on him… if you ever feel the need to go sweat in public, that is."

Jake grinned. This evening was far different from his arrival yesterday. He knew without asking that Ruby was the one who'd organized this. He remembered that about her from his father's funeral. He hadn't even known Blessings had a bed-and-breakfast until Ruby introduced Rachel Goodhope, but she was nice. She'd made sure to let him know that the dining room at the B and B would be open to the public on Thanksgiving, which was good to know for the people like him who had nowhere else to go.

"We're going to leave now," Ruby said. "Enjoy your supper, and if you need anything, all you have to do is ask."

Jake followed them to the door, giving each a quick hug and a thank-you for what they'd done, and then he stood on the porch and waved as they drove away.

As he was standing there, the school bus went by on its way into town. Jake thought of Laurel's little girl, Bonnie, riding that bus and guessed Laurel would be scurrying around now, tending to her family. He glanced in that direction and then chided himself that they were too far away to see, went back inside, and closed the door.

After the chatter of three women, the silence of his house surrounded him like a warm blanket on a cold night. It was the peace he'd sought. The healing he needed. He turned on the lights and then went to the kitchen and began filling a plate with whatever took his fancy. He poured a cup of coffee and started to sit down in the kitchen to eat, then changed his mind and carried it to the living room. He wanted a little conversation with his meal, but he didn't want to have to participate, so he turned on TV and kicked back to watch as he ate.

The mood inside Laurel's trailer was far from peaceful and a long way from quiet, but it was home. Bonnie was changing out of her school clothes and hurrying out to feed Lavonne before it got dark, and Laurel had white beans and a ham hock heating while she tried to scrub a ketchup stain off of one of Bonnie's white socks. It was business as usual at her house.

She was in the middle of scrubbing at the stain when she flashed on the scene of finding Adam's body and how hard she'd scrubbed before she'd gotten the blood off the carpet in her bedroom. The memory was jarring and, as she looked down at the sock and noticed the stain was gone, she wished she could wipe away the one from her memory as well.

Then Bonnie came running into the house from doing her chores, bringing life and a cold gust of air with her, and Laurel turned loose of the sadness. "Mama, it's not school tomorrow, right?"

"That's right. Tomorrow is Saturday, why?" Laurel asked.

"I told Lavonne that I'd make her a new nest. I just wanted to make sure."

Laurel smiled. "So Lavonne is getting a new nest?"

"Well, just new straw and grass and stuff like that. She likes the box nest on the wall. She said it keeps the cold air off her feet when she sleeps."

Laurel was used to listening to Bonnie's chatter, but the mention of cold air reminded her that she did need to winterize the little coop, so she and Bonnie would both be hanging out with Lavonne tomorrow.

———

Jake spent a good portion of the evening dividing the food into smaller portions, saving some of it to eat for the next few days and putting the rest in the old chest freezer in the utility room. Tomorrow was Saturday, but he didn't have a schedule. It was quite the luxury not to have to report for duty on base or clock in at some business. Having this much freedom was the trade-off for experiencing it alone. He couldn't help but wish his dad were still here. There were so many things they could have done together—so many things Jake could have done for him. But such was life, and Jake figured he'd lived through being blown up for a reason, so he would figure it out on his own.

He went to bed with a hopeful attitude and a full belly, and then he fell asleep and dreamed, and in the dream he bled and died.

He woke up bathed in sweat and shaking, then glanced at the clock and groaned. Only 4:00 a.m. It was too early to stay up, but if he went back to bed, he'd never fall asleep. And he didn't want to take any sleeping pills. They kept him locked into the nightmares longer. He thought of the three-layer coconut cake, put on a pair of sweatpants, and went barefoot to the kitchen. Turning on the kitchen light chased away the lingering memories of the nightmare. Cutting a big piece of the cake and pouring a glass of milk to go with it was powerful medicine.

He sat in silence, savoring each bite and remembering the nights he'd done this with his mother. She'd had insomnia, and he'd had a hollow leg, as his daddy used to say. As a kid, Jake couldn't remember ever being completely full, and a nighttime raid for a snack had been commonplace. He'd had the best conversations about his life at this table with her.

He took a bite of cake and lifted it in a toast.

"To you, my sweet mama. Thank you for the lessons."

After that, he went back to bed and slept without dreaming until sunlight coming through the cracks in the blinds woke him up.

He spent the morning setting up his email and Wi-Fi and then caught up on waiting messages. Most of them were from buddies. Some were still in uniform while others, like him, were no longer in service.

—⁓—

Laurel had winterized the chicken coop by pushing some hay bales around the outside for windbreaks while Bonnie put fresh hay in Lavonne's nest. The fact that they'd gathered another egg had been a huge source of excitement, and Bonnie had carried it into the house and put it in the refrigerator while Laurel finished up outside.

She was on her way inside when she met Bonnie coming out. "Where are you going?" Laurel asked.

"Just outside to play," Bonnie said.

"Okay, but stay close to the house."

If Laurel had paid more attention, she would have noticed Bonnie didn't answer as she ran past her mother. She wanted to go visit Mr. Lorde's son like she used to visit Mr. Lorde.

—⁓—

The day was cool, but the sky was clear. Jake had tired of being inside and got on his dad's tractor and dragged up a couple of fallen trees from the woods. He was sawing up the logs into two-foot lengths before splitting them into firewood when he saw a shadow on the ground behind him. He turned around, a little surprised by the visitor, and quickly let off the throttle and killed the chain saw.

Bonnie Payne was sitting on an upended bucket. "Hi!" she said when the engine stopped running.

He grinned. "Hi. Does your mother know where you are?"

"My mama lets me play in the creek."

"You are a ways from the creek," Jake said.

"I know, but I came to see your daddy all the time."

That surprised Jake a little. His dad had become a little cranky in his old age, but he must have had a soft spot for his youngest neighbor. "What did you and my dad do when you came to visit?"

She shrugged. "Mostly, I just watched him work. I used to watch Daddy work, but that was before he made himself die."

Shock rolled through Jake so fast it made the hair rise on the back of his neck. "Your dad killed himself?"

She nodded. "Mama had to clean up the bedroom afterward. Mama cleans houses for people in Blessings so she knows how to do it."

Jake was speechless. Laurel must have been the one to find him. Now he understood what the cold vibe he felt from her was all about.

"I'm sorry," Jake said.

Bonnie sighed. "Me too."

Jake glanced at the time. He didn't want her in trouble, and he didn't want to be in trouble with Laurel, either. "I think you need to get back before your mother starts to worry, don't you?"

Bonnie shrugged and then launched herself off the stump. "Mr. Lorde used to give me a treat before I left."

"What did he give you?" Jake asked.

She pointed toward the orchard. "Sometimes an apple from those trees."

"It's too late for apples now. They're all gone. How about a stick of gum?" he asked, as he pulled a pack from his pocket.

She held out her hand. "Yes, please."

He let her pull a stick from the pack and then waited while she peeled off the paper and popped it in her mouth. She handed him the wrapper and waved as she ran toward the creek.

He watched until she was completely out of sight and then wondered if he should call and let Laurel know she was here, only to realize he didn't know her number.

He started the chain saw and resumed what he'd been doing, but he couldn't get the image of Laurel finding her husband's body out of his head, imagining her shock and the horror of cleaning up blood from the bed where they'd slept—imagining the grief and, eventually, her anger—because anger always followed death for the ones who'd been left behind.

<div align="center">~~~</div>

Laurel was just about to go down to the creek to check on Bonnie when she saw her emerge from the tree line and come skipping toward the house. Bonnie saw her mother and waved.

Laurel waved back and then continued on her way to the cellar to store the last jars of jelly she'd made the other day. When she came up, she walked toward the chicken coop where Bonnie was playing with Lavonne. She could hear Bonnie talking to the hen as if she were one of her school friends. If life had been different, Bonnie would have had a sibling by now—someone else to play with besides a chicken. Then Laurel saw Bonnie was chewing gum and frowned. She never bought gum because it was bad for her teeth.

"Bonnie, where did you get that gum?" she asked.

"From Mr. Lorde."

Laurel's heart skipped a beat, and when she spoke, panic tinged her voice. "You went all the way up to the Lorde property?"

Bonnie looked up then nodded. "Yes, you always let me go see Mr. Lorde."

Laurel's voice rose an octave. "But he's not there anymore, and his son is. I didn't tell you it was okay to go there."

Bonnie was confused and it showed. "But, Mama, he's nice just like Mr. Lorde, and he's like my daddy."

"He's nothing like your father, and you don't know anything about him. I'm telling you now, you are not allowed to do that again, do you hear me?"

Bonnie's chin trembled and her eyes welled with tears. "He's lonesome, Mama. If I can't go visit, who will be his friend?"

"He has his own friends. You do not go back to that place again. Promise me."

Tears rolled as her shoulders slumped. "I promise," she whispered, then took the gum out of her mouth, dug a little hole with her fingers, and buried it as solemnly as if she'd buried the man who'd given it to her.

"Come into the house now," Laurel said. "I'll make lunch."

"I'm not hungry," Bonnie said.

"Come into the house anyway," Laurel said and held out her hand.

Bonnie got up, but wouldn't hold her mother's hand and walked into the trailer house on her own. Even though Laurel knew she'd hurt Bonnie's feelings, she was convinced she was in the right. She followed her daughter inside, locking the door behind her as she went.

By nighttime, Laurel just assumed Bonnie had gotten past her upset. When she began helping her get ready for bed, her usual chatter was absent. A little surprised that she was still reacting to the scolding she'd received, after several minutes of trying to engage her in conversation, it became obvious that no amount of talking was going to help.

Satisfied that it would pass, Laurel sat down on the side of the bed to hear Bonnie's prayers, but instead of saying them, she stopped and looked up. "I can do this by myself, Mama."

Laurel blinked. Bonnie waited.

The rejection was both unexpected and shocking. Laurel got up and walked out of the room on shaky legs, but instead of closing the door all the way, she left it ajar, then stood in the hall to listen.

"God bless Mama, and God bless Daddy, wherever he is. God bless Lavonne because she's my best friend, and God bless Mr. Lorde. Mama doesn't like him, so it's up to you, God. Please don't let him be sad that I can't go visit anymore. Amen."

Laurel reeled like she'd been slapped, then went into her room and closed the door. She stood in the middle of the room while the pain in her chest grew with every breath.

Yes, she knew Jake, but her daughter did not, and yet Bonnie's reaction to meeting him had been an instant attraction. Maybe it had to do with missing her father. Maybe it had to do with missing Mr. Lorde. In fairness to Bonnie, Laurel had never had a question of worrying about her daughter visiting the old man, but she'd taken an instant distrust to the son with no reason other than Jake had been discharged from the army just like Adam. She was afraid of Jake because, in the end, she'd been afraid of Adam, too.

She sank onto the side of her bed and then clasped her hands in her lap and closed her eyes. She could still see the blood splatter on the wall, the blood-soaked bed and bedclothes, and the pool of blood on the floor beside her house shoes. She'd seen all that, but she wouldn't look at what he'd done to himself. The pain inside her had been so severe she'd been unable to cry. Instead, she'd called the police, sat down on the front steps to await their arrival, and thanked God Bonnie was spending the night at her grandparents.

Looking back, she supposed it was why Adam had chosen that night to do it, knowing Bonnie would be gone. Her hands were shaking from the memories. She had so many unanswered questions. She felt so betrayed by how it had happened. Why the hell had he done it in their house—in their bedroom—in the bed where they'd made Bonnie? Why had he defiled that, too?

It had taken every spare penny she had to buy another bed and mattress, repaint the walls, and scrub the carpet. If she'd had the money, she would have moved them both out of this trailer and left all the bad times behind. But that was not an option.

She had to accept that what she'd gone through had damaged her in much the same way war had damaged him. She didn't trust that life wouldn't kick her again when she was down. She didn't trust Jacob Lorde because he reminded her of Adam. She was so tired of being afraid. Why was this happening again, just when she was beginning to get a handle on making the best of their situation? And what was she going to do about Bonnie? Laurel's fears had driven the first wedge between their mother-daughter relationship, and it felt like a knife in the heart.

Finally, she got up and went through the house to lock up and turn off the lights. She peeked in Bonnie's room and saw her sleeping with her panda bear again. Probably because Bonnie felt like she'd been bad like Panda was bad. Laurel sighed. She had to find a way to fix this.

—⁓—

It threatened rain all Sunday. Jake thought about going to church but was uneasy he would get cornered in the congregation, so he checked email, answered a few messages, paid a few bills online, and then there was nothing left to do.

When his dad died, he hadn't stayed long enough after the funeral to deal with any of his father's belongings, and while he wasn't looking forward to it, he decided to begin with his dad's clothing.

The room was cold, so he left the door open and moved to the dresser and started emptying the drawers of his dad's socks and underwear. The stack of neatly folded handkerchiefs brought a lump to his throat. His dad never left the house without one in his pocket. He took a deep breath and put them on the bed with the rest of his dad's things.

And so it went until the dresser and chest of drawers were empty and the things packed away. He took the clothes hanging in the closet out on hangers, laying them across the foot of the bed, and then stacked the boxes of shoes nearby. Once he'd finished, he made a call to a church he knew that kept a charity room full of clothing for people in need. They were thrilled with the donation and agreed to a pickup date.

When it came time to eat, he took out some of the food the ladies had brought him. There was so much, he thought about sharing it with Laurel and Bonnie. But again, reminded himself he didn't know her number and wasn't sure where she lived, even less sure of a positive reception. So he watched football, ate some more, and fell asleep in his dad's recliner.

All of a sudden, a clap of thunder came so loud and close that it rattled the windows. Jake woke abruptly, his heart pounding so hard he couldn't think. He leaped out of the chair, looking frantically for his weapon and a place to take cover. He was running through the living room when he stubbed his toe on a leg of the sofa. It was the pain that pulled him out of the hallucination. It wasn't sand beneath his feet; it was a hardwood floor, and he wasn't somewhere outside in the desert. He was in a house—his house—and there was rain blowing against the windows.

"Oh lord," he said softly.

What he'd heard was weather, not war. The rain had finally arrived.

Still shaken from what had happened, he went from room to room in an aimless manner, looking for answers to questions he had yet to pose. This was home. He'd grown up here, but the people who'd made it special were gone. When he was younger, he'd always imagined working somewhere around Blessings and raising his own family here. He'd expected to grow old in this house, but not alone. The way he was now, there was a very good chance no one would want him. Sometimes he didn't even want himself.

He walked through the kitchen, then out onto the back porch to face the wind. When the rain blew under the porch roof and onto his legs, he didn't move away. The chill air was refreshing, and the bad dream was fading. He shoved both hands through his hair and tried not to feel sorry for himself. He was alive, for which he was grateful.

He glanced toward the barn to the ricks of wood he'd cut. It wasn't enough for the entire winter, and as soon as everything dried up, he'd have to cut some more.

Thinking of the wood made him think of Bonnie Payne, which made him think of Laurel. Such a pretty face, but with sad eyes and lips too tightly clenched. Maybe she was afraid to open them too wide for fear some of that sadness would come out in a scream.

He sighed, shoved his hands in his pockets, and went back in the house. Her husband—a veteran like him—had killed himself. He could not imagine the horror of walking in on something like that. So what if she seemed a little cold toward him? He represented everything she'd lost.

Another clap of thunder sounded, making him flinch. Angry with his inability to control his emotions, he strode back into the living room and turned on the television. Maybe if it was loud enough, it would drown out the thunder *and* the memories.

And Sunday passed.

Chapter 4

LAUREL HAD OVERSLEPT AND WAS RACING AROUND TRYING to play catch-up and get Bonnie ready in time to catch the bus. Bonnie was dragging her heels, clinging to Laurel and whining about not feeling good and wanting to stay home. Laurel felt certain the only thing wrong with Bonnie was that she was upset about being angry and didn't know how to resolve it. Bonnie's mother was her touchstone, and Laurel'd never failed her before, but Laurel knew she'd failed her now, and she had to fix it.

"I'm sorry you are upset with me," Laurel said.

Bonnie ducked her head.

"It's okay," Laurel said. "I need to say sorry for yelling at you. I reacted without thinking it through, okay?"

Bonnie shrugged.

"You know how much I love you, right?"

Bonnie nodded.

"And everything I do is done to keep you safe and happy. I promise I will never yell at you again, okay?"

Bonnie nodded.

"Can I have a hug?" Laurel asked.

Bonnie threw her arms around her mother's neck and started crying.

"It's okay, honey. It's okay," Laurel said as she hugged and kissed her. She held her until she'd calmed down and then kissed her one more time. "So how about getting the rest of your stuff on, and let's get up the road to catch that bus, okay?"

"Okay, Mommy. Can I have peanut butter and jelly in my sandwich today?"

Laurel grinned. "May I, and yes, you may. I'll make the lunch if you finish getting dressed. And I'll drive you up the driveway to catch the bus so you won't have to stand in the rain, okay?"

"Yay!" Bonnie cried, and just like that, everything was back to normal.

Laurel was a little bit shaky as she headed for the kitchen, but the knot in her stomach was gone. It didn't feel good being on the outs with her baby girl.

A short time later they were at the end of the drive in her old pickup, watching the yellow bus as it came around the curve.

"There's the bus!" Bonnie cried, and started to jump out.

"Wait," Laurel said. "I'll walk you to the door. Let me get the umbrella."

The bus came to a stop. Laurel held the umbrella over Bonnie as she helped her through the mud, then across the blacktop to the bus. The driver grinned as he opened the door for Bonnie to get in. "Morning, Mrs. Payne. Nasty weather we're having."

"Yes, it is, Mr. Fisher. Bye, Bonnie. I'll see you this evening. Have a good day!"

"Bye, Mommy. Can we have pancakes for supper?"

Laurel laughed. "We'll worry about that later," she said and blew Bonnie a kiss before running back to her truck.

She was soaked by the time she got inside, but she

was satisfied that Bonnie was warm and dry. She drove back to the trailer house and then ran inside, shivering as she went. She changed into old, dry clothes and got busy with chores she'd been putting off.

It was nearing 10:00 a.m. when her phone rang. She pulled it out of her pocket and then frowned when she saw it was from the school. "Hello?"

"Mrs. Payne, this is Mrs. Smith."

When Laurel heard the first grade teacher's voice, her heart skipped. "Is something wrong?" Laurel asked.

"It's not life-threatening by any means, but Bonnie slipped on a wet spot on the floor and cut her chin."

"Oh no!" Laurel cried.

"She needs stitches, I'm sure. We have her lying down and are keeping an ice pack on the cut, but she needs to see a doctor."

"Yes, yes, of course. I'll be right there. Tell her that I'm on the way, okay?"

"I certainly will, and I'm so sorry I had to call with bad news, but I'm sure she will be okay once she gets treatment. Drive carefully."

"I will, and thanks."

Laurel disconnected, put the phone back in the pocket of her jeans, and then raced to her bedroom to get her purse. She changed out of her tennis shoes into her old cowboy boots, put on her raincoat, grabbed her purse, and headed for the door. Her hands were shaking as she locked the door behind her and then made a run for the truck, splashing through the puddles as she went.

She was almost at the truck when she saw the carcass of a dead cat about halfway down the drive. She threw up her hands and started screaming and cursing. Of all times for her sorry-ass brothers-in-law to harass her! Why they felt the need to punish her for their brother's suicide was beyond her. It wasn't the first time, and she was sure it wouldn't be the last.

And while she didn't have time for this, she couldn't let Bonnie see a dead animal. It would send her into a tailspin. She grabbed the tail and threw it as far across the road as she could fling it. When it landed in the bushes on the other side of the road and out of sight, she ran back to the truck.

Now she was so mad she was shaking as she headed out of the drive. Trying to make up for lost time, she accelerated, and as she did, the truck began fishtailing in the mud. Once she made it to the blacktop, it leveled out. Soaked to the skin, she still breathed a sigh of relief and headed for town.

About a mile up the road, the truck began to pull hard to the left. In a panic, she just kept driving, and was right in front of the Lorde driveway when she had to stop. She knew without looking that the left front tire was flat. She wanted to cry, but now was not the time to lose it.

She jumped out of the truck, saw the flat and groaned, then climbed into the bed of the pickup. She unfastened the spare; tossed it, the jack, and the tire iron onto the blacktop; then climbed out and began loosening the lug nuts before she jacked up the front end of the truck.

The rain felt like icicles down the back of her neck, and it was running out of her hair and down into her eyes, but the first lug nut wouldn't budge. No matter how hard she tried, she didn't have the strength to break it loose.

"Damn it!" she screamed, and gave it one last push.

When she did, her hand slipped off the lug wrench and she skinned her knuckles on the blacktop. Now she was bleeding. "God help me," she muttered, and got a firmer grip on the lug wrench and started over.

———

Jake's night had been little more than a collage of bad dreams that were still with him through a morning shower and breakfast. The rain was still coming down, which meant whatever happened today would be inside this house, so he got out a dust mop and began cleaning floors.

He had just finished in the living room and was pushing furniture back in place when he happened to glance out the front window and saw a pickup stopped on the road in front of the house. When he realized it was Laurel Payne, he grabbed a coat and his pickup keys, jumped in the truck, and headed up the drive to see what was wrong.

When he parked his truck at the end of his drive, he saw the flat tire and jumped out on the run. Laurel saw him drive up, and when he ran over to where she was working, she was relieved. "Can I help?" Jake asked.

She stood up. "I can't get this lug nut loose, and I've got to get to town. The school called. Bonnie's been hurt. They said she's going to need stitches and—"

Jake gently gripped her shoulders. "Take my truck and go do what you have to do. The keys are in the ignition. I'll fix your flat and we'll trade later."

Laurel was so relieved she began to shake. "Thank you, oh, thank you," she said as she grabbed her purse out of the front seat of her truck and ran across the road.

Jake watched her drive away and then grabbed the lug wrench and got to work.

Truman Slade saw Adam Payne's widow coming into Blessings in Jake Lorde's red pickup truck and frowned. Jake hadn't wasted much time striking up a relationship with his neighbor, or maybe they'd had something going on long distance all this time. At any rate, she was driving around town in that shiny red truck like she owned it.

The first thought that went through his mind was, what could he do with this knowledge? And just like that, his good intentions of bettering his life were forgotten at the thought of revenge. He wanted to get back at Lorde for all the years he'd spent in prison. Maybe he'd find a way to hassle the little lady instead. He was fine with whatever it took, as long as it bothered Jake Lorde.

He watched her until she turned off Main and headed down the street toward the school, then he drove away with his groceries, ready to settle in his house and wait for the weather front to pass.

Laurel was cold and breathless as she ran through the parking lot in the rain, and then dripped water all the way to the office.

Mavis West, the school secretary, saw her walk in and grimaced. "Girl, you are soaked."

"I had a flat on the way into town," Laurel said. "Where's Bonnie? Is she okay?"

"We moved the cot out of the front office this year. She's in the back. I'll go get her."

"May I come with you?" Laurel asked.

"Sure. Follow me," Mavis said.

Laurel left wet tracks all the way down the hall and then into the little alcove where Bonnie was lying. One of the teacher's aides was sitting with her, and when Bonnie saw her mother, she started crying all over again. "Mommy, I fell, and it made me bleed all over my clothes," she cried.

For a moment, it felt to Laurel as if the walls were beginning to spin. Blood on the clothes, blood on the floor beneath the cot, blood on her daughter's hand.

Like Adam. Blood everywhere.

Then she took a deep breath and knelt to get a closer look at the cut and tried not to let her concern show. It was very deep, and from the shape of her clothing, she'd already lost a lot of blood.

"I know, baby. I can see. We're going straight to the doctor and get you all fixed up," she said, then helped Bonnie into her raincoat, slung the backpack over her arm, and scooped Bonnie up into her arms.

Bonnie recoiled slightly. "You're wet, Mommy."

"I know. It's raining very hard, and I had a flat tire. I'll tell you all about it on the way to the doctor, okay?"

Mavis handed Bonnie her ice pack. "Here, honey. Keep this on your chin, okay?"

Bonnie nodded, and then they were gone.

Mavis watched Laurel walking away and thought to herself that the young woman was too thin, and then she shrugged off the thought and went back to work.

———

They were both wet again by the time Laurel settled Bonnie into the front seat of Jake's truck and buckled her in.

"Where's our pickup? Whose truck is this?" Bonnie asked as Laurel got in behind the wheel.

"I had a flat in front of Mr. Lorde's driveway. He traded vehicles with me so I could come take care of you. We'll trade back later after we get home, okay?"

Bonnie was mildly interested in the truck, but hurt too much to dwell on it.

"What is the doctor going to do to my chin?" she asked.

"He'll put some medicine in it to make it numb so you can't feel what he's doing, and then he'll stitch it up, sort of like how I stitch up the hems in your shirts and dresses."

She moaned and then whimpered. "I don't want him to do that. I don't want my chin hemmed."

Laurel sighed. Chalk up that poor choice of words to how rattled she was.

"It will be okay. I promise. I'll be right beside you the whole time."

Bonnie wasn't convinced and sniffled and cried all the way to the ER. By the time they got parked and Laurel carried her into the building, she felt like crying, too.

"I need a doctor. My daughter fell at school and cut her chin," Laurel said.

The receptionist's eyes widened at the sight of so much blood on the little girl's clothes, then looked at Laurel. She was pale and soaked and visibly shaking. Instead of taking pertinent information first, she made a judgment call.

"I'll get a wheelchair and—"

"I'll carry her," Laurel said.

The receptionist nodded. "Follow me. I'll get your information after we get her settled."

Laurel did as she was directed and was relieved when she could finally lay her daughter down. As soon as Bonnie was on the bed, Laurel took off her coat and tossed it on the floor against the wall, out of the way. Even though her shirt was damp and sticking to her skin, shedding that wet, heavy coat felt better.

The nurse was helping Bonnie off with her raincoat, taking off her rain boots as another nurse came and covered her with a clean, heated blanket. The warmth alone was enough to ease some of Bonnie's discomfort and she finally quit crying.

Laurel stood next to the bed, holding Bonnie's hand as a doctor came in to assess the wound.

"Hello, young lady. My name is Dr. Quick. What's yours?"

Bonnie sniffled. "Bonnie Carol Payne."

Dr. Quick smiled, then glanced at Laurel. "Are you her mother?" he asked.

"Yes, I'm Laurel Payne. Bonnie fell at school. I think she's going to need stitches."

Bonnie began to whimper again. "Don't want you to hem my chin," she cried.

Laurel grimaced. "That's my fault. I was trying to explain what might happen and used an analogy that morphed into this."

Paul Quick chuckled. "I guess there is a small similarity between tailors and surgeons. We both stitch. Now let's take a look at this marvelous chin," he said, and motioned for his nurse to wash out the wound, which elicited another round of wails and tears.

Dr. Quick seemed immune to the noise and continued his examination. "Bonnie, I'm going to check your teeth and make sure none of them are loose, okay? And this won't hurt a bit, I promise. I just need to put my finger on each tooth in front and make sure they are nice and snug in there."

Bonnie looked at the finger he was holding up.

Dr. Quick grinned. "Yep, that's the one. Now I need you to open your mouth so I can see your teeth."

Bonnie reluctantly opened, but not wide. Before Laurel could urge her to open wider, Dr. Quick took care of the problem in a most ingenious way.

"Oh! Hello, tooth! You look quite fine! Oh, you say your name is Martha? Hello, Martha, nice to meet you."

Bonnie's eyes widened. She didn't know her teeth had names. Interested in spite of herself, she relaxed her jaw enough that the doctor checked the first two teeth on the top.

"Ah, hello down there," he said, as he felt along the teeth on the lower jaw. "I'm Dr. Quick. I'm here to make sure you're still properly in place. Oh? Really? You say you never get out of place? That you mind your manners very well? That's wonderful! What's your name, by the way? You say they call you Miss Helen? So nice to meet you, Miss Helen."

Dr. Quick glanced at Bonnie. She was totally into the discussion going on inside her mouth now, and so he kept up the patter until he was convinced her teeth were sound. "So, it's been nice talking to all of you. Most happy to report you are all fine."

When he took his finger out of her mouth, Bonnie looked at Laurel. "Mama, did you know about Miss Helen and Martha?"

Laurel shook her head. "No, I did not."

Dr. Quick smiled. "No worries. Only doctors can talk to teeth. All they need you to do is brush them good every day. Okay?"

Bonnie nodded.

Dr. Quick smiled, but knew this moment wasn't going to last. "Now we're going to numb the area around the cut and then put you back together, Miss Bonnie. Are you ready to be a brave girl?"

"No, I don't want to be brave," Bonnie said, and dissolved into tears.

Bonnie was wailing and Laurel wanted to cry with her. "Just do what you have to do, Dr. Quick. I'll hold her head still and talk to her while you work."

So Laurel stood at the end of the bed behind Bonnie's head and held it still while Dr. Quick and his nurse went to work.

When he stuck the needle in the cut to deaden it, Laurel was already talking to Bonnie, telling her not to move, and as soon as Dr. Quick was through with this one thing, her chin would quit hurting. Bonnie didn't buy it, and her fears were justified. Her shriek echoed all over ER when the needle went into her chin. It made Laurel sick to her stomach to know her little girl was scared and in pain, and she began talking even faster about Lavonne, wondering if she'd laid another egg, and telling her how kind Jake was to let her drive his truck, and they should make him some cookies as a thank-you.

By the time the numbing had taken place, Bonnie was exhausted. She was teary-eyed during the stitching but had quit crying and screaming, for which everyone in the ER was truly grateful.

Then, finally, they were done. Dr. Quick dropped

the needle and sutures on the tray and motioned for the
nurse to bandage the chin. "We're through," he told
Bonnie, as he patted her knee.

"Mommy, I want to go home now," Bonnie said.

"Soon, honey. We're almost ready. Just rest."

Bonnie sighed, her eyes closed, and she fell asleep
from the exhaustion.

~~~

Jake soon had the flat in the back of Laurel's truck and
was headed to town to get it fixed. The spare was missing
a lot of tread and he hoped he'd make it in before it went
flat, too. He couldn't quit thinking about how frantic
Laurel had been and hoped her little girl was okay.

As soon as he reached Blessings, he went straight to
Tire Supply and drove up to the garage. After a quick
explanation of what he needed, they drove the truck
inside, fixed the flat, and put it back on the truck, then
put the spare in the truck bed.

Jake watched, and when they started to put the jack
and lug wrench in the bed also, he stopped them and had
them put those two items behind the front seat instead.
He'd tell her later what he'd done, so she wouldn't think
they were missing, but having those loose in the back
of a truck bed made them too easy to steal. The spare
tire was there in the open, too, but at least Adam Payne
had rigged up a system to fasten down the spare with a
couple of big wing nuts.

He paid for the flat and drove home, wondering how
the Payne girls were faring. Even after he was home, he
hovered anxiously at the front windows, watching for
that red truck to appear. When it finally did, he was so

relieved that he stood and watched them drive by before it dawned on him that he needed to follow. He grabbed his coat and her truck keys and headed out the door on the run.

~~~

Bonnie had fallen asleep and was slumped against the console.

Laurel couldn't quit shaking and periodically brushed a hand over Bonnie's head just to reassure herself she was okay. She was all the way past the Lorde house before she thought and then groaned.

"Dang it," she mumbled, then glanced in the rearview mirror and caught a glimpse of her old truck coming over the hill behind her. *Good. He's following me home.*

When she came around the curve and saw their trailer, home had never looked so good. She took the turn down her muddy drive and then drove all the way to the trailer and parked.

Now, with the engine off and the rain still falling, the quiet within the cab was intensified. If Jake hadn't been so close behind her, she would have burst into tears just from the relief that the worst was all over. When she remembered her house key was on the key ring in her truck, she dug the extra key out of her purse, but she was shaking so hard she didn't think she could carry Bonnie up the steps.

Before she could panic again, Jake Lorde had pulled up beside her. She watched as he got out and ran to the passenger side of the truck. She unlocked the door and when he opened it, his presence invaded the space.

"Is she okay?" he asked.

Laurel nodded. "Eight stitches."

Jake frowned. Laurel was shaking like a leaf. "If you'll open the front door, I'll carry her inside for you."

The relief she felt was huge. Again he'd come to her rescue and just in time. "Yes, okay," she said, then got out, making sure she took all of their things from his truck as she went.

She stumbled up the steps, unlocked the door, and then held it back, waiting for them to come in.

Jake had seen the blood all over Bonnie's clothes from the corner of his eye and had done everything he could to focus on something else, but then he had to unbuckle the seat belt. Even though she still had on her raincoat, he saw enough to send him straight back to war. If it hadn't been for the rain running down the back of his neck, he might have stayed there, but getting caught in a rainstorm in the desert didn't happen. He took a deep breath and closed his eyes, and when he opened them again, he saw the trailer and his dad's truck, and the panic was fading.

As he unbuckled her seat belt, she began to wake up. "Hi, Bonnie, it's me, Jake. I'm going to carry you into your house, okay?"

She nodded.

He needed to get her in without getting her any wetter and then thought about the blanket behind the seat. He grabbed the plastic pack it was in, shook it out inside the truck, and laid it over Bonnie just before he picked her up. "Okay, baby girl, let's get you in out of this rain," he said softly.

He picked her up and saw the look of trust in her

eyes just before he pulled the blanket over her head. It reminded him of how he felt the summer he grew six inches. Like he'd discovered the secret to becoming a man.

He carried her up the stairs and into the house with ease. "Do you want her in her bedroom or down on the sofa?" he asked, as Laurel hovered behind him.

"I think to her bedroom," she said. "I've got to get her cleaned up and in dry clothes."

"Lead the way," he said, and then followed Laurel through the living room and down the narrow hall into the first room on the left.

When he laid Bonnie down, Laurel started to remove the blanket to give it back to him, but Bonnie grabbed it with both hands, loudly objecting.

"No, Mama, it's magic. It will make me get well faster."

"Now, Bonnie, this belongs to Mr. Lorde. You can't—"

"Please, let her keep it," Jake said.

Laurel turned around to argue, then stopped. The plea in his eyes was so similar to the look in Bonnie's that it made her shiver. "If you're sure," she mumbled.

"I'm sure," he said, and then winked at Bonnie, who was still clutching the blanket with both hands.

He handed Laurel her car keys. "There was a small nail in your tire. It's fixed, and your spare is back in place. I put the jack and lug wrench behind the seat, though. Having it loose in the truck bed is an invitation to get it stolen."

"Thank you. How much do I owe you?"

"Nothing. Consider it payback for the ride home the other day."

She shivered. The keys were still warm from his

hands. As difficult as it was for her, she made herself look at him. "You were a godsend today. I owe you."

He sighed. The wall she kept between herself and the world was still up, but she was peeking over and he knew that was tough. "You owe me nothing, and you are most welcome," he said.

There were paper and crayons on the desk in Bonnie's room, and he paused long enough to write the number of his cell phone. "That's my number. Call anytime you need help. It's what neighbors do, you know. I'm going to go now so you can get your girl settled. I'll let myself out."

Laurel nodded and then held her breath as she listened, tracking the sound of his footsteps through the house, and didn't breathe again until he was gone. Then it was back to the business of tending to Bonnie, and she got too busy to think about how empty the house felt without him in it.

Chapter 5

JAKE DROVE HOME THROUGH THE DOWNPOUR, THINKING HE should have said something more, but couldn't imagine what it could have been without saying too much. There was something about Laurel Payne that seemed as broken as he felt. And little Bonnie had lost the man who had meant the most to her—her father. What irony that he was grieving a similar loss.

The closer he got to his house, the less interested he was in being alone, so he kept driving all the way into town and wound up on Main Street. He'd skipped lunch waiting for Laurel to come back, and the thought of eating something at Granny's Country Kitchen was appealing. He parked at the curb and ducked his head against the rain as he ran toward the entrance. Once inside, he paused in the small foyer to shake the water off his coat, then carried it in with him.

Lovey was working at the cash register and smiled when she saw him walk in. "Welcome!" she said, and came out from behind the counter to give him a quick hug. "Nothing has changed around here. Sit where you want. The girls know this is on me."

"That's really kind of you. It sure smells good in here."

"Beef tips and noodles on special today. Comes with your choice of cherry cobbler or coconut cream pie."

"That will hit the spot," Jake said, and paused a moment to check out the room, then chose a booth against the wall. He was headed toward it when someone called out his name.

"Jake! Hey, Jake! Come sit with us," Mike Dalton said.

Jake saw Mike and Peanut Butterman sharing a table and gladly accepted the invitation.

Peanut grinned as Jake sat down. "Welcome home, Jake."

"Thanks, Mr. Butterman."

"Oh no…call me Peanut, please."

"How's it going?" Mike asked, as he gave Jake a quick pat on the back. "LilyAnn told me you were back."

"It's good to be back. How does it feel knowing you're soon to be a father?"

Mike beamed. "Scary. Exciting. Nervous."

"I can only imagine," Jake said.

The waitress arrived bringing a glass of water and the coffeepot. She refilled coffee cups, filled one for Jake, and took his order before she left.

For the time Jake was inside Granny's, he could almost convince himself he'd never left Blessings. The people were still as friendly, just a little older, some a little heavier and grayer, but still people from home.

It was well after 4:00 p.m. before he left town. Rain was letting up, and he felt more optimistic about the future than he had in months. He stopped at the mailbox to get the mail before driving on to the house.

The house was chilly when he walked in, and so he turned up the thermostat on his way to the utility room, where he hung up his wet coat and took off his wet boots. He laid the mail on the kitchen table as he went to change clothes, and once he had on dry clothes, began to go through the mail, all of which was addressed to *Resident*. It was too soon for any forwarded mail to catch up, so he checked messages on his laptop. There was one from a soldier from his unit, and as soon as he opened it and read the first words, his heart sank.

Hate to be the bearer of bad news, but—

Jake read the message, typed a quick reply, and then got up and walked onto the back porch. His gut was in a knot and there was a pain in his chest growing with every breath.

Joaquin DeSosa.

He couldn't imagine him dead. He'd kept morale up in the unit when everyone was worn down and homesick. He knew dirty jokes and knew everyone's story— where they came from, who they loved, how many kids the married ones had.

Jake shoved both hands through his hair and felt the scars beneath his fingers. Joaquin was the one who'd saved his life.

"Son of a bitch," Jake said softly, and then stepped off the porch and started toward the barn.

The rain was gone but the air was still damp. The ground sank beneath his feet but he kept on walking. He went into the barn, got an ax, a sledgehammer, and the iron wedge his dad had used to split the logs, and walked out to the stack of logs he'd sawed up. He rolled one out of the stack, set it on end, and went to work.

Tears soon mixed with sweat but he kept on working, using his pain as energy, and hammering the splitting wedge into log after log until he looked up and realized it was getting dark. His arms were aching by the time he had the tools put up and the split wood stacked into ricks.

The sky was still overcast, so there was no brilliant sunset to end the day—just a gray sky to match his mood.

"Rest in peace, DeSosa. God knows you've earned it," he said and mentally marked off one more soldier down.

His dark mood didn't get any better with the passing of time. The thought of food turned his stomach, and so he took a hot shower, put on some old sweats, and settled on the living room sofa to watch some TV.

Hours later he was still awake and his belly was grumbling. He opted for some popcorn and a cold drink, and ate the popcorn one handful at a time, standing on the back porch in the dark.

The sky had cleared. Stars were visible from every angle. He had vivid memories of summer nights and lying out in the yard, looking at the sky when he was a kid. His mama always said to make a wish on a falling star, and no sooner had he remembered that than he saw movement from the corner of his eye. He caught himself holding his breath as he counted the seconds the star kept burning until it blazed out and disappeared. Even though it felt childish, he wasn't going to waste the opportunity. He thought for a moment and then closed his eyes. The wish was heartfelt although nearly impossible, but he'd already beat the odds once by living through war.

The air was getting colder. It was time to quit stargazing. He tossed the last of his popcorn into the yard and went inside. The warmth was welcome, enough so that he decided to try and get some sleep. He thought about taking one of his sleeping pills and then, again, chose not to do it.

The house was locked tight, the thermostat turned down. Lights were out, bed turned back. All he had to do was get in. Instead, he gripped the posts at the foot of the bed and leaned forward. "You are just a bed, not a fucking time machine, so do not take me anywhere but to sleep. Understand?"

Satisfied that he wasn't getting an argument, Jake kicked off his shoes and stripped, then crawled into bed naked. He pulled up the covers and then rolled over on his side. Exhausted from splitting wood and heart-sick from the emotion of losing a good friend, he said a quick prayer and closed his eyes. Within minutes he was asleep.

"Get up, damn you! Come on, Lorde, you gotta stand up. You're too fucking big for me to carry and I'm not dragging your ass through this fire. Get up! Get up!"

Jake moaned. He could hear DeSosa's voice, but the words didn't make sense. Something was wrong with his head, and his legs wouldn't work.

"I'm dead."

DeSosa screamed. "Like hell! You're not dead until I kill you myself! Do you hear me? Get up, damn it. Get up. You still owe me five dollars."

Jake sat up with a jerk and threw back the covers. He was on his feet and looking for his friend before he opened his eyes. Then he saw the room, remembered where he was, and was awash with grief all over again. DeSosa was gone.

He glanced at the clock. At least an hour before sun-rise. Night was over enough for him.

~~~

Laurel was exhausted. She'd cooked pudding, thinking it would be easier for Bonnie to eat if she didn't have to chew, but Bonnie was in a mood and cried anyway. She was still weepy and wanted to be held, even after Laurel had given her pain pills, and so she wrapped Bonnie in Jake Lorde's blue-and-green-plaid blanket, then sat down in the rocker with her.

Bonnie clutched the edge of the blanket as Laurel rocked, and even after she fell asleep, the blanket stayed. Laurel put Bonnie in bed and then went to the kitchen and sat down in the warmth and the light to call her mother. In all of the chaos, she'd forgotten to let her know about Bonnie.

The call began ringing, and Laurel knew her mother would answer on the third or fourth ring. Even if she was sitting beside the phone, Pansy Joyner believed if you answered a cell phone too fast that the call would stop, and there was no way they could convince her she was wrong.

Sure enough, when Pansy answered, it was on the fourth ring. "Hello?"

"Hi, Mama. Are you and Dad staying dry through all this rain?"

"Oh yes, we've been inside all day, although it's driving Benny crazy. Are you all okay?"

"That's actually why I'm calling," Laurel said. "I got a call from school today that Bonnie had a fall and cut her chin. She had to get stitches, and she's pretty unhappy right now. I'm a wreck, as you can imagine."

"Oh no! How many stitches did it take?"

"Eight, and the cut was deep. She's going to heal okay, but it's going to be a cranky few days ahead."

"Oh, I'm so sorry. That just makes me sick. Is she awake? Can I talk to her?"

"She's asleep, thank goodness. I had to rock her to get her easy, and she won't eat, I guess because it hurts to chew."

"Maybe some soup?" Pansy said.

"I cooked pudding. She didn't even want that."

"Well, well, I'm sure she'll be some better tomorrow. You're keeping her home from school?"

"Yes."

"Do you need me to come stay with her?"

"No, but thanks for offering. This is her first big injury, and I feel like I need to be with her."

"I'm sure you're right. Well, you know we're here if you need us. Love you both."

"Love you, too, Mama. Good night."

She hung up, wondering as she went through the house, locking doors and turning out lights, why calling her mother always felt like a duty. Probably because Pansy was so critical about everything. She loved her parents very much, but they weren't always the easiest to deal with.

The house was dark except for the night-light in Bonnie's bedroom as Laurel crawled into bed beside her daughter and covered them both. She'd already canceled her cleaning jobs tomorrow and would call school in the morning to let them know Bonnie would be absent. The only important thing in her life was getting her baby well. She rolled on her side, snuggled Bonnie close against her, and closed her eyes.

When she fell asleep, she dreamed in increments, seeing only the darkest bits of the past and watching it all unfold as if she was an observer, not a participant.

Something exploded inside the house. Laurel dropped

*the laundry she was putting into the washing machine
and ran, screaming Adam's name. Once she reached
their bedroom, she realized it wasn't an explosion but
a gunshot, and it was obvious why he hadn't answered.*

*The gun was lying on his belly with two of his fingers
still curled around the grip. The blood. The blood. It was
everywhere. How did one small piece of lead do so much
damage to a body?*

*Someone was screaming and begging God to take it
back. She didn't know until she grabbed the phone to
call the police that it was her.*

*People are everywhere now, walking through her
house with plastic footies over their shoes, so they won't
contaminate the scene. When they swab her fingers for
gun residue, as if they believe she would have done this
to someone she loved, she can't quit sobbing.*

*Someone called her parents. They arrived in obvious
shock. She could see their lips moving but didn't hear
a word. Her mother dried the tears from Laurel's face,
and her daddy wrapped her in his arms and held her
while the people kept going in and out of the trailer,
carrying things away in plastic bags, as if they'd been
shopping at the mall.*

*Sometime later, a doctor gave her a pill even though
she wasn't crying anymore. She handed it back and
told him Adam needed it more, so they could put him
back together.*

*Then two men emerged from the shadows in her
dream pushing a gurney into the living room and then
pushing it in circles because it was too wide to get down
the hall. They carried the body bag with Adam's remains
to the gurney, but it didn't register that her husband's*

body was in it. She was standing in the doorway, watching the ambulance and the police cars driving away when she heard someone crying.

She turned to look and saw Bonnie. She frowned. Bonnie wasn't there. Where had she come from?

It was Bonnie crying out in her sleep that woke Laurel from the nightmare.

"You're okay, baby," she said softly and pulled her close and tucked in the covers.

Bonnie settled, but Laurel was afraid to close her eyes again for fear sleep would take her back to where she'd been. She didn't often dream that anymore and guessed it was Bonnie's accident that had resurrected the memories, just like she knew Bonnie's tearful state had less to do with pain in her chin and more to do with the pain of all her losses.

She'd tried talking to Bonnie about death when Adam died and then when Mr. Lorde passed away. Bonnie became afraid her mother was next. It had taken weeks for that fear to fade, and now, it had all come back with the pain of the accident.

A tear rolled down Laurel's cheek as she kissed the top of her daughter's head.

Poor little girl. You've seen the dark side of life at a very young age. I pray the future is kinder to the both of us.

In spite of her determination not to go back to sleep, Laurel dozed. It was almost 8:00 a.m. when she woke up again, and it was because Bonnie was trying to crawl over her to get out of bed. "What do you need, honey?" Laurel asked.

"I need to go to the bathroom, Mommy."

Laurel quickly got out of the way and then helped unwind her from all the covers. She watched her make a dash for the bathroom across the hall and then looked down at the clothes she'd slept in and went to her bedroom to change.

———

It was close to noon when Laurel took the apricot pie from the oven. Bonnie was hovering nearby waiting for its exit because when it was done they were taking it to Jake. It was a thank-you pie, Mommy said, and she wanted to go see him.

"Can we go now?" Bonnie asked.

"Not until I make sure he's home," Laurel said, and sent a quick text. Are you home? We have something for you.

The answer came quickly. Yes.

Laurel sighed. Now she was committed. She thought about putting her hair up but wanted to get the delivery over with, so she pulled it back into a ponytail and grabbed their coats.

"Let me see your chin first," she said as she was buttoning up Bonnie's coat.

The bandage had come off in her sleep, but the stitches looked fine. Once Bonnie found out why she was making the pie, she'd gotten over her weepy spell, too.

"It doesn't hurt much, Mommy."

Laurel kissed her little girl's cheek. "I am so glad," she said, and then put the hot pie in a carrier and grabbed her purse. "I'm going to put the pie in the pickup first, and then I'll come back and get you. The ground is so muddy, I don't want you getting your feet wet, okay?"

Bonnie nodded, then stood in the doorway holding Laurel's purse as she took the pie to the truck. A few moments later, she was back for Bonnie. They locked the door, then Laurel swept her into her arms and carried her to the truck to begin the short journey up the road.

Bonnie was full of chatter, and Laurel just let her talk and kept her gaze on the road. She was slowing down to take the turn into the driveway when another vehicle came over the hill. She waited with her turn signal on and glanced at the driver as he passed, but without recognition, then turned off the blacktop and headed for Jake's house.

Jake was standing at the window when he saw them coming, and then he saw the other car coming over the hill. He didn't recognize the vehicle and was too far away to see the driver, and then let it go, focusing on the arrival of his company, unaware Truman Slade's foray into his life had just begun.

Jake walked onto the porch, then jogged down to the truck and opened the door for Laurel to get out. As soon as he helped her down from the truck, she leaned back inside to get the pie carrier while Bonnie walked across the seat and straight into Jake's arms.

"Good morning to the both of you," Jake said. "Let's get inside out of the cold."

He started to put Bonnie down and then felt her grip tighten on the back of his neck and looked into her eyes. The yearning for more was there, and then she pled her case.

"So my shoes don't get muddy, Mommy said."

"And a good idea it is," he agreed, and carried her to the porch before he put her down, and then followed them into the house.

"We brought a thank-you pie," Bonnie said.

"That's great," Jake said, but his gaze was locked on the length of Laurel's hair and thinking what it would be like to wrap his hands in it when they made love. Then she turned too quick and caught him staring, and he blurted out anything but what he was thinking. "I just noticed the length of your hair. Been growing it long?" He stifled a groan and stuffed his hands in his pants, hoping that didn't sound as stupid as he felt.

"I've never worn it short," she said.

"Wow," Jake said, nodding and smiling. "That's amazing. Well now, let me take a look at that thank-you pie. It's my favorite kind," he said, and winked at Bonnie as he moved toward the counter.

"It's apricot," Laurel said.

"Mmmmm, the perfect dessert to go with lunch. I made chili and was going to make some cornbread to go with it, but I can't find Mom's recipes. Dad used them from time to time, and I don't know what he did with them."

Laurel hesitated and then took off her coat and draped it on the back of a kitchen stool. "I can show you," she said.

"Only if you guys will stay and have lunch with me," Jake added.

"Yay!" Bonnie cried. "I love chili and cornbread."

Laurel sighed. She was outnumbered and arguing would be rude. "So I see the bowl. Where's the cornmeal?"

Within minutes they had cornbread in the oven, and Bonnie was sitting on Jake's knee showing him the stitches in her chin. Then he took her hand and lifted it to his head.

"Put your fingers right here," he said. "Now what do you feel?"

He could feel her little fingers tracing the ridges of scars and knew when her eyebrows knitted that she was confused.

"What are those?" she asked.

"They're scars. I had stitches too once, but they're gone, and my head is all healed."

"Can I see?" she asked.

"Bonnie, really—" Laurel began.

"No, it's all right. I introduced the subject," Jake said, and then lowered his head.

Laurel's heart began to pound as she watched her daughter part his hair and trace the scars. There were so many she was surprised she hadn't noticed them before, but then realized his hair was long enough to hide most of them. She imagined him wounded and bloody—like Adam had been bloody, except Adam had wanted to die and Jake had obviously fought hard to live. She frowned and looked away, uncertain how she felt.

And then the timer went off.

"Cornbread's done!" Jake said, and lifted Bonnie off his knee and went to the stove.

"What can I do?" Laurel asked.

"Butter's in the refrigerator. Would you put it on the table, please?"

Happy to have something to do, she did as he asked, and then found the drawer with cutlery and got place settings for three. Within minutes they were all seated at the table with a bowl of chili and a piece of cornbread on each of their plates.

"The chili might be a little bit hot, so test it before you take a big bite. And I don't mean hot with spices, hot from the fire. I know it's not a manly thing to admit, but I'm not a fan of spicy food."

And with that admission, the meal progressed.

Laurel found herself comparing Jake to Adam and Adam to Jake while they ate. It took her quite a while to admit they were nothing alike, and she should have nothing to fear. But that was easier said than done. She didn't mind being neighborly, and she guessed it was okay for Bonnie to visit now and then, but that's where it ended. She didn't want the responsibility of loving anyone ever again.

Jake could tell Laurel was weighing the pros and cons of being a friend. He understood her reluctance. He felt the same way. What he'd imagined his life would be like and what he was now capable of doing were two different things.

When Bonnie stopped chattering to take another bite, he ventured a quick question. "So, you clean houses for extra money?"

Laurel frowned. "Not extra money. For a living. Life insurance isn't worth a plug nickel when you take yourself out."

Jake refused to let her go down that angry road again. "I would guess that being self-employed works for you since you want to be home by the time Bonnie gets out of school?"

Laurel looked a little taken aback and then nodded. "Yes, it actually is a plus. I make my extra money selling craft items online, mostly crocheted things, when I have the time to make them, that is. It's been a while since I started anything new."

"Good for you," Jake said. "I'm going to have to come to terms with a job as well, but thought I'd get settled in a little better before I start."

"Do you know what you want to do?" Laurel asked.

"I used to think about law enforcement. Not sure that's the thing for me now since I'm a little gun-shy. I guess it's all still up in the air."

He got up to refill their coffee cups and then added another ice cube to Bonnie's glass of water. She smiled when it clinked against the side of the glass and then had to take a quick sip.

"Whoa Nellie, that's good and cold, just like I like it," she said.

Jake blinked, and when he laughed out loud, Laurel shivered. He was a very compelling man.

"That's straight out of my father's mouth," Jake said.

Laurel grinned.

Bonnie giggled, happy that everyone else was happy, too. "I'm ready for thank-you pie," she said.

Jake grinned. "So am I. Want ice cream on yours?"

Unsure of the rules of eating in a strange home, Bonnie looked at her mother. "Mommy, do I want ice cream on my pie?"

Laurel laughed. "Probably."

"I'll put a little bit on it, just in case," Jake said.

Laurel cleared the table of their dirty bowls and plates while Jake cut the pie. She wouldn't let herself think of how comfortable it was to share a meal with him. It was a meal and nothing more. And so they ate and laughed some more, and when the dishes were done, they went home.

Jake stood in the doorway and waved until they were

gone and then shut the door and tried not to think of how quiet and empty the house seemed without them in it.

———∼∼∼———

Truman Slade had been watching Jake's house from the row of trees above the creek, and when he saw the Payne woman leaving, he took off running, trying to get back to his truck before that woman and her kid got home. He'd parked on the other side of the creek, behind their house, and snuck up to where Jake Lorde lived to get the lay of the land, so to speak. If he was going to make life miserable for Lorde, he needed to find his weak spot, and it would appear that was the woman and the girl.

The ground was soft from the recent rain, so he'd been forced to walk in the creek to keep from leaving footprints. Running back, not only his feet were wet, but his pants were pretty much soaked from all the splashing. His side was hurting, his breath coming in short, painful gasps. He was so out of shape it was pitiful.

Finally, he saw the fork in the creek that would take him to where he'd parked and lengthened his stride. Even as he left the creek and began climbing up the creek bank, he could hear Laurel Payne's truck coming to a stop at the trailer. He grabbed for a tree root to steady himself, and the root came away in his hands. He fell all the way down the bank and into the water, making an even bigger splash.

Cursing beneath his breath, he climbed back out and made a run at the bank, attacking it with both momentum and an increasing panic. He didn't want to be caught on the premises before he even got started.

He slipped and cursed again, then began grabbing at

bushes, roots, and saplings, anything he could hold to pull himself up, until finally, he was out of the creek and on the other side. He quickly disappeared within the trees and breathed a sigh of relief only after he was back on the blacktop and taking the long way home.

He reached down to turn on the heater and then remembered it didn't work. So he cursed again at the futility that was his life and drove faster, anxious to get out of the wet clothes and be warm again.

Chapter 6

JAKE WOKE UP THE NEXT MORNING THINKING OF Laurel and Bonnie. He wondered if she was going to school and if she was still suffering much pain, and on impulse, sent Laurel a quick text. How is your patient today? Is she still hurting?

The text back was quick and brief and did not impart the surprise Laurel had when she'd seen his pop up. She's better. I think afraid to go back to school because that's where she got hurt, but she'll be fine once she's there. Thanks so much for asking about her. Gotta go. Bus is coming.

And sure enough, within five minutes, the big yellow bus drove past his house, so he started his day, but Bonnie Payne's fear and sadness stayed with him.

That night as he was going through email, a couple more from the old unit emailed him the same news about DeSosa, which aggravated the emotional wound again. One mentioned DeSosa was not only getting a Purple Heart posthumously, but also a medal for valor for when he'd saved the lives of Jake and two others that day.

Jake shoved the chair back and strode angrily to his room, dug his duffel bag out of the closet, and then unzipped an inner pocket and pulled out a flat box. His hands were shaking. He felt like throwing up as he opened the box with his Purple Heart and then angrily tossed it on the bed. "I don't need a damn medal for staying alive. DeSosa earned his and this one, too," he muttered, and then tossed the bag back in the closet and walked out of the room, leaving the medal on the bed.

He worked outside all day, doing more repairs, and also hauled up another couple of deadfalls to saw up for firewood later, unaware Truman Slade watched everything he was doing.

That evening he was replacing a portion of the floor in one of the granaries when he heard Bonnie calling his name. "I'm in here!" he yelled, and then jumped out of the grain bin as she came running inside carrying a small sack.

In usual Bonnie fashion, she began talking the moment she saw him. "Mommy said I could bring this to you, but she said I have to come right back home. I can spell 'cherry' because it's my favorite pie, and Lavonne laid a green egg today."

Jake stifled a grin as he sat down on the granary step, and when she arrived, she promptly crawled up in his lap and handed him the sack. "Before I look in the sack, I want to hear you spell 'cherry.'"

Her eyes widened, excited that she was going to perform, and rattled it off.

"That's great. You are a good student. Your mommy must be very proud of you."

Bonnie nodded, making her windblown curls bounce. "Look in the sack," she said. "You'll love it. It's my favorite candy ever."

He peeked in and saw a handful of faintly grubby gummy bears. He'd purposefully eaten dirt when he was a kid just to see what it tasted like, and he'd swallowed a goodly portion of a desert on the other side of the world, so a little more dirt on candy would not hurt him.

"Since they are your favorite, I want you to pick one out for me."

"Okay," she said, and dug through the candy, then pulled out a green one. "This one is sour apple. It's not my favorite, but I think it will be yours."

He opened his mouth, and she put it on his tongue. He made a big face because it was sour just to hear her giggle, then chewed it up. "Ummm, you were right. This is going to be my favorite flavor of gummy bear ever. Now you eat one."

"No. These are for you. I have some in my pocket for me," she said, and pulled one slightly fuzzy gummy bear out of her pocket. "Just a little bit of tissue on it," she said, and licked off the fuzz, then popped it in her mouth.

Jake laughed out loud and gave her a quick hug. "How's the chin?" he asked.

She tilted her head back so he could see.

"Everything okay? Doesn't hurt too much anymore?"

"No, it doesn't hurt, but I have bad dreams."

He frowned. "Why?"

She shrugged.

"Is everything okay? Is someone bothering you at school? Is your mommy okay?"

She nodded.

"What is it that makes your dreams bad?" he asked.

She cupped her hand against his ear and then whispered, afraid to say it too loud. "I can't remember what Daddy looked like anymore, and I think he's mad at me. I hide in my dreams because I don't want him to know."

What she said broke his heart. "Oh, honey, your daddy will never be mad at you. He can't be. It's a rule that he won't ever be mad, okay?"

"A rule? Really?"

"Really, now thank you for the candy, and you better head home before it starts getting dark."

"Okay," she said, and slid out of his lap.

He walked her to the end of the doorway, watching until she disappeared into the trees, then reached into his hip pocket for his phone and called Laurel.

When she answered, she sounded breathless, and he closed his eyes against the fantasies that evoked. "Hello?"

"Hey, it's me, Jake. Just wanted you to know Bonnie is on her way home. Thank you for letting her bring me the candy."

Laurel breathed an easy sigh. When she'd seen who was calling, she'd thought something had happened to Bonnie.

"You're welcome. I hope she's not a bother, but when she gets a notion, she can be very insistent."

"She's not a bother at all." He hesitated, then knew he couldn't keep this to himself. "Hey, I feel like I need to tell you something she said, but I don't want you to think I'm intruding."

Laurel's pulse kicked. "What did she say?"

"I was asking her if her chin still bothered her, and she said no, and then pretty much out of the blue she said she was having bad dreams. Do you know about this?"

"No," Laurel said, and sat down in the nearest chair before her knees went out from under her. "Did she say why?"

"She can't remember what her daddy looks like anymore, and she's afraid he's mad at her. She says she hides from him in her dreams so he won't find her."

"Oh my God," Laurel whispered, and then choked back a sob. "No, I didn't know this."

Jake sighed. "I know about being scared to go to sleep. I just couldn't let this slide without telling you. I also need to tell you that I said it was a rule that daddies could never be mad at their children. Just so you know when she pops up with that statement and you wonder where it came from."

Laurel couldn't see the floor for the tears in her eyes. "Thank you for that, and for the call, and for…for…for being you."

He heard her disconnect, put the phone back in his pocket, swallowed past the lump in his throat, and stared across the pasture for a while, thinking about a little girl and another dead soldier. All of a sudden, he knew what he was going to do with that Purple Heart.

Laurel couldn't come out and ask Bonnie about the bad dreams without giving away the fact that Jake had told her, so she kept waiting for a moment to work it into the conversation. Before she knew it, the week flew by until it was time to take Bonnie back to the doctor to have the stitches removed.

Laurel raced through work. Bonnie's stitches came out today, and she was dreading a repeat of the day they'd put them in. Instead of riding the bus home, Laurel was picking her up at school, and she needed to hurry. Hoping to set a good tone for the visit, she stopped at the pharmacy on Main to pick up a snack for her to eat on the way to the appointment.

LilyAnn Dalton was at the front register checking out a customer when Laurel walked in. "Afternoon, Laurel!" LilyAnn said.

Laurel waved and went straight to the candy aisle, chose a small bag of gummy bears, then grabbed a soft drink from the cooler on her way to check out. The other customer was gone, and LilyAnn was waiting when Laurel set her purchases on the counter.

"Will that be all?" she asked.

"Yes, thanks," Laurel said, and handed her a five-dollar bill, trying not to think that she was spending that much money on what her mother called junk when money was always so tight. "When's the baby due?" Laurel asked as LilyAnn counted back her change.

LilyAnn rolled her eyes. "Not soon enough," she said. "It's a toss-up every day as to which swells faster, my feet or my ankles."

Laurel nodded. "I remember, but the end result is well worth it, even the first few months of sleepless nights."

LilyAnn grinned. "Have a nice day."

"You too," Laurel added, and left as quickly as she'd arrived.

She was on her way to where she'd parked when someone called out her name. She stopped, then turned and saw Jake hurrying her way with a sack in his hand.

"Hi!" he said. "I'm glad I saw you. I've been carrying this around with me for days, and when I saw you go into the pharmacy, I came running. I haven't been able to quit thinking about what Bonnie told me, and I have something I think might help."

"We weren't been able to have much discussion on the subject. She clams up when she doesn't want to talk, and I didn't push it. I'm actually on the way to school to pick her up, and I'm dreading it. She gets stitches out today, and I bought snacks in hopes it sets a good tone."

"Then my timing is perfect," Jake said, and handed her the sack. "This is for Bonnie."

Laurel pulled a stuffed bear out of the sack, and then when she saw what was pinned on the bear's chest, she gasped. "No, Jake! You can't give away your—"

He stopped her with a look, and then his voice was shaking from emotion and anger. "You don't understand. I'm somewhat fucked for life because of PTSD and the inability to have one good night's sleep anymore. They gave this to me for living, and the man who saved my life is dead now. They shouldn't give out medals for staying alive. Stuff like this belongs to the ones who didn't come home. It's just how I feel. Now Bonnie needs to feel safe, and this might help. Just tell her that his name is Brave Bear and that he got his medal because in Toyland he did some very brave things, and now that he's come to live with her, he will keep her from being afraid."

Laurel was speechless. Her emotions were in free fall, and she wanted to throw her arms around his neck because she felt his torment and sorrow as surely as if it had been in her. And the thoughtfulness of what he'd just done was beyond anything she would ever have expected.

She clutched the bear to her chest. "Thank you, Jake. Thank you so much. This is amazing."

He shrugged. "Hey, I remember being scared and I was a grown man. It's tough to be little and have to go through the hard stuff. You've both had your share."

He felt emotion welling and didn't want to cry. Tears came so damn easy these days, so he bolted. "I'll see you around," he said, and walked away.

Laurel saw the slight limp in his walk and the way he held himself stiff and upright, like he was waiting for another blow, and it hurt her heart to know he was sad like Adam. It was also scary.

Adam's suicide had come out of nowhere. She'd been oblivious to the signs until after he was gone, and now she saw signs everywhere. Jake Lorde was a good man, but he was damaged goods, and in her experience, that made caring about him dangerous.

She was still shaking as she glanced at the time and then made a run for the truck. She set Brave Bear beside her as she drove toward school and glanced down once at the stuffed toy and grimaced. "I could have used a brave bear a time or two in my life," she muttered, and then drove into the school parking area and parked.

She got out at a jog and ran to where other parents were waiting, and didn't have to wait long before the doors opened and teachers emerged with their classes. One group went toward the buses while another group moved to a different location to be picked up by parents, and she saw Bonnie in the crowd.

Good. She remembered to give the teacher my note.

Laurel waved.

Bonnie broke into a big grin and tugged her teacher's sleeve, then pointed. The teacher saw Laurel and waved as she let Bonnie go. Moments later, Bonnie hugged her mother and started talking. "Walk and talk," Laurel said, as she took Bonnie by the hand and led her to the truck, then lifted her into the seat.

The moment Bonnie saw the bear, she stopped talking. The reaction surprised Laurel. She thought Bonnie would be excited.

Bonnie pointed. "Mommy, who's that for?"

"He's for you. Jake gave him to you. He said his name is Brave Bear. He said the bear did some very brave things in Toyland, and so they gave him a medal. That means Brave Bear is a hero. Jake said to tell you that anytime you feel afraid or sad to hold Brave Bear close because his job is to help you feel safe."

Bonnie picked the bear up and hugged him in such a solemn moment Laurel didn't know how to react. She slid behind the wheel and closed the door, then leaned over and buckled up Bonnie and her bear.

"What do you think?" Laurel asked.

Bonnie's eyes were wide, her voice almost shaking. "Jake doesn't want me to be afraid anymore," she said.

Laurel reached out and brushed flyaway curls from Bonnie's forehead. "I don't want you to be afraid either, my sweet girl. You know that, right?"

Bonnie nodded.

"And you will talk to me anytime you are afraid, okay?"

Bonnie hesitated and then held the bear against her chest as she looked at her mother. "Sometimes I have bad dreams."

Laurel's heart was breaking, but she couldn't let on that she already knew that and knew why. "Sometimes I do too," Laurel said. "What do you dream about?"

Bonnie shrugged, hugged the bear, and then blurted it out. "I dream about Daddy."

"Well, so do I," Laurel said. "And my dreams aren't happy either."

Bonnie's surprise came out in her voice. "Really, Mama? You have bad dreams about Daddy, too?"

Laurel nodded. "What makes your dreams bad?"

Bonnie lowered her voice. "I can't remember what he looked like. Do you think that will make him mad?"

Laurel sighed. "No, he would never be mad. Do you want me to find a picture of him to hang in your room?"

"Maybe," Bonnie said.

"Well, whatever you decide…. Don't worry about it, okay? You know there's a rule that daddies can't be mad at their children, right?"

Bonnie smiled. "That's what Jake said."

"Well, he's right, and even though he's not a father, he would still know all the rules because he's a guy."

Bonnie nodded, then laid the bear in her lap and began tracing the shape of the medal with her fingertip. "What does this medal mean, Mama?"

"It's called a Purple Heart. They give it to soldiers who are wounded or who died during a war. It stands for bravery."

"I love Brave Bear," Bonnie said. "Can I take him inside the doctor's office when they take out my *siches*?"

"Stitches, and yes, I think that's a great idea."

"I won't be afraid then," Bonnie said.

Laurel squeezed Bonnie's little hand. "Honey, it's okay to be afraid of something, but facing it anyway because you have to…that's what it means to be brave."

Bonnie hugged the bear again.

Laurel handed her the little bag of gummy bears and opened the soft drink and put it in a cup holder in the console between them. "Let's go get this over with, what do you say?" Laurel asked.

Bonnie popped a gummy into her mouth and then leaned back in the seat with Brave Bear riding shotgun beside her. "Yeah. Over with."

Laurel took a big, deep breath and then exhaled slowly. God, how she loved this girl.

An hour later, they were in an examining room in the doctor's office, waiting for him to come in. Bonnie was sitting on the exam table with Brave Bear in her lap. She hadn't uttered a word in almost five minutes, which was so not Bonnie. Laurel couldn't help but worry that a meltdown was imminent. Then the door opened, and Dr. Moses, Bonnie's regular pediatrician, came in.

"Good afternoon!" he said, dropped Bonnie's file onto the table beside her, then plopped down on his rolling stool and wheeled it up to the exam table. He eyed the stuffed bear, and when he realized that Purple Heart was real, he spun toward Laurel, still pointing at the bear. "Really?"

She nodded. "She's been having a hard time and a friend gave it to her."

Dr. Moses turned back to Bonnie. "I'm sorry stuff's been rough lately. I understand you're here to have some stitches removed?"

Bonnie sighed. "It really hurt when the doctor hemmed my chin. Is it gonna hurt like that when you take them out?"

Dr. Moses grinned. "Hemmed it up, did he?"

She nodded.

"So let's take a look first, okay?"

She tilted her head back without hesitation, but Laurel saw her take a firmer grip on the bear. The door opened behind Laurel, and the doctor's nurse came in carrying a small tray with what he would need to do the job.

"Oh, these look great!" Dr. Moses said. "They shouldn't hurt much at all. Are you ready?"

Bonnie held Brave Bear tight. A tear rolled down her cheek, but she didn't budge. "I will sit very still."

"I want you to lie down so your neck won't get tired, okay?"

She nodded and didn't argue when the nurse laid her back.

"You're doing great, sweetheart," Laurel said.

"Thank you, Mommy."

"So, here we go," Dr. Moses said, and, without wasted motion, swiftly clipped the first stitch and pulled it out. Then another, and another, and Bonnie hadn't moved or let out a peep.

Laurel was amazed and grateful all at the same time.

Dr. Moses snipped another, removed the stitch, and laid it on the tray his nurse was holding. "One more and we're done," he said, and before Bonnie could blink, it was gone. "The end!" He laid the surgical scissors on the tray and then wiped the area with an alcohol swab to clean it.

"That's it," Dr. Moses said. He helped Bonnie sit up, then leaned down and very ceremoniously shook the bear's paw. "Good job, sir! She was very brave."

Bonnie ran her finger along the scar and then looked at Laurel. "It feels just like the ones on Jake's head!"

Dr. Moses looked over at Laurel. "Jake Lorde?"

She nodded.

The doctor glanced at the Purple Heart again. "Okay then," he said softly, clearing his throat.

"Can we go now?" Bonnie asked.

"Yes, you may," Dr. Moses said, and helped her

down from the exam table. "You and Brave Bear take
it easy, okay?"

Bonnie nodded.

Laurel took Bonnie by the hand. "Is the nurse
bringing the charge sheet here, or will it be up front
at the desk?"

"No charge," Dr. Moses said.

"Really?" Laurel asked.

"Yeah, really," he echoed. "If the hospital puts 'em
in, taking them out is on the house."

"That's good news for today," Laurel said, leading
Bonnie out the door and then out of the office.

The doctor's nurse arched an eyebrow. "You are such
a softie," she said.

Dr. Moses shrugged. "Not really," he said.

"Yeah, really," she said, echoing his words only
moments earlier.

Dr. Moses pretended to frown and pointed toward the
door. "Go find something to sterilize," he muttered.

He could hear her giggling all the way down the hall.

When Laurel and Bonnie went one way after school,
Jake went another, all the way down Main Street to
The Curl Up and Dye. He needed a haircut, but hadn't
bargained on a roomful of women in various stages of
having their hair colored, curled, and cut. The Curl Up
and Dye definitely lived up to its name, and to his relief,
he wasn't the only man waiting for a haircut.

Peanut Butterman was kicked back in a chair, waiting
a turn. Like Jake, he was a walk-in, which meant you
waited until they could work you into their schedule,

and since Jake didn't have anything else to do, he didn't mind the wait.

Back in the work area the Conklin twins, Vera and Vesta, had seen him come in. Although neither of them was married, they both had high admiration for the opposite sex.

Vera was into body shapes and couldn't help admiring Jake's long legs and wide shoulders, while Vesta was more into looks and kept cutting glances at Jake's handsome face.

Vesta poked her sister's arm and arched an eyebrow.

"I saw him," Vera whispered. "Looks a little bit like that actor, Chandler Tate."

Vesta rolled her eyes. "Channing Tatum, you goof, and yes, he does, only bigger."

"Yes, bigger and better," Vera added, and then grabbed the curling iron and started putting curls into her client's hair with speedy precision.

Vesta was closer to done and was the first to finish. "The next one's mine," she crowed, thinking it was Jake.

"And that would be Peanut Butterman," Vera stated.

"Well then," Vesta muttered, and walked her client to the front so she could pay. She kept eyeing Jake as she waited for her client to decide which credit card she was going to max out and then finished the transaction. "Alrighty then. You're up next, Peanut."

Peanut followed her, eyeing Ruby as he took a seat, and then leaned back in the shampoo chair so Vesta could wash his hair. Vesta was scrubbing away when Peanut let out a big sigh and then closed his eyes. "Dang, Vesta, that feels so good I could let you do that all day long."

Everyone turned to see what wonderful thing Vesta Conklin was doing.

Vesta's eyes widened as a pink flush rolled up her neck, but she was grinning from ear to ear. "Well, I do what I can," she drawled, and deepened the intensity of her scrubbing.

When Peanut groaned again, all the women grinned.

Jake was sitting up front smiling, reminding himself not to open his mouth once they started on him, and as fate would have it, the next stylist free turned out to be Ruby.

Ruby collected her money, then glanced at Jake as her client left. "Hello, Jake. Did you come in for a haircut?"

"Yes, ma'am," he said, then stood up and followed her back.

Ruby seated him in a shampoo chair next to Peanut, put a towel under his neck, and turned on the water to get it at a good temperature. "Are you settling in okay?" Ruby asked.

"Yes, all things considered, I'm doing pretty good," Jake said.

"That's good to hear," she said, and began washing his hair, and then within seconds felt so many scars beneath her fingertips that it scared her. She stopped immediately. "Uh...I... Did I hurt you?"

It took Jake a couple of seconds to figure out what she meant. "Oh no, those scars are old. Don't worry."

"Right," Ruby said, and finished the shampoo and rinse, then moved him to her chair for the haircut. "So what are we doing here?"

"Same haircut only shorter...at least an inch shorter."

"Got it," Ruby said, and then ran her fingers through

his hair in several different directions to see how it had been cut before she picked up her scissors.

She combed off a section, then began cutting, and the more she cut, the more rattled she became. The scars were everywhere, some thicker than others, some jagged, some shaped like half-moons. She could only wonder what other scars he had beneath his clothing. It was a shocking and visible reminder of an ongoing war so far away.

The twins knew something was wrong because Ruby was never this quiet. Even Vesta, who'd been halfheartedly flirting with Peanut, had the good sense to stop talking.

Then Peanut went up front to pay, and when the doorbell jingled as he left, Ruby lost her composure. Quiet tears rolled with every snip of her scissors, but Jake didn't know it. "Sweet lord," she finally muttered, and laid down her scissors. "Excuse me just a moment, Jake. I need to blow my nose."

He thought nothing of it until he glanced up and saw the tears. "Hey, Ruby, those aren't about me, are they?"

She waved a hand and disappeared into the back room.

"Well, hell," Jake muttered, and glanced at the other women. "Sorry I freaked everyone out here. It's just that I've lived with them long enough that I don't think much about them anymore."

Ruby came back wiping her eyes and blowing her nose, her voice rising with every step. "Well, I'm thinking about them for you, okay? What happened, Jake? Who did this to you and how?"

Jake grimaced. "Not a who, it was a what…an IED…a bomb buried on the road. Our transport ran over it. All but three of us died. Some guys in the transport behind us pulled us out before we got burned. It was bad, and now it's over."

Ruby picked up her scissors and began again with more purpose. She was over the shock and had moved on to furious. "I am sorry. I am so sorry," she said, *snip, snip, snip*. "If women were running the countries of the world, this stuff wouldn't be happening." *Snip, snip, snip*.

Jake grinned. "I have no doubt that you are right. If you want to run for president, you have my vote."

"We'd vote for you, too," the twins said.

Mabel Jean, the manicurist, came in the back door with an empty deposit bag. "Receipt is in the bag," she said, and laid it on Ruby's station, then gave Jake a big smile. "Hi, Jake. Good to see you back."

Jake winked. "Thank you, Mabel Jean."

Ruby muttered and huffed and snipped and snipped until she was done. She handed him a mirror and turned him around so he could see the back. "Looks great, Ruby. I can't see even a hint of one scar."

Ruby exhaled on a big sigh. "Good, because that was certainly my intent."

Jake stood up and hugged her. "I'm sorry I upset you."

Ruby poked a finger against his chest. "You didn't cause it. I cried because you suffered it. There is a big difference. And don't start pulling out money because this is on the house. I'll take your money next time, when you don't have to sit and listen to me bawling. Okay?"

"Okay," he said, and waved at the twins and Mabel Jean as he left.

As soon as he was gone, Ruby went up front and locked the door, then turned the *Open* sign to *Closed*.

"I'm calling it a day," Ruby said, and began gathering up wet towels and sweeping up the hair around her station. "I couldn't listen to another woman sit in my chair and complain about the sale on shoes that she missed or the fact that someone in Ladies Aide told a lie about her. Not after witnessing the suffering Jake Lorde must have endured to be with us today."

The twins gave her a hug. "Go home. We'll finish cleaning and lock up."

Ruby sighed. "Thank you. I believe I will. My heart hurts tonight even more than it did when I found out my no-good husband was cheating on me."

She grabbed her purse and went out the back door without looking back.

Chapter 7

A FOX PAUSED NEAR THE BACK PORCH OF TRUMAN SLADE'S rental house, sniffing around the trash barrel, then caught the scent of a rabbit on the air and trotted past it without investigating.

Truman had gone to bed hours ago for lack of anything better to do and was sound asleep beneath the covers, oblivious to the activity going on in the attic. It went on for some time until the scratching and scurrying about became loud enough in the ceiling above his bed that it woke him. He rolled over on his back, naked as the day he was born, then sat up and listened, trying to figure out why he was awake.

When the scratching sounded again, he groaned. "Damn squirrels! Get the hell out of my attic!" he yelled, then got out of bed, picked up one of his tennis shoes, and threw it at the ceiling. It hit with a solid thump and then dropped back to the floor with another thump.

Silence!

Truman listened until all was quiet again, then he crawled back into bed, punched his pillow a couple of times, turned it to the cool side, and stretched out. He was almost asleep when the scratching resumed, and Truman took it as a personal affront.

"Well, son of a bitch," he yelled, and flew out of bed in a rage. He stomped through the house on his way to the kitchen to get the broom, turning on lights as he went. He grabbed the broom and stomped back through the house, poking the ceiling with the broom handle as he went. When he got to his room, he leaped up onto his bed and began thrusting the broom at the ceiling like a knight doing battle with a sword.

Thump went the broom handle against the Sheetrock—*thump, thump, thump,* over and over. *Bam* went the headboard against the wall as he used the bed to catapult him higher. *Bam, bam, bam,* bouncing the headboard against the wall as he came down.

After several minutes of that, he paused to listen and thought he could hear the hasty exit of tiny feet, so he repeated the move one last time to make sure whatever it was didn't stop running. *Thump, thump, thump.*

Bam, bam...crack and *boom!*

All of a sudden, Truman was flat on his back. The bed frame was broken and the bed was on the floor. Truman still held the broom in an upward thrust but in a less-than-heroic state. Being naked had its drawbacks and this was one of them. Because of a squirrel, he had broken his damn bed. He laid the broom on the floor, pulled the jumble of covers back over his shoulders, and rolled over.

Beds were overrated anyway. He'd slept on the floor half his life, and he'd do it again. If he'd turned the lights on in the bedroom, he would have seen what he'd done to the ceiling. More than once the broom handle had pierced the Sheetrock, and when it had, he'd yanked downward with some force to pull it free. Now there were nearly a dozen holes in the Sheetrock and a notice-able sag in the ceiling.

And Truman was, once again, sound asleep. He

was dreaming about squirrel hunting with his brother, Hoover, who was in the state penitentiary doing twelve to twenty for armed robbery.

In the dream, Hoover had just taken aim at a big, fat squirrel. Truman was already imagining how good squirrel and dumplings would taste when Hoover shot. The crack of the rifle was loud, but in the dream the squirrel hadn't moved.

He punched at his brother's shoulder.

What the hell, Hoover? Did you miss?

Then he heard the crack again, only Hoover wasn't holding his rifle, and they were no longer at the creek. He thought he heard Hoover yell, *run, Truman, run,* then the ceiling above his head fell in.

When a large portion of the Sheetrock landed on top of him, along with what had passed as the squirrel's nest, Truman screamed. All the while he was trying to get out from under the debris, he could hear the squirrel's angry chatter for having been displaced. Just as he pushed the Sheetrock aside, the squirrel that had been on top of it dropped onto his bare belly, then spun out so fast trying to get away that Truman wound up with a dozen angry scratches in his skin.

He got up cursing. His belly was burning, his bed was dirty, not that it had been all that clean before, but there was now that huge hole in the ceiling. His landlord was gonna have himself a fit, and then most likely kick him out, which meant Truman just needed to keep his mouth shut and his rent paid up, and the landlord might never know.

In the meantime, Truman put on some pants and then tossed the Sheetrock on the back porch, dragged his mattress into the empty bedroom across the hall, then shook out the sheets and remade the bed. He was looking for something to doctor the wounds on his belly when he heard the scratch of the squirrel's claws on the floor in the hall.

"You just wait until I get me some ammunition for my gun," he yelled. "I'll blast your furry ass to kingdom come."

The squirrel didn't seem worried, and Truman was hurting too much to give chase. Like it or not, until he could get to town to get a live trap, it appeared he was going to have to put up with a roommate.

~~~

Ruby Dye was at the lumber and hardware store shopping in the display aisle for towel rods. The one in the bathroom at The Curl Up and Dye was loose and kept falling to the floor. She was debating with herself between a wooden rod and a metal one when she realized the two men in the next aisle over were talking about Jake Lorde. She heard the words "payback," "make him sorry," and "get rid of him for good" and she gasped. Those sounded like threats against his life!

Desperate to find out who was talking, she hurried down the aisle and then peeked around the end cap to see who was on the other side. She recognized Truman Slade immediately and remembered years earlier it was Jake's testimony that had sent him to prison, but she didn't know the other man. She pretended to be looking for something on the bottom shelf and, instead, snapped a picture of the two men with her phone.

They walked away, unaware they'd been overhead

and photographed, while Ruby hightailed it back around the aisle, grabbed the wooden towel rod, and made a run for the front to check out.

She got to her car and then didn't immediately get in. She didn't know what to do. She guessed the police wouldn't do anything because all she did was overhear a threat. Unless something actually happened to Jake, the police couldn't do a thing. She was trying to decide the best way to handle this when Peanut Butterman drove up beside her and parked.

As she watched him get out, she thought to herself what a good-looking man he was. Reminded her a little bit of a young Clint Eastwood.

Then he saw her and smiled. "Well hello, Miss Ruby. How are you this fine day? I must say I like that hair shade you're sporting. Are those turquoise highlights in your pretty auburn hair?"

For a moment, Ruby forgot what she was bothered about and unconsciously touched her hair to make sure everything was in place. "Yes, they're highlights. They aren't permanent, you understand, but I feel it's my duty to advertise my skills in every way I can, and the young girls these days are all about wearing crayon colors in their hair."

Peanut nodded while eyeing her trim figure and earnest face. He liked Ruby Dye, and he couldn't say that about a whole lot of other people.

"Well, I better let you be on your way," he said.

Then she remembered her dilemma. "Peanut, may I ask you something?"

"Sure thing. Ask away."

"I was inside the store just now when I overheard two

men talking about Jake Lorde. One was making some threatening comments that sounded like Jake's life could be in danger. I snuck around and snapped a picture of them. I recognized Truman Slade, but don't know the other man. How do I report this? Is there anything I can do?"

Peanut's eyes widened as he tried to picture Ruby Dye sneaking anywhere. She stood out in a crowd no matter where she was.

"May I see the photos?" he asked.

She quickly pulled them up on her phone. "Yes, that's Truman alright. Even if you showed these to the law right now, there's not anything they can do. It's just hearsay until something happens."

"Then what can I do?" Ruby asked.

"I don't want you to do anything, because if people find out what you heard and start talking, it could put you in danger down the road."

Ruby shuddered. She hadn't thought of it in that way.

Peanut patted her arm. "Why don't you send the picture to my phone? I'll talk to Deputy Pittman and see what he says."

He gave Ruby his cell number. She attached the photo, and moments later the picture popped up in a message. Now it was saved to his phone.

"Okay, got it," he said. "Don't worry. I'll make sure the proper people find out about this. Even if they can't do anything about it now, they'll know it happened. If Lon needs to talk to you about it, he'll call you."

Ruby breathed a sigh of relief. "Thank you, Peanut. You have taken a load off my shoulders. Thank you so much."

"You are most welcome," Peanut said, and then opened the car door for her so she could get in.

Ruby drove off with a wave.

Peanut watched until she was gone.

"Yes, she is a fine figure of a woman," he said, and then thought of what she'd told him and got back in the car and headed for the police station instead.

He knew the police chief was in the hospital getting his gall bladder out, and Deputy Lon Pittman was, for the time being, acting chief. It occurred to him that Lon might be out of the office so he called the precinct, confirmed Lon was in, and told the dispatcher to let him know he was on his way.

--- ~~~ ---

Lon was standing in the front office talking to the dispatcher, Avery James, when Peanut walked in. "Hello, Peanut. Give me a second," Lon said, and finished giving Avery needed information, then turned to Peanut. "Avery said you wanted to see me?"

"Yes."

"We can talk in the office." He led the way back. "Have a seat," he said, and dropped into the chief's chair. "So, what's up?"

Peanut related what Ruby had told him, then ended by showing him the picture on his phone.

Lon frowned. "Truman Slade is a blight on Blessings," he muttered. "However, unless he takes action, there isn't anything we can legally do."

Peanut nodded. "That's pretty much what I told Ruby. I also told her not to talk about this to anyone. If Truman got wind of it, I wouldn't put it past him to try and intimidate her just to keep her quiet."

"What I can do is take this report," Lon said. "Also, if

you'll email that picture to me, I'll include it in the report. Then if he does try something, it will be on record."

"What's the email address here?" Peanut asked.

Lon wrote it down and shoved the pad across the desk so Peanut could see it. Peanut emailed the picture while he was sitting there and then dropped his phone back in his pocket.

"So, that's done, and I have an appointment in about fifteen minutes, so I guess I'd better get back to the office. Thank you for hearing me out. I'll let Ruby know."

"I hope this all comes to nothing," Lon said.

Peanut nodded. "So do I. Jake Lorde has been through enough."

~~~

Jake pulled up to the gas pumps at Ralph's on the edge of town and killed the engine. He pulled a credit card out of his wallet, then got out and moved to the pumps. He swiped the card, waited for approval, and then began refueling. While he was standing there, Laurel Payne drove by.

He waved.

She waved back and kept driving.

It made him wonder how the trip to the doctor had gone, and then he frowned. He was letting himself get too involved in someone else's life, and there was no future in it. He already liked Laurel Payne. He'd even spent time letting himself imagine what being in a relationship with her would be like. He already had more than he could handle. He didn't want to fall in love with a woman he couldn't have. And then the pump kicked off, and he hung up the hose and drove away.

He stopped at the mailbox to pick up his mail, and to his dismay, the postman had accidentally left two letters in his box that belonged to Laurel. If they'd just been circulars or some kind of ads, he would have set them aside and given them to her at another time, but damn it, they were probably bills—that needed to be paid on time.

He sighed, backed up the truck, and drove toward her house.

Laurel was unloading her truck when Bonnie came bouncing out of the house. She'd already changed out of her school clothes and fed and watered Lavonne and was looking for something else to do when she glanced up at the mailbox. Only recently had she grown tall enough to reach it and be trusted not to let important mail blow away.

"Mommy, can I go get the mail?"

"*May* I, not *can* I, and yes, you may. Hang on tight to everything, okay?"

"I will!" Bonnie shrieked and off she flew.

Laurel started to tell her to slow down and then stopped and smiled. She watched her running with such abandon. It was how every child should live—with total joy. If she fell, she would get up because that's how she would learn.

"Ah, God, help me do this right," she said, and then saw a pickup coming over the hill and frowned. It was Jake Lorde, and he was slowing down.

She saw him stop and get out, and she started walking toward the mailbox. Bonnie was getting too attached to a man who would be nothing but a friend. She walked faster, wanting to know why he'd come again so soon.

Maybe it had to do with the bear, maybe not, but she wanted to know.

————————

Bonnie broke into a big grin when she saw Jake's truck, and when she saw him stop and get out, she waved. "Hi, Jake! I'm getting the mail!"

He smiled. "Good job, and I brought some more. The mailman accidentally left them in my box. Here, take these to your mommy."

"Okay!" she said, and headed back to the house.

Jake saw Laurel coming, and short of being rude, he had to wait.

"I got the mail," Bonnie said.

"Put it on the table," Laurel said.

"I will, Mama," Bonnie said, and kept going.

Laurel didn't ask Bonnie what Jake said. It didn't matter. It's how Jake answered her that was going to count.

Jake didn't know what was going on, but he didn't like the expression on her face. He suddenly felt like she was a stranger. He stuffed his hands in his pockets and leaned against his truck. When she stopped in front of him, he took a deep breath.

"Postman left some of your mail in my box."

She blinked. "Oh. Well then, thank you."

"No problem," he said.

Now she felt awkward. She'd come at him with attitude, and he'd seen it.

"Bonnie really liked Brave Bear. It made all the difference when Dr. Quick took out her stitches."

"Then he's doing what he was meant to do. Sorry if I startled you."

"No, it was nothing like that. I just—"

"You don't have to explain yourself to me, Laurel. She's your daughter. It is your job to make sure she's safe at all times. I would think less of you if you didn't. I know you're busy, so I'll be on my way."

Laurel felt like she'd just broken a new toy. Whatever trust and relationship they'd been working on was gone, and it was her fault.

"Thank you again. You've been nothing but kind, and I guess I'm a little raw about people thinking I can't take care of myself. You know?"

Jake sighed. He did know. That's pretty much how people had been treating him before he came home. He'd had hopes of this being different, but like the scars in his hair, he could hide them, but they didn't go away.

"It's all good. No problems. Call if you need me," he said, then turned around in her driveway and disappeared over the hill.

Laurel took a deep breath and turned around. Her old truck was still there, waiting to be unloaded. The trailer still needed repairs, and winter was coming.

Bonnie came around the corner of the house carrying Lavonne and waved.

Laurel waved back, ignored the ache in her chest, and started walking.

—∞—

Truman Slade unloaded the piece of Sheetrock he'd bought and carried it into the house. His buddy, Nester Williams, grabbed an armload of two-by-fours and followed him inside.

"Wow, it's a mess in here," Nester said.

"Wait till you see my bedroom," Truman muttered. "Damn squirrel tore it up. It's in the house somewhere. Keeps tearing up my stuff."

"In the house?"

"Yeah. It fell in when the ceiling fell. I can't catch it."

"Maybe you could just leave the door open for a while. It might run itself outside."

Truman shrugged. "I guess."

Nester didn't see any doors opening themselves, but he didn't live here and wasn't going to get involved. He'd offered to help patch up the ceiling, and that's where his helping stopped.

"So, let's get this started. I have a date tonight," Nester said.

Truman frowned. "I haven't had a date in months."

Nester shrugged. That wasn't his problem either. "I'm going to get my tools."

Truman leaned the Sheetrock against a wall in the hall, then went to the utility room and opened the back door. The place needed a little airing out, and if the squirrel left in the process, so much the better.

Chapter 8

LAUREL FELT BAD ALL EVENING ABOUT HOW SHE'D BEHAVED. She didn't know what was wrong with her. One minute she was grateful for Jake's help and compassion, and the next thing she did was treat him like a pariah after all he'd done for them. She was ashamed of herself.

So while Bonnie was taking a bath and getting ready for bed, Laurel mixed up some cookie dough and put it in the refrigerator to cool. She heard Bonnie moving from the bathroom to the bedroom and went to put her to bed. The first thing she saw when she entered was Brave Bear on her pillow. He was obviously here to stay.

"Did you brush your teeth?" Laurel asked.

Bonnie nodded and opened her mouth to show her, as if looking at her teeth would be evidence enough, but she could smell the minty toothpaste.

"Good job, honey. Now hop in bed. Tomorrow is going to be a big day at school. First-graders get to wear their Halloween costumes to school, and then you will have a costume parade through the other classes."

Bonnie giggled. "I'm going to be the best panda bear ever!"

Laurel smiled, thinking about the costume she'd made out of black sweats and a black sock cap. Adding a little face paint to finish the look wouldn't take long in the morning. She wished she could go to school on class party days and be one of the parents who got to help host the party or, like tomorrow, go to watch the parade with the other mothers, but she had to work.

"You'll be great. Now get to sleep, okay?"

"Okay," Bonnie said, and tucked Brave Bear beneath her chin and closed her eyes. "Don't turn out all the lights," she added.

"I won't," Laurel said, leaving the night-light on and closing the door.

She went back to the kitchen and turned on the oven and began getting the cookie pans ready. As soon as the first pan went in, she set the timer, filled the other two sheet pans with cookie dough, set them aside, and began cleaning up the dirty dishes.

By the time the last pan came out of the oven, she had cleaned the kitchen and written checks to pay the bills that had come in the mail. They were a bitter reminder of her earlier faux pas. Hopefully, the cookies would be a sweet recipe for forgiveness.

Finally, the cookies were cooled and packaged to give away, and she was stretched out in bed, too tired to turn over. The lights were out, and she was listening to a faucet drip when she fell asleep.

She woke once and went to check on Bonnie, but she was still asleep. After a quick trip to the bathroom, she went back to bed. The alarm wouldn't go off for another three hours.

The next time she woke up, she could hear Bonnie in the hall. She groaned. The alarm wasn't due to go off for another twenty minutes, but Bonnie was obviously excited about costume day because she was up.

At the last minute, Bonnie insisted her panda bear should have a fat belly, and so Laurel tied an old throw pillow around Bonnie's waist and called it done. Bonnie was so entranced with her look that she kept patting it.

"Mommy, how do I look?" Bonnie asked.

"You look amazing," Laurel said. "Let me get my phone to take a picture." She took a half dozen and then stopped. "That should be enough. We'll send one to Granny and Gramps, okay?"

"Yes!" Bonnie said. "And send one to Jake, too, okay?"

"I'll be sure to show him," Laurel said. *If he'll ever talk to me again.* Then she glanced at the clock. "Okay, kiddo, it's time to head up the road. The bus will be here any minute. Grab your backpack. Your lunch bag is inside it."

"Are you gonna walk with me?"

"Absolutely. I wouldn't make a little panda bear walk to the bus stop alone."

Bonnie giggled, and out the door they went with Laurel carrying the backpack and Bonnie practicing her fat-belly walk. Laurel laughed all the way to the mailbox and then got teary as the bus drove away, thinking of what beautiful moments Adam was missing.

Once back at the trailer, she loaded everything she would need in the truck, then went back for the cookies before she locked up. Just thinking about facing Jake again made her sick to her stomach, but Laurel was anything but a coward. She'd messed up. It was her job to fix it.

***

Jake tried to sleep, but he couldn't relax. Between being blindsided by Laurel and sick at heart about DeSosa, he was too angry to sleep. He'd emptied an entire pot of fresh coffee between 10:00 p.m. and midnight, pulled a pie from the freezer, then opted against eating it and put it back.

He'd paced the halls, then wandered into his dad's bedroom, thinking he might find solace. Instead, it was as empty as his life. The longer he was up, the colder the house became, until he either had to turn the thermostat back up or build a fire. He opted for the fire. It took a little while to carry in the firewood and even longer for the fire to start, giving off heat enough to warm the room, but it was both cheery and comforting.

He locked up, turned off all the lights, threw a quilt and a pillow on the floor in front of the fireplace, and then stretched out. Slowly, the warmth seeped into his body, and his muscles began to relax. He was getting sleepy, so he pulled the afghan off the sofa beside him and covered up. He was watching the flames gorging on a trio of oak logs when he fell asleep, and the next thing he knew it was morning.

His body was stiff as he got off the floor, but by the time he'd folded up the quilt and afghan and tossed the pillow on the sofa, his mobility was better. He went into the kitchen to make coffee and was thinking about breakfast when he heard the school bus go by. It reminded him of Bonnie, which reminded him of her pretty mother, which made his heart hurt all over again.

He was about to scramble some eggs when his phone pinged a text, and when he checked it and saw the picture of Bonnie dressed as a panda bear, he grinned. He was still smiling when he heard a car pull up. He put the eggs back and went to the living room, then was shocked to see Laurel getting out of her truck.

A few moments later, she was at the door. She knocked. He took a deep breath and went to the door, and the moment he opened it, she started talking.

"I made cookies. They are my peace offering and the 'I'm sorry I was an ass' letter I didn't know how to write. All I can say is I'm sorry for how I treated you. I have a chip on my shoulder because I'm a single mother. I'm always afraid someone will think I'm not doing a good job. You just got in the way of my very damaged ego, okay?" She thrust the box forward. "Will you accept my apology?"

Jake felt the knot in his stomach unwinding and smiled in spite of himself. He was impressed that she so quickly acknowledged her mistake and was so willing to apologize. He didn't know any women like that.

He narrowed his eyes, pretending to give her question a lot of consideration, then pointed at the box. "The picture was a good start, so I might. What kind of cookies did you bring?"

"Chocolate walnut."

"Okay then, we're good," he said, and took the box out of her hands. "Breakfast has been served. Do you have time to come in and eat a cookie with me?"

She grimaced. "No, and I wish I did. I have two houses to clean before school is out, so I need to stay on a schedule. Maybe another time?"

"Absolutely," he said.

She hesitated and then extended her hand. "Friends?"

When he grasped her hand, he felt the calluses on her palm. He was thinking about how tough she was, and then she smiled. It was tentative and brief but it touched his heart, and then she was gone. He watched until she disappeared over the hill and then took the box into the kitchen, refilled his coffee, and opened the lid.

The scent of chocolate rose to meet him as he took the first bite, then closed his eyes in appreciation of how good they tasted. If this was how Laurel said *I'm sorry*, she could be mad anytime she wanted.

Truman's night wasn't much better than Jake's. He and Nester had fixed the ceiling. The tape and bed job was drying, but he wasn't going to repaint. The digs weren't high-class enough to worry about all that.

He'd tried to fix his bed frame, but the wood had shattered, and one of the metal pieces on the side was severely bent. So he'd swept the insulation out of the floor, dragged his mattress back into the room, and called it done.

Then he'd set the live trap he'd borrowed from Nester in the kitchen and gone to bed. He was so tired he slept the entire night without waking, and by the time the sun was up, so was Truman.

After a quick trip to the bathroom, he went to check the trap, and then crowed with delight when he saw the beady-eyed critter staring back at him.

"Ha!" he said, slapping his leg. "Caught you, you little bastard. I oughta make stew and dumplings out of you, but I'm not in the mood to cook, so this is your lucky day. I'm taking you with me today when I go see what Jake Lorde is doing. I'm gonna let you go so far away from me that you'll never find your way back, and then see what I can do to ruin his day."

Jake had a half dozen cookies and two cups of coffee under his belt before he finally left the house. Having made peace with Laurel made him feel better about everything. Even though he had more wood he could split and there were still repairs to be done in and around the barn, he wanted to do a little exploring today. Bonnie made the trip from her house to his by using the creek as her highway, and he was curious to see it. Just in case he saw some overgrowth that he wanted to take down, he took the ax. He'd played in that creek as a kid, but there was no telling what it looked like now.

The heavy frost that had been on the grass when he got up was fading, but enough was still there that he could see where small animals had moved through the area, disturbing the crystals on the grass as they'd passed. He saw rabbit tracks. A small dog or a fox had been behind the rabbit, and when he got into some loose dirt, he even saw wild turkey tracks. He smiled as he kept moving toward the creek, completely comfortable with the environment.

As he got closer to the creek, he finally saw a small trail through the grass and guessed it was where Bonnie came and went. Once he reached the top of the creek bank, he stopped to look down and was surprised by how far it was to the water. There must have been a big flood through here in the last five or ten years because he didn't remember it being like this.

When he started down, he grabbed on to some overhanging branches, using them for balance as he moved down the bank. Once he was down, he was surprised by how quiet it was. Sound was muffled by the heavy growth of bushes below and the forest above.

The water wasn't deep, less than two feet, and was running swiftly over the rocks. He paused to test the solidity of the creek bed and almost slipped on a moss-covered rock. Once he regained his footing, he began moving up the creek, looking for signs of animal dens or dangers of which Bonnie wouldn't be aware.

When he saw an unusual grouping of rocks, he stopped for a closer look, only to realize it was something Bonnie had built. When he saw that she'd written her name in red crayon on one of the flat rocks, he smiled. It made him remember trying to build a dam across the creek when he was about ten, and that it had washed out every time it rained. And now, another generation later, a little girl named Bonnie had made a similar pile of rocks and had the foresight to mark it with her name.

On impulse, he hacked a small limb from a branch and then stuck it in between the rocks to let her know another traveler had passed by her marker. He smiled, knowing her imagination would take her places he had never thought to go, and then kept walking.

It took almost ten minutes to get from where he'd come down to the creek to the little path Bonnie took out of it. He could see the indentation in the bank where she'd slipped and slid going up and coming down so many times that she'd almost made a rut. And he could tell which trees and bushes she used for handholds by the lack of leaves where she'd gripped them so tight she'd stripped them off.

On impulse, he exited the creek on the same path,

expecting to see their trailer house when he got to the top, only to realize there was still a considerable amount of tree growth between the creek and their home. He frowned, thinking of how long the land had been neglected to allow that much growth into what had once been pasture, then reminded himself it was none of his business and went back down the same way and began retracing his steps, this time going downstream with the flow.

He was about halfway home when he heard something snap in the woods up on the far side of the creek bank. He stopped to listen, thinking it was most likely a deer moving through the brush. But then it dawned on him everything had gone quiet. Except for the sound of the water flow, he heard nothing.

The hair suddenly rose on the back of his neck, and he gripped the ax handle a little tighter. He knew this feeling. It had been with him many times in the desert while going through bombed out villages looking for snipers.

He was being watched.

"Who's there?" he called out, as he did a slow three-sixty turn where he was standing. "I know you're there. Either speak up, or get the hell off my land!"

He strode into the water and was halfway across with full intent of going up the other embankment when he heard the sudden flurry of footsteps running through the forest, crushing the dead leaves as they went. He stopped, his grip tightening even more in frustration, knowing he'd been right. Someone had been watching him. He thought of Bonnie running up and down the creek in all innocence. Was the watcher just someone out hunting, or was there a more sinister reason for staying obscured?

Jake waited a few seconds more until he was certain there was no one around and then waded out of the water and headed for home.

───※───

Truman Slade's heart was hammering so hard he thought he was going to pass out. He'd been too confident of himself and nearly got caught. When he got back to his truck, he wasted no time leaving. He'd already let the squirrel loose, and his business here was done. He spun out as he accelerated and didn't look back.

───※───

Laurel's last job for the day had canceled because the owner was sick in bed. After rescheduling the cleaning job, she realized she might just make the parade. She knew it was going to be just before the kids went to lunch, so she hurried to the school and parked, then ran through the parking lot and into the office.

Mavis West looked up as Laurel entered the office, breathless and windblown. "Mrs. Payne? Is everything alright?"

Laurel nodded. "Am I too late to see the first-graders costume parade on their way to the lunchroom?"

"Why no, you're not too late at all. They are at the far end of the building lining up. I think there are at least a half dozen other parents to walk along with them. Clip this visitor pass onto your jacket and head that way. Just drop it off here before you leave."

"Oh, thank you," Laurel said, and then clipped the pass to her jacket as she headed toward the far end of the hall.

As soon as she turned the corner to go toward Bonnie's classroom, she saw Mrs. White trying to get them lined up and quiet. Bonnie saw her and began jumping up and down and waving. Laurel waved back, glad she'd made the effort to come. Bonnie looked so happy.

The teacher turned, saw Laurel, and smiled. "You're just in time. We're about to begin our parade."

"Mommy, Mommy," Bonnie cried.

Laurel gave her a quick hug and then put a finger to her lips to indicate *quiet* and tried not to laugh. The black sock cap was still on Bonnie's head, but it had become twisted, and the ears were running perpendicular on her head like a Mohawk haircut, rather than side to side like ears. The face paint was still in pretty good shape except for the black nose, which had obviously been blown a time or two. She could see where little fingers had used a tissue and smudged it.

Bonnie was so hyper she was shaking. "You can hold my hand, Mommy. Lissa's mommy is holding hers."

"Then that's what we'll do," Laurel said quietly. "Let's take a deep breath and remember to be quiet. Remember, panda bears can't talk."

Bonnie's eyes widened and seconds later, she went from giggly girl to fat, little panda bear before Laurel's eyes.

One mother tapped Laurel on the back and whispered near her ear, "Did you make Bonnie's costume? It is adorable."

Laurel turned around. "Yes, I did, and thank you."

"Okay, children! We're walking, we're walking," Mrs. Smith said, and clapped her hands as she began moving them along.

Bonnie was in full panda mode, and Laurel felt like she was walking on air. The cost of the black sweats and sweatshirt—ten dollars. The utter joy of being a part of childhood all over again? Priceless.

Thirty minutes later she parted company with her daughter, promised she'd see her at home, and when Bonnie went to the lunchroom with her class, her lunch bag in her hand, Laurel headed back to the office to turn in her visitor pass.

Mavis saw her coming, got up from her desk, and ran to a side table to get a flyer.

Laurel was still smiling when she walked in and handed Mavis the pass. "Was it a success?" Mavis asked.

"Rousing," Laurel said.

"Here are a couple of flyers for the fall festival this coming Saturday. Didn't want you to forget about it."

"Oh, I won't forget," Laurel said. "I'm manning the kissing booth. Bonnie volunteered me."

Mavis chuckled. "Well, you'll be glad to know that no real kisses are traded. They have several sizes of big red stickers in the shape of lips. Depending on the size of the kiss they buy, you choose which sticker to put on their cheek."

"I know," Laurel said. "Believe me, if it had been real ones, I would have already vacated the job."

"Well, take these anyway," Mavis said. "Maybe you have a friend or neighbor who might like to come. All the money goes into buying things for the elementary school, you know."

"Sure, okay," Laurel said, and took the flyers with her as she exited the office.

She stopped at the Piggly Wiggly for a few grocery items and, to her horror, ran into Adam's sister, Beverly, in the cereal aisle. Her in-laws had refused to believe Adam had been suffering severe depression and to this day still blamed her for his suicide. She wanted to turn tail and run, but she didn't.

"Hello, Beverly," Laurel said.

Beverly Westfall gave Laurel a cold look and then turned her back.

Laurel sighed and tried not to care. It was hard enough losing Adam without losing his family. It was as if they had channeled grief into rage and targeted her because she was still here and Adam wasn't.

She reached for the cereal she wanted, dropped it in her basket, and started to move on when Beverly suddenly grabbed her arm.

"Turn me loose please," Laurel said.

"It's not fair. Adam shouldn't be dead. You should have—"

Laurel flashed on the suicide scene, and then the rage on Beverly's face, and lost it. She yanked away from Beverly's grasp and leaned forward, making sure no one else would hear what she was going to say.

"You are right! It's not fair! Adam shouldn't have put that gun in his mouth and pulled the trigger. It splattered his brains and his blood all over our bed, and the wall, and the floor, and I had to clean that up. Yes, he was depressed, but he wouldn't take the meds the doctor gave him and chose to quit going to his psychiatrist. I'm pretty pissed off myself. He left his daughter

Chapter 9

JAKE WORKED THE REST OF THE DAY AT THE BARN, BUT couldn't quit thinking about the trespasser down at the creek. He wasn't sure what to do about it or whether to even mention it to Laurel. She was already touchy about anyone interfering with her parenting skills, and he didn't want her to think he was judging her for letting Bonnie play there, so he decided to stay watchful but say nothing for now.

By the time he quit to go eat, it was close to suppertime. He'd worked all the way through lunch without giving food a thought. So he decided to call it a day and put away his tools, then walked up to the mailbox to get the mail before going in for the night.

The first thing he saw when he pulled out the mail was the flyer.

"Oh wow. The fall festival. I can't believe they're still doing that," he mumbled, and then glanced through the other mail as he headed back to the house.

Some of his regular mail was finally catching up with him because he noticed the yellow forwarding stickers on the envelopes. Once he was inside, he tossed it all on the kitchen table and then went to wash up. He had food in the freezer and some leftovers in the refrigerator. All he'd had today were Laurel's cookies, and as much as he wanted to just sit down and fill up on them again, he knew he needed more than sugar in his system and opted for scrambled eggs and toast.

It didn't take long to make them, and he ate while reading the flyer again, then tossed it aside. It was silly to think about going to something like that. The place would be crowded. There's no telling what might be going on that could set him off, and he didn't want to embarrass himself. He started to throw it away, and then on impulse just pushed it aside. There were still a few days before the weekend. He'd give it some thought.

Laurel wasn't the only one trying to come to terms with what had happened at the Piggly Wiggly today. Beverly Westfall had been shaken to the core by the torture in Laurel's eyes and the rage in her voice. She'd never once thought about what Laurel had seen or what she'd gone through when Adam died. All she'd thought—all any of their family had thought—was that Adam was gone. He'd come home from a two-year tour of duty without suffering a wound. None of them had grasped the depth of his depression, and when he'd suddenly killed himself, their mother had been the one to assume it was because Laurel had surely hurt him in some way.

Her suppositions had ranged from falling out of love while he was gone to asking him for a divorce. She'd surely broken Adam's heart. None of them had ever wondered if what he'd done had broken hers.

Beverly knew she needed to warn the family about Laurel threatening a lawsuit. None of them had the money to pay a lawyer if they had to go to court, but she needed to tell her mother first. It was up to her how the rest of this played out because she was the one who had started giving Laurel the cold shoulder.

Beverly sat at the kitchen table and made the call, uncertain how she would broach the subject. And then her mother answered, and she started talking.

"Hey, Mom, how's it going?" Beverly asked.

"I'm okay. I canned pumpkin today. You know how I am. I like my own pumpkin when it comes to baking."

"Yes, so do I, but I still have some in the freezer from last year, so I'll use that up before I do any more. Say, Mom, I need to tell you something, and you need to hear me out before you start arguing, okay?"

Adele Payne frowned. She didn't like the tone of this conversation. "I'm not making you any such promise," Adele said. "Just start talking."

Beverly sighed. "Whatever, but don't say I didn't warn you. I saw Laurel at the Piggly Wiggly today."

Adele gasped. "I don't want to hear a thing about that bitch. My Adam is dead because of her! Why would you think I'd—"

"Mama!" Beverly shouted. "Stop talking and listen. She said hello. I didn't answer. So when she started to go past me, I grabbed her arm and started in on her, and she freakin' lost it."

"What do you mean?" Adele asked.

"She pretty much told me off. Told all of us off. Said she was mad at Adam for killing himself. She was mad that he left Bonnie without a father and left her to raise their girl alone. She said she had loved him. She said we had all loved him, and none of that had been enough. She said he'd quit going to see his shrink, quit taking the medicine they'd been giving him for depression, and what he did was the result."

Adele was shaking. "I don't believe it! My Adam wouldn't—"

"Well, actually, Mama, he did do it. We all know that. The law knows it. Every bit of evidence proved he killed himself. What we didn't know, because she kept it to herself, was that she was the one who had to clean all that up. Adam's blood and brains were all over the room and their bed and everything. She was so enraged by what he'd done to her—to their family, to their own bedroom—that she could hardly get it said to me. I know what I saw, and I know what I heard, and after today, I'm not blaming Laurel for what happened to my brother. The war happened to him, Mama, and we're gonna have to accept that."

"I won't! I don't have to accept any such thing!" Adele screamed.

"Well, you do need to know that Laurel gave us all fair warning. If one of us ever says anything mean to her again, or accuses her of something, she says she will file harassment charges against us, and then everyone in Blessings will know what kind of people we are. Are you ready for that?"

Adele's silence was telling. "She said that?"

"Yes, ma'am, and her voice was shaking, and her face was all crazy looking. I think she's been pushed to a breaking point, and I, for one, do not want to wind up in court against the widow of a soldier who took his own life. She'll have public sympathy if nothing else."

Adele was silent again to the point Beverly thought she was going to hang up. "Mama?"

"I'm here," Adele said. "I'm just thinking. I guess I can speak for myself when I say I'll leave her be, but I can't speak for Adam's brothers."

"That's all well and good," Beverly said. "But you better tell your sons to start digging in their pockets for spare change, because she'll haul their asses to court and make them pay. Just leave her alone, Mama. She's grieving. I saw it. She's grieving, and we left her to grieve it alone."

"She's got her people," Adele muttered.

"We were her people, too," Beverly said. "Bonnie is our blood. We haven't seen her in nearly two years, and because of how we've been treating her mother, she not only lost her daddy, but she lost all of us. I don't know how that makes you feel, but I'm feeling pretty damn low about myself."

"I don't want to talk about this anymore," Adele said.

"Fine. Don't say I didn't warn you, and if any of you wind up in jail, don't call me to bail you out."

Beverly was shaking when she hung up the phone, but talking to her mother like that always made her nervous. Adele Payne was a cold, hardscrabble mountain woman who lived by "an eye for an eye" code, even when it didn't apply.

"Lord, lord," Beverly muttered, and went about her business. She'd done her duty. The rest of this mess was up to Adele.

Adele frowned when she realized Beverly had disconnected. She didn't like to be hung up on. She also didn't like what she'd just been told. It changed the whole concept of how she'd been grieving. Who would she blame if it were not the fault of Adam's wife? She couldn't blame her own son. She'd raised him in the Bible ways and taught him—taught all of her children—that it was a sin to take your own life. If she accepted that Adam had killed himself, then she would have to accept that in her belief, he put his soul in eternal damnation. For Adele, that would have been a black mark against her for raising a child to do such a wrong. She wasn't sure what to do about all this, but it appeared she needed to warn her two other sons about that woman's threat just the same.

~~~

Truman was still in Blessings when the sun went down. He and Nester were at the Blue Ivy Bar shooting pool and taking turns buying beer. They were both on the way to being drunk, and May, the barmaid, was about ready to kick them out. She'd warned them twice already to quiet down, and they had turned around and gotten into an argument with another pool player. Rather than trade blows, the player chose to pay up and leave.

May was watching them closely, waiting for an excuse to throw them out, when another customer came in and sat at the bar. She took his order and then glanced toward the back again and could tell by the frown on Truman's face that he was losing. It would be too much to hope that if he did, he'd just go home.

"Hey, May, you got some pretzels to go with this beer?" the customer asked.

"Sure thing, Billy," she said, and scooped up a dish just for him.

As she set the pretzels in front of him, she heard Truman yell, "Oh, hell no!" and then something cracked.

She looked up just as Nester dropped to the floor.

"Oh, good grief," she muttered, grabbed the phone, and made a call to the Blessings police.

"Blessings PD," the dispatcher said.

"This is May at the Blue Ivy Bar. Truman Slade and Nester Williams are both drunk as skunks, and Truman just laid Nester out with a pool cue."

"I'll get someone right there," the dispatcher said. "Do we need an ambulance?"

"Well, Nester's down and not moving, so I'd say yes."

She rolled her eyes at her customer and grabbed the baseball bat from beneath the bar, just in case Truman decided to bring the fight to her.

Billy, her customer, frowned. "I'll take care of him for you, May."

"No. The cops are on the way. Let's stay out of it if we can."

Billy nodded, but he had the sense to take a different seat so he wouldn't have his back to the drunks. Within moments, they heard a siren, and then a second one. May breathed a sigh of relief. Police and the ambulance were on the way.

―᚜᚜―

Clyde Inman was a new officer with Blessings PD, although he'd been in law enforcement going on ten years. He'd been on the job less than a month and was still feeling his way around with locals, but drunks in a bar were the same all over.

He pulled up to the bar and wasted no time going in. The woman behind the bar pointed. He saw one man holding a broken pool cue and a man with a bloody face on the floor, and headed to the back of the room with his hand on the handle of his gun.

"Sir! Put the pool cue down and turn around."

Truman started to bluster and argue, but Inman was no fool. He grabbed the pool cue before it became a weapon, spun Truman around, and pushed him face-down on the pool table. He had one of Truman's arms pinned against his own back and was reaching for the other one when the EMTs came in.

"Back here," he shouted, as he handcuffed Truman in nothing flat and dragged him out of the way.

The EMTs began examining Nester. "He's got a good pulse," one said.

Inman grabbed the handcuffs with one hand and Truman's belt with the other and physically aimed him toward the door.

"Walk toward the exit, sir."

"Am I under arrest?" Truman asked.

"Yes, you are."

"What for?"

"Assault, drunk and disorderly, and anything else Ms. May decides to tack on. Keep walking."

"But Nester was cheatin', damn it!"

"And so you broke a pool cue over his head. He's going to the hospital, and you're going to jail. The end."

Truman groaned. "Aw, man!"

May watched them go with a frown. She hated getting on the wrong side of Truman Slade. It would be just like him to return for payback because she'd called the cops.

They carried Nester out next on a gurney.

"Is he gonna be okay?" she asked, eyeing all the blood.

"His nose is broken. Pretty sure he has a concussion. I can't speak to anything more," the EMT said, and then they were gone.

May sighed. "Just rest easy, Billy. I'm gonna get the mop and bucket and start cleaning up all that blood."

"I'll get the broken pool cue and reset the pool table for you," Billy offered.

"Thanks, but you just sit and enjoy your beer. This shit is part of owning a bar."

~~~

Truman was booked and in a cell sleeping it off when Nester came out of X-ray. He'd come to long enough for the doctor to reassure him that he wasn't going to die, after which the doctor proceeded to reset his broken nose. Nester passed out from the pain, and the doctor had him admitted because of a concussion. It was not how either Truman or Nester had envisioned ending their day.

~~~

Jake spent the next two days splitting wood, and after breakfast Friday morning, he headed straight to town. He needed to get the chain sharpened on his chain saw and stop by the hardware store to pick up some chain-saw oil.

He was driving by Ralph's gas station at the edge of town when he saw a black wreath hanging on the door and a sign below it. He knew before he even stopped to read it that it was bad news, and it was.

Ralph Sinclair was dead!

According to the message his widow had put on the door, Ralph had died of a heart attack yesterday. She had closed the station indefinitely and thanked everyone for condolences. He got back in his truck with a heavy heart. Ralph had been a good guy he'd known all his life. He sure hated to hear this news.

He thought about it all through the morning as he dropped off the chain to be sharpened and stopped at the hardware store for the oil. He ran the rest of his errands without lingering to visit. The news was all anyone wanted to talk about, and he wasn't one who liked to discuss death like some people discussed the weather.

He thought about the station again as he passed it on his way home, wondering what was going to happen. If it closed down, there would be only one place left in Blessings that sold gas.

He got home, put up what he'd purchased, and then went into the house and made a call to Peanut Butterman.

His secretary, Betty Purejoy, answered. "Mr. Butterman's office, Betty speaking."

"Hello, Betty, this is Jake Lorde. By any chance is Peanut in?"

"Why, yes, he is. Just a moment, and I'll put you through."

Jake waited only a few seconds before Peanut answered. "Hello, Jake! What can I do for you?"

"I just got back from town and saw that Ralph Sinclair had passed and the station is closed."

"Yes! Sudden heart attack," Peanut said. "Let it be a lesson to all of us. We never know when it's going to be our time."

"That's for sure," Jake said. "Look. I saw on the notice Mrs. Sinclair had up that the station is closed indefinitely."

"Yes. She's likely going to be moving to Savannah. That's where their only son and his family lives. Why?"

"Is she going to sell the station?"

"Are you interested in buying it?" Peanut asked.

"I might be if the price is right and there is no lien against the property."

"Well now," Peanut said. "I'm handling the estate, so I can certainly find out. I can't answer you now, but give me a couple of days, okay? It's a tender subject right now. Mrs. Sinclair is devastated, as you can imagine."

"Yes. It's why I was calling you. I would never have asked her such a thing at a time like this. I appreciate you getting that information for me. Call my cell when you know something," Jake said, and then proceeded to give Peanut his number.

He disconnected, leaned back in his dad's recliner, and stared out the window to the road beyond. The silence of the house wrapped around him like a hug from an old friend. It felt like he'd just taken the first step back into the real world.

Saturday dawned clear and cold.

Laurel had a thousand things to do today before the fall festival kicked off this evening. Her parents had planned to go and help look after Bonnie while she manned the kissing booth, but a call from her dad last night changed that. Her mom was down with the flu, and neither of them would be able to go. She'd been sorry for her mom, and then a little worried for herself. Now who could she ask to look after Bonnie? She was going to have to play it by ear when they got there and hope one of the other mothers would let Bonnie tag along with them through the festival. Granted, it was all indoors at the high school gymnasium, but there were a half dozen ways to get in and out of the building, and Bonnie was too young to be on her own.

She glanced out the window to see if Bonnie was still playing with Lavonne, and then began mopping the kitchen floor. If she stayed outside playing until the floor dried, it would be a first. She kept glancing out as she worked, making sure she knew where Bonnie was at all times, and the next time she looked and didn't see her, she put down the mop and stepped outside.

"Bonnie! Bonnie Carol! Where are you?" she yelled.

"I'm in the front yard, Mama," Bonnie called.

Laurel walked around to the front of the house and was stunned to see her sister-in-law, Beverly, standing beside her car with Bonnie in her arms. Beverly saw the look on Laurel's face and immediately put her niece down and started walking toward the house, talking as she went.

"Don't be mad. I didn't come to make trouble. I haven't been able to get what you said out of my mind."

Laurel touched Bonnie's head as she stopped beside her mama. "Go play inside for a while, okay?"

Unaware of the undercurrents, Bonnie happily did as she was told. As soon as she was out of hearing distance, Laurel looked up.

"Say it fast and get off my property," Laurel said.

Beverly sighed. "I deserve that and more. I admit it. But I came here to apologize. Understand I'm not speaking for anyone else, but I want you to know that I am so sorry for how we treated you. I have no excuse. I let...

No, we all still let Adele Payne run our family like we were children. We mostly do it because she's too damn hard to fight with, but Adam's death was a shock and we didn't think of anyone but ourselves. I am so sorry. Can you forgive me?"

Laurel was stunned. This was the last thing she expected to come out of Beverly's mouth.

"Forgive you? I don't even know if I believe you," Laurel muttered.

Beverly's shoulders slumped. "Well, I just wanted you to know, okay? I'll be going now. Would you call me if you ever needed help?"

"No," Laurel said.

"Why?" Beverly asked.

"Once, I needed help washing my husband's blood and brains off the room I still sleep in, and what I got was a phone call from your mother screaming that I killed her boy. I needed help when it came time to pay for burying him. It took everything we had in the bank to pay it off, and it left me completely broke. I needed help when there was nothing to eat in my kitchen but a loaf of bread and a jar of peanut butter. My parents found out and brought us food. I needed help when the bank foreclosed on the car loan and repossessed it. I'm driving my daddy's old farm truck and grateful for it. I clean houses for a living and sell my crocheted pieces when Bonnie needs school clothes. I figured it out by myself. Just because you suddenly got a guilty conscience does not mean I want any of you back in our lives. You weren't here when it mattered. It's good you don't hate me, and that's enough."

Beverly's eyes welled, but she didn't cry. Truth hurt. "You don't trust me, do you?"

"If you were me, would *you*?"

Beverly sighed. "No. We put you through two years of hell."

Laurel didn't comment.

Beverly eyed Laurel closely, looking for the shy, tenderhearted woman she'd been when Adam married her. "You're not the same woman. You speak your mind without hesitation."

Laurel shrugged. "Adam killed her. I'm all that's left. Now, if you'll excuse me, I was mopping the kitchen."

She turned around and walked into the trailer with her back ramrod straight and her steps long and sure. She heard the car start up and drive away, but she didn't bother turning around. Just thinking about Adam's family made her shudder. They were mean and vindictive, and no matter what Beverly said, Laurel didn't trust any of them one bit.

She finished mopping, threw out the mop water, and then, as soon as the floor dried, made lunch. She called Bonnie to come eat, but when she didn't answer, she went to look for her and found the door to her room shut. She looked in and saw Bonnie playing school. Brave Bear was sitting at the table with a doll and a stuffed giraffe. Panda Bear was in the corner.

She grinned. "Lunch is ready, Bonnie. Didn't you hear me call?"

"No. Sorry, Mommy."

"Go wash your hands and then come to the kitchen, okay?"

"Okay, but I need to ask you something," Bonnie said.

"Ask me what?"

"Who was that woman who was here this morning? The one who picked me up?"

Laurel's skin suddenly crawled. "You don't remember her?"

"No."

"Then why did you let her pick you up?"

Bonnie shrugged. "I thought I knew her, but now I don't."

Laurel sighed. "It's okay. She is your daddy's sister."

Bonnie thought about it a few moments and then shrugged. "Oh. What are we having for lunch?"

"Fried potatoes and baked beans and wieners."

"Yum. I like that."

Laurel smiled. "So do I. Now hurry before it gets cold."

Bonnie skipped out of the room. Laurel glanced at Brave Bear sitting at attention and frowned. "We could both use a Brave Bear today. I might be wishing you were real."

Chapter 10

TRUMAN LEFT THE POLICE PRECINCT MINUS HIS USUAL ATTI-tude and plus a mental note to himself never to go back to the Blue Ivy Bar. The booze they served was lethal. He had an assault charge pending. Nester had a hospital bill and a broken nose. He was pretty sure he and Nester wouldn't be hanging out anymore.

He walked all the way down to the police impound-ment, paid a hundred dollars to get his truck released, and drove home a chastened man. He knew about Ralph Sinclair dying and the store closing down. He knew tonight was the fall festival in town, but once he got home, he wasn't leaving again until he ran out of food.

Whatever plans he had for revenge on Jake Lorde were put on simmer. He wasn't quitting, but he needed to recharge.

Jake was in the barn when he thought he heard a car coming down the drive. He stepped out to look and saw a FedEx delivery van pulling up. When the driver got out with a box, Jake gave a yell to let the man know where he was and then waved.

The man stopped, acknowledged Jake's wave, and started walking toward him. They met near the back corner of the yard.

"Delivery for Jacob Lorde."

"I'm Jacob Lorde."

"Sign here, please," the man said.

Jake signed the delivery sheet. The driver handed him the package and drove away.

Jake glanced at the return address as he headed toward the house and then stumbled when he saw the last name. *DeSosa.*

The skin crawled on the back of his neck as he went back to the house. He took it to the kitchen, cut away the wrapping, and took the lid off the box. Tears welled the moment he saw the bottle of tequila. The plane ticket taped to the bottle was puzzling, but the letter in the envelope explained it all.

> *Jacob Lorde, my name is Sophia. You do not know me, but I know you. My husband, Joaquin, spoke of you in every letter he sent home, and in every email message, and even when we Skyped. You were the brother he never had.*
>
> *He told me once that if anything ever happened to him, I was to send you a plane ticket to his funeral, a bottle of tequila, and to remind you that you still owe him five dollars from your last card game.*
>
> *As you can imagine, my heart is broken, but fulfilling a wish for him is almost like holding him in my arms once more. The time and date of Joaquin's memorial service is at the bottom of this letter. The address of our home is beneath it.*
>
> *No pressure, but I hope we see you soon.*

"Well damn," Jake said softly, then checked the

calendar against the date of the service. There was no question of *if* he would go. He had to. He had a debt to pay.

He was getting ready to go online and find a hotel to stay in when his cell phone rang. "Hello."

"Jake, this is Peanut Butterman. Just wanted to fill you in on the status of Ralph's. Mrs. Sinclair *is* going to sell. After the funeral, she'll see about getting it appraised so she'll know what to ask for it. It's likely to be a month or more before all of this happens. I told her you had interest in the property if she did, and she was pleased that it was you. There is no lien on the property, and she will sell it as is. Further details will be forthcoming, but I wanted to let you know where this stood."

Jake was encouraged by the news. "Thank you for the information. Please let me know when it's about to go on sale. I would like to know what all is included in the selling price and possibly make an offer."

"Will do," Peanut said. "Have a nice day. Oh, by the way. Don't know if you're aware of it or not, but this is the evening for the fall festival. It's still as big a deal in Blessings as it ever was, and if you're in the mood, you'd have a good time. Fun for all ages."

Jake thought of the flyer in his mailbox, and now, a second invitation to go. It seemed as if the universe was telling him to go.

"Oh yes, I remember it well. I just might do that, and thanks for the reminder."

"See you there," Peanut said, and hung up.

Jake remembered going with his parents when he was a kid. It had actually been a pretty fun time for everyone. They used to have a big bingo area, an old-fashioned cakewalk, and lots of game booths set up. He wondered if Laurel and Bonnie were going and then frowned. He needed to stop basing his plans on hoping they would overlap hers and decided to go anyway. He didn't have to stay if it didn't feel right, but if he was thinking about starting a business that catered to the public, he should start mingling with them.

However, he had a funeral to attend, so he went online, found a hotel very close to Sophia DeSosa's address, and booked a room for two nights. Today was Saturday. The funeral was next Wednesday, so if he arrived Tuesday before noon, it would give him time to go to their home and pay his respects. The memorial service was the next afternoon at 2:00 p.m. He would fly home Thursday morning. Maybe it was a good thing. Facing the facts of one's life always made it easier to accept.

He was thoughtful and a little bit sad as he went back to the barn. After repairing the second granary, he headed for the house for a late lunch.

By 6:00 p.m. that evening, Jake was on his way to town and only semi-anxious about stepping out of his comfort zone. By the time he arrived, the parking lot at school was packed. He finally found a place to park and headed toward the gym. The noise from inside was spilling out as he neared the building. A couple of teenage boys ran past him and darted inside. He followed them through the open doors and was immediately swallowed up by the slowly moving crowd of people stopping at the booths.

Instead of feeling out of place, he saw dozens of people he knew and almost immediately saw Mike and

LilyAnn. They pulled him into their midst and began plying him with bites of funnel cake and playing games at the booths. By the time the cake was gone, they were all licking powdered sugar from their fingers. Full of sweets and getting tired, LilyAnn wanted off her feet. She and Mike wandered off to sit down, while Jake moved on.

He saw kids crowded around the cakewalk, waiting their turn to play musical chairs, and remembered playing that when he was in middle school. The prize was usually a cake, or in this instance, an extravagantly decorated cupcake, after which they started over again with a different set of players.

Jake was watching the kids squealing and running as they pushed and shoved to get to a chair before the music stopped. All of a sudden, there was a scramble for chairs, and he saw a flash of red and blue and then grinned when he realized it was Bonnie Payne. She came from behind a big boy and slipped into the chair just before he sat down—right in her lap.

Everyone laughed, but the boy was out.

Fascinated with the intensity of the look on Bonnie's face, he watched from the sidelines as the game played on until Bonnie won. When they announced her name, she threw her hands in the air as if she'd scored a winning touchdown and strutted her way to the winner's table to pick out a cupcake.

Jake watched her go for the one that looked like a little, fat pumpkin. They put it in an equally small carryout box, and as soon as she had it, she went in the opposite direction, straight across the gym floor. He wondered where she was going and then saw Laurel manning the kissing booth, and his heart skipped a beat.

She was taking money and handing out kisses as fast as she could, with a line of men halfway across the floor waiting for their turn. Before envy had time to burn, he saw the men walking away from the booth with big grins and red stickers on their cheeks in the shape of a woman's lips. He was wondering how she'd react if he showed up at the booth when Bonnie saw him.

"Jake!" she squealed, and ran toward him through the crowd, then launched herself into his arms. "You came! Did you see me win a cupcake?"

"I sure did," he said. "You're really fast."

"I know!" she said, and then wiggled to be put down and grabbed him by the hand. "I have to go tell Mama where I'm going next, or she will worry. Grandma was supposed to walk around with me tonight, but she's sick. I told Mama I was a big girl and would be 'sponserble.'"

Jake's grin widened. "And where are you telling Mommy we're going?"

She pointed to a booth where stacked bottles were knocked down with baseballs, and then he saw the prizes. The walls were lined with all kinds of colorful glass bead necklaces. To a six-year-old girl, the jewelry must have looked like it came out of a pirate's treasure chest.

"I thought you might like to play that game," she said, as she gave him a considering glance.

"It does look like something I might enjoy," he said.

She beamed. "Then let's go tell Mommy."

Jake let her lead him across the gym floor to the booth. Laurel had just put a red kiss on Lon Pittman's cheek when they walked up.

"Mommy! Look who's here!"

Laurel was laughing when she turned around, and

then she saw Jake, and all of a sudden, she had stars in her eyes. She'd never seen him dressed up like this. The pants were dark, his shirt was pale blue. He had on a black leather bomber jacket and dark boots, and the thought went through her mind that he was beautiful.

"Oh! Hi!" she said.

"We're gonna go win me some diamonds and rubies," Bonnie said.

"She has high expectations," Jake said, and then grinned. "We will be right over there at the bottles and baseball game, okay?"

"Uh, yes, sure, and thanks for letting me know," she said.

The next guy in line was getting impatient. "Hey, Miz Laurel! It's my turn. How about a real kiss?"

"Sorry, I have to get back to work," she whispered, then turned around and frowned at the old man who was waving a five-dollar bill in the air. "Buzz Higdon, what would your wife say if she heard you say that?"

His wife stepped out of the crowd. "She'd say kiss him at your own risk. His false teeth are likely to slide out."

The crowd roared with laughter, and Buzz grinned.

Laurel took his money, put a big red sticker on his cheek, and gave him a wink.

Buzz turned as red as his shirt. His wife laughed, and the crowd was clapping.

Jake did not want to walk away, but it was clear that Bonnie was on a mission, and while he couldn't wipe that smile off of Laurel Payne's lips, he could make her daughter happy.

He read the sign on the booth and plopped down two

dollars. The man handed him three baseballs, told him the rules, and then stepped aside to give Jake a fair shot.

Jake moved Bonnie so that he could see her from his peripheral vision and then eyed the stack of bottles. He knew the ropes. The bottles were always weighted and were far harder to knock off than it would appear. But he'd been lobbing grenades and carrying a good portion of his weight in gear for years. He had this in the bag.

"Okay, Miss Bonnie. Rubies and diamonds it is," he said, and fired a baseball into the stack so hard that they scattered in three different directions.

"Wow," the man said, eyeing Jake with new respect. "You've just won your pick of necklaces from this wall."

"I still have two more balls," he said. "Set 'em back up and let's see if I can do that again."

The man laughed and restacked the bottles.

Jake fired a second baseball into that stack so fast that when it hit, it sounded like they had shattered.

The crowd that had gathered around them clapped and cheered.

"He just won you another necklace, little lady," the man said.

"I have one ball left. Set 'em back up," Jake said.

Bonnie was so excited she was dancing from one foot to the next.

Jake winked at her as the man reset the bottles one last time.

"Can he do that again?" the man cried, knowing it was going to draw a bigger crowd and more men would be wanting to try and match what Jake Lorde was doing. "Stand back, everybody! This one's gonna be a barn burner, I can tell."

Jake threw the last ball into the stack with such force that the bottles shot sideways.

The man whooped!

Bonnie was squealing and clapping.

The crowd cheered.

Laurel couldn't see what was happening, but she knew the squeals were Bonnie's and people were laughing and clapping. It had to be something good.

A few moments later, Bonnie came flying back to the kissing booth wearing three very ornate necklaces. One was made of red glass beads, the second one of silver beads, and the third one was clear glass—as close to diamonds as Jake Lorde could get.

She looked up at the man standing behind Bonnie.

God bless you, Jake Lorde. No girl ever forgets the first man to give her diamonds. You just gave my baby a night she'll always remember.

"That's wonderful!" Laurel said. "Now, my sweet girl, why don't you come sit in the booth with me for a while."

Bonnie cheerfully agreed, anxious to inspect her jewelry closer. Laurel got her situated, and when she looked up, Jake was gone. She tried not to feel let down and got on with her job.

But Jake hadn't gone far. He still couldn't believe he was standing in line at a kissing booth just for the opportunity to be up close and personal with Laurel Payne for a few moments more.

One by one the men moved up, then moved on, until there were only two ahead of him, and she still didn't know he was there. And then there was only one man between him and Laurel. His heart was pounding, and he wanted to touch her, but he was absolutely certain that wasn't allowed.

He already had a twenty-dollar bill in his hand. He didn't know how big the sticker would be for that much money, but the way he figured it, the more surface she had to stick down, the longer it would take for her to do it.

He grinned at the disconcerted look on her face when she saw he was next in line.

"How much will this buy me?" he asked softly, and slid the twenty-dollar bill across the counter.

Her smile slid sideways as her face turned red.

Jake leaned forward like all of the other men had done so she could reach their cheeks, but Laurel had forgotten what to do. She was just standing, staring into his dark brown eyes, and reminding herself to breathe.

"Kiss him, Mommy!" Bonnie cried.

Laurel gasped and then fumbled for another set of stickers, ones with bigger lips—redder lips. She peeled one off and then reached out to put the sticker on his cheek.

Jake felt her fingers on his face, and when she began pressing the sticker down so it would adhere, he slowly turned his head so that her fingers were now on his lips.

"Oh, I'm sorry," she said, as she yanked her hand away.

"I'm not," he said softly, and then backed up and walked away.

Laurel was so rattled that she couldn't think what to do next. If it hadn't been for Bonnie's constant input and instructions, she would have embarrassed herself. Every time she got a chance to look around, she looked for Jake. But when she didn't see him again, she assumed he'd gone home.

Then, in the midst of all the excitement, the sounds of sirens brought the noise inside the gym to a momentary halt. Seconds later, someone received a phone call, and then another and another, and word soon spread that there had been a terrible wreck on the road just past Ralph's.

Laurel's heart sank.

That's the road she lived on—the road Jake lived on—and he was gone. Was it *him*? Did Jake drive away from the festival only to get in a wreck? She was in a panic. If she hadn't put that flyer in his mailbox, chances are he wouldn't have known to come. What if he was hurt? Or worse? She couldn't let herself think of what might have happened.

—⁓—

Jake bought a corn dog and ate it while he was walking around. He saw plenty of people he knew, but it was quickly apparent going solo to these things had a downside. There was no one to laugh with or share the moments with. After playing a couple of games of bingo and listening to two ladies bickering beside him, he quit the game and got up. Peanut Butterman waved at him from the far side of the room, but he was playing auctioneer, selling homemade pies to the highest bidder.

Jake was walking out of the gym when someone's car backfired out in the parking lot. He jumped like he'd been shot and was looking for a place to take cover when it dawned on him where he was. After that, he knew it was time to go home before he embarrassed himself.

He was still shaking when he drove out of town. Despite the chill of the night, he rolled down the windows in the truck and let the cold air blow on his face.

He had just passed Ralph's station when he thought he heard thunder, then realized the sky was clear. Seconds later, a bright-orange fireball appeared on the horizon, and once more, his skin began to crawl. As he topped a hill, he saw two cars in flames and someone standing, highlighted against the blaze. He called in the accident and then sped up.

When he arrived, he saw it was a young woman he'd seen standing, and she was staring blankly into the flames. He left his truck lights on and got out on the run. Blood was running from a cut in her forehead and across her cheek.

"Ma'am, you need to step back from the fire," Jake said gently, took her by the arm, and led her a safe distance away. "What's your name?" he asked, as he helped her sit down.

"Melanie Payne. Where's my husband? Where's Luke?"

"I'll go look," he said, hoping the husband was not someone still in the fire.

He ran back to look and found a man lying on the side of the road. Jake began feeling for a pulse and checking for obvious injuries.

"My wife, where's my wife?" the man kept mumbling.

"What's your name?" Jake asked.

"Luke Payne. Where's my wife? Where's Melanie?"

The name startled Jake. He knew this man. It was Adam Payne's older brother—Laurel's brother-in-law.

"She's safe, Luke. She's sitting by the fence. Where do you hurt?"

"My head, my leg. It wouldn't hold me up no more."

Jake felt both legs and then grimaced. There was a bone sticking out the side of his right leg. This was serious, even life-threatening. Where the hell was the ambulance?

"Do you remember what happened?" Jake asked as he took off his belt and quickly made a tourniquet between the man's hip and the broken bone.

"Car came over a hill…both in the middle of the road. We hit. I don't remember nothin' else."

Jake looked up at the burning vehicles and felt the scene beginning to go in and out of focus.

"My wife. Where's my wife?" Luke kept asking.

"She's okay. Don't move," Jake said, and then heard a siren, and then a second one, and he began to shake.

He was on his knees with his head down, trying to stop the world from spinning, when he thought he could hear someone else screaming for help. He checked the tourniquet again and then forced himself to get up and began circling the burning vehicles, looking for another victim.

The sirens were louder now, and the heat from the fire was making him sick to his stomach. It was too much like coming to after the IED explosion and thinking he was going to burn to death. Even though he could still hear someone screaming, he was losing hold on reality. Part of the time, he thought he was the one screaming, and then he heard the voice again.

"Help! I'm here!"

Jake reeled where he stood, then bent over and grabbed on to his knees to keep from losing it.

It's not me. Focus, damn it. Someone needs help.

The sirens were a constant scream now. Help was imminent. He dropped to his knees and put his hands over his ears, willing that sound to stop, and it wasn't until he turned his back to the blaze that he was able to see into the darkness.

"Here, I'm here," a man cried, and lifted a bloody arm into the air.

Jake got to his feet and stumbled toward him.

"Help me," the man said again, and grabbed Jake's wrist.

"Where are you hurt, man?" Jake asked.

"My back. I can't feel my legs," he said, and then started weeping. "The ones in the other car?"

"They are both alive," Jake said, and then heard the ambulance arriving. "Help is here. Don't try to move. I need to tell them where you are. What's your name?"

"Darrell Ames. I took a wrong road and got lost."

"Hang tough, Darrell. I'm going to get help."

Jake got up and ran from the blaze so fast that he startled the firemen on the scene.

"What the hell?" one of them yelled.

"There's another victim back there," he yelled, pointing beyond the fire.

The fireman turned and yelled at the EMTs. "You have another vic over here!"

The second ambulance was already pulling up when Jake ran toward the ones already on the scene. He dropped to his knees beside the EMTs and noticed Luke was unconscious.

"Is this your belt?" an EMT asked.

"Yes, it's all I had."

"Probably saved his life," the EMT said.

Luke swiped a shaky hand across his face. "His name is Luke Payne. His wife, Melanie, is over there by the fence. She has head wounds. There's one more victim on the far side of the fire. He says he can't feel his legs."

The EMT grabbed his radio and called in a request for a third ambulance, then divided up the help that was already there. He sent one EMT to Melanie, while two others ran toward the fire to the third victim.

Jake got up and walked away. He was still sick to his stomach, and he wanted to go home, but he'd been first on the scene and needed to stay until the highway patrol arrived so they could take his statement.

He was barely hanging onto sanity as he walked toward his truck to wait. Smoke was in his eyes, and there was a lump in his throat. He'd heard the fear in Darrell's voice. He might never walk again, and all because he'd lost his way. Jake knew about being lost. It was a damn scary feeling, even for a grown-up.

Jake got into his truck, and the moment he shut the door, the chaos outside became muted and the silence within enveloped him. He saw the big red sticker he'd stuck on the dash and without thinking stroked the surface—right where Laurel's fingers had been.

He closed his eyes, picturing the smile on her face, the curve of her lips, the gentle way she had of moving through the world, and then thought of the strength in her grip. He wanted to love her, but wouldn't go there. Anything between them beyond friendship was bound to fail.

One ambulance left, and then the second was about to pull out when the flashing lights of a highway patrol car finally appeared in his rearview mirror.

"Thank you, Lord."

He took a deep breath and got out of the truck.

Laurel was exhausted. The fun had long since worn
off the event. All she'd been told about the wreck was
that two vehicles hit head-on and were burning. She
fought tears after that, until finally, another fall festival was over.

Bonnie had fallen asleep on a blanket inside the
booth, and Laurel was waiting for Mavis to come get the
money from her event so she could leave. When Mavis
finally showed up, Laurel handed her the cashbox.

"I didn't count it, but it's full," she said.

"Great news," Mavis said. "We'll have a complete
accounting by tomorrow. It will be in the next issue of
the *Blessings Tribune*. Thank you for volunteering."

"My pleasure," Laurel said. "So, I'm heading home
now, okay?"

"Yes, you're finished," Mavis said, then eyed Bonnie.
"Can I help you get her to the car?"

"I can manage, but thank you," she said, and proceeded to carry Bonnie out of the gym.

She stretched her out in the seat of her truck and then
buckled her in before she started home. All the way
through town, she kept wondering about the wreck site.
It bothered her to think of the possibility of Jake being
hurt again, and it bothered her that she cared. Was he
already in a hospital bed somewhere, or had he come
all this way across the world just to die a few miles
from home?

She kept on driving, but the farther she drove, the
more anxious she became. She began smelling smoke
before she came up on the wreck site. Both vehicles

were still there. One was a truck. One was a car. They were both charred and smoldering, and a rural fire truck was still on-site to make sure no fires flared up.

She wanted to stop and ask who'd been in the wreck, but she didn't have the guts to hear bad news and then try and get her and Bonnie Carol home.

When she came over the hill above the Lorde farm and saw a light on in the house and then saw his truck parked beneath the carport, she burst into tears and cried the rest of the way home.

Chapter 11

JAKE DIDN'T REMEMBER THE REST OF THE DRIVE HOME AND was in such a daze that he almost drove past his own house. By the time he got inside, he was shaking. He thought about taking that bottle of tequila to bed, and then opted for a cold shower instead.

Later, he crawled into bed naked and pulled the covers up to his chin. "Please God, help me," he said, and closed his eyes.

He flashed first on the fire, and then the blood on the victims. He could feel himself falling into the pit where nightmares reigned when another face superimposed over the darkness. Her eyes were gentle, her voice was soft, and she was reaching toward him.

Laurel.

He slept.

———

It was morning before Laurel saw the dead dog lying in her front yard. She was getting dressed and had glanced out her bedroom window when she saw it. She sighed. It appeared her in-laws had paid her another visit in the night. They seemed to think that anything dead would remind her of what Adam had done. So one would assume Beverly's visit in an attempt to make peace had not spread to the rest of the family.

Bonnie was still asleep, and Laurel needed to get rid

of the carcass before she woke up. So she grabbed a
pair of gloves and got a shovel from the back porch and
hurried to the front yard.

It didn't take long to ascertain the dog had been dead
longer than twenty-four hours, and since it wasn't there
when they'd left for the fall festival, someone had to
have dumped the carcass here. The ground was still soft
enough for the last rain to make digging easy, and so
she quickly dug a shallow grave near the bar ditch. She
ran back, grabbed the carcass by the tail, dragged it into
the hole, and then covered it up. By the time she was
finished, she was nauseous and shaking, but the deed
was hidden from Bonnie, and that's all that mattered.

She went back inside to clean up and make Bonnie
some breakfast. After this, putting food in her mouth and
keeping it down was pretty much impossible. Maybe
she'd feel better after church, but it was a horrible way
to begin the day.

Adele Payne spent the night at the hospital in
Blessings. Her daughter, Beverly, and her son David
and his wife, Trisha, had been with her until daybreak.
At that point, they'd gone to Beverly's house to sort
out all of the children who'd been left with Beverly's
husband, Garrett.

Luke and Melanie had three boys, ranging in
age from ten to fifteen. Beverly decided to keep the
youngest one with her three children, and David and
Trisha were taking the two older ones home to stay
with their two.

Once Luke came out of surgery and they learned he

was going to live, their relief was huge. But Melanie, who seemed at first to be the least injured, had fallen into a coma around midnight and had yet to wake up. She had a brain bleed, and her prognosis wasn't good.

Adele had led them in prayer all night, convinced that God would answer her prayers because she considered herself a true and faithful servant. It was only after they were gone, and she was alone, that the doubts crept in. First Adam, now Luke and Melanie. It seemed as if her family was being punished, but for what?

And their biggest question—the one thing they had talked about all night and had yet to understand—why were Luke and Melanie even on that road? They hadn't gone to the festival, and their home was on the other side of Blessings. Yet something had led them to a place that brought them to such harm. Maybe when she was able to talk to Luke, she would find out. For now, the only thing she could do was keep praying.

⟶

Jake woke up before daylight, took a cup of coffee onto the back porch, and waited for sunrise. He took a sip and then held it between his hands to keep them warm.

The sky was gray.

The air was still.

Every time he exhaled, a tiny cloud of condensation lingered around his chin just long enough to mark the chill of the day. He took another sip of coffee and thought of what lay ahead.

Going to Joaquin DeSosa's funeral would be walking back into the past. But that was a selfish thought, and this wasn't about him. It was about paying a debt.

He owed DeSosa more than five dollars. He owed him his life.

He finished his coffee just as the sun sent a spray of violet hues above the horizon, followed by a wash of colors in a thousand shades of pink. He lifted his cup to the display and toasted the angels heralding the day set aside for God.

"You have outdone yourselves," he said, and then waited for the sun to remind him there was a whole new day on the way with the opportunity to do something new—something better.

The sun came up like always, and Jake thought how the sunrise on his land was so much better than the sun rising on a land at war. Now that the ceremony was over, he went back inside.

The bottle of tequila mocked him. *Drink me. I'll make you forget.*

But DeSosa's intent was a gesture of remembrance—to remember he had lived—and Jake knew it. So he bypassed the tequila for the pantry, got a box of cereal and then milk from the refrigerator, and ate standing up.

He was debating about going to church or putting the brush hog on the tractor and clearing some brush between the barn and the creek when his cell phone rang. It was Laurel.

"Hello, neighbor, what's up?" Jake said.

Laurel's voice was shaking a little, which alerted him it wasn't just a neighborly call.

"I hate to ask, but do you have a gun?"

His belly knotted. "Dad's rifle is here, why?"

"Bonnie went out to feed Lavonne this morning and came running back inside crying. She said there was a big possum that scared her, but when I went out to look I saw a raccoon instead, and it's sick, Jake. I think it has rabies, and I don't have a gun or anyone who lives close enough to call for help."

He frowned. A rabid animal was nothing to take lightly.

"I'll be right there," he said.

He thought of the handgun he'd brought home, but he had no intention of ever buying ammo. Then he ran to his dad's room. He'd seen the old rifle when he was cleaning out the closet and was pretty sure there was a box of ammo on the floor beside it, and there was.

He grabbed it all and headed out the door. He kept thinking about the fear in her voice and told himself whatever hell he might fall into from shooting a gun again, it was nothing to leaving her or Bonnie in this kind of danger.

She was standing on the front porch when he drove up. He got out on the run, loading the gun as he went. "Where is it?" he asked.

She pointed. "See that old shed past the chicken house?"

He nodded.

"It went in there, and I think it's still there because there's no back door out."

"Stay here," he said, and took off at a lope.

"Be careful!" she cried, and then ran back into the trailer and out onto the back porch just as Jake reached the shed.

"Mommy, I wanna see," Bonnie said.

Laurel turned around. Bonnie was standing in the doorway.

"No, baby. Go back to your room. Get Brave Bear, and say a prayer for Jake to stay safe."

"Okay, Mommy," Bonnie said, and disappeared.

Laurel closed the back door. The less Bonnie heard, the better. She saw Jake hesitate in the doorway, and then he walked inside. Her heart was pounding.

Be okay, be okay, please be okay.

All of a sudden, she heard a loud thud, and then a big commotion sounded inside the shed. She was imagining the worst when she heard two gunshots. And then nothing.

"Jake?"

He didn't answer.

"Jake, are you alright?"

He still didn't answer.

She couldn't stand the suspense any longer and ran down the steps and out across the yard. She was afraid of what she would see and yet she had to face it. It was her fault that he was even here.

She reached the doorway, hesitated just a moment to let her eyes adjust to the darker view, and then saw Jake leaning against the wall. The boar raccoon was huge, and it was dead. She breathed a sigh of relief, and then saw the expression on Jake's face and her heart sank. She'd seen Adam zone out like that more than once and had not known at the time what was happening. She knew now, and the gunfire was probably responsible.

She looked for a few moments until she saw the rifle. It was lying on a worktable beside him.

Oh God, please help me do this right.

"Jake, it's Laurel. Can you hear me?"

He hadn't moved and she was afraid to touch him.

"Jake! The raccoon is dead. Come out into the light."

—m—

Jake saw the raccoon the moment he stepped into the shed. It was one of the biggest boars he'd ever seen, and Laurel had been right to call. He'd seen animals with rabies before, and he would bet money this one had it.

The raccoon reacted to his presence with a hissing growl and then came at him, knocking over a large stack of wooden crates. His first shot was on target. The raccoon dropped, but was still kicking when Jake shot again. He knew it was dead.

Then the raccoon disappeared, and the jumble of trash inside the shed became a bombed out village. He was waiting for more bombs to fall when he heard someone calling his name.

He looked around for DeSosa and then saw someone standing in the doorway. At first, all he saw was a silhouette, and then when his name was called again, he knew the voice.

Laurel? Is that you?

"Jake, please look at me," Laurel said.

And so he did. Reality came back with her presence. He took a deep, shuddering breath and then pointed at the carcass.

"Don't touch it. Rabies."

"Oh my God, I just knew it," Laurel said, and walked into the shed, took him by the hand. "Let's go out into the light, okay? I'll call the veterinarian and find out who to call to come get it."

He picked up his rifle, and by the time he was out of the shed, his focus was settling. Sunlight caught in Laurel's hair, turning the auburn highlights into streaks of fire. He started to touch it—just to see if it was as hot as it looked, but he did not, and then she stopped and turned to face him.

"I know what it cost you to fire that gun. You are a man above most, Jacob Lorde, and while I continue to thank you, somehow it doesn't feel like enough."

"Let it go, Laurel. It's dead and you and Bonnie are safe, and that's all that matters."

Laurel's eyes suddenly welled.

Jake saw the tears and groaned. He laid the gun in the grass and took her into his arms. "It's okay. Really," he said, and just held her.

It had been a long time since Laurel had let a man touch her, and the fact that he was just as big a risk to love as Adam didn't seem to matter. Not now. Not when she was so tired of being the only one in charge.

The back door banged. Bonnie was standing on the porch. "Mommy, are you okay?"

"She's okay, honey," Jake called. "She just got scared. Come here. She needs more hugs to feel good again."

Bonnie flew down the steps, ran to where they were standing, threw her arms around Laurel's legs, and hugged her tight. "It's okay, Mommy. Brave Bear took care of me, and Jake took care of you." She looked toward the shed apprehensively. "Is that big possum dead now?"

Laurel wiped her eyes and then picked Bonnie up in her arms. "It was a raccoon, and yes, it's dead now. It was sick, and so we can't go anywhere near it. Let's go inside so Mommy can call someone to come get it, okay?"

"Okay," Bonnie said, and wiggled out of Laurel's arms and ran back toward the house.

Laurel couldn't face Jake, but he didn't care. He tilted her head up to meet his gaze.

"I'm leaving Tuesday for L.A. I'll be back sometime Thursday. Just wanted you to know, in case you wondered where I'd gone."

"Is everything okay?" she asked.

He sighed. "Going to a memorial service for a buddy who didn't make it home. It's a long story, but the bottom line is, it was an invitation I couldn't turn down."

"I am so sorry," Laurel said.

"Yes, so am I," Jake said. "So, I was thinking about church earlier, but I'm not in the mind-set for sitting still. However, I don't want to spend the day alone at the house. I think I'm going to have Sunday dinner at Granny's. I don't suppose you and Bonnie would like to go with me?"

A thousand reasons why she shouldn't went through her head, but she heard the need for company in his voice. "That would be a treat," she said. "What time?"

"How about I pick you up about eleven thirty? We won't be too early, but we will still beat the church crowd."

"Okay. We'll be ready," she said, and then she put a hand on his arm. "Thank you again for coming to help."

"That's what friends are for," he said. He picked up the gun and walked away.

Laurel watched him drive away with a knot in her stomach. She'd just agreed to go to Sunday dinner with him. Granted, Bonnie would be along, but that didn't change the fact that it felt like a date. Then she sighed. He'd come when she'd called. The least she could do was reciprocate. He'd lost a friend and was sad. He didn't want to be alone. So when he'd asked

her a favor, there was no way on God's earth she could
have refused. Right?

"Mommy! Lavonne is scared. Come inside, and call
someone to get that possum."

Laurel grinned at the little sprite standing on the
back porch. "Yes, I'm coming," she said, and ran back
to the house.

———— ∾∾ ————

Luke Payne woke up an hour after his wife, Melanie, died.

Adele was bordering on hysterics and had called the
family back in. Melanie's people all lived in Florida, and
it would take at least a day before they could get here.
She was sitting at Luke's bedside, waiting for David and
Beverly to return and help her make decisions. She didn't
think it was a good idea to tell Luke anything about his
wife until he was more stable.

She'd heard the nurses talking about the driver of the
other car. He'd broken his back in the wreck and would
live out his life in a wheelchair.

Adele and the family had already been told that the
vehicles hit head-on coming over a hill, so both drivers
were obviously at fault. There would be no blame to lay
except upon themselves.

She was watching the clock and listening to every
breath that Luke took when he began to stir. He'd
already awakened once, enough to answer a couple of
the nurse's questions. Now that he was coming to again,
Adele hoped he would answer some of hers.

He groaned.

Adele got up and leaned over the bed to pat his arm.
"Mama's here, Luke. You are going to be okay."

His eyelids fluttered. "Mel'nie," he mumbled.

Adele fought back tears. Bless his heart. He was asking for his woman. He was a widower and didn't know it.

"Luke, it's Mama. I'm here, Son. I'm right here."

He took a slow breath and then groaned as he exhaled. "Hurt."

"I'll call the nurse," Adele said, and pressed the Call button.

"Yes, ma'am. How can I help you?" the nurse said.

"My son is awake and in pain. Do you have something to help him?"

"I'll check his chart," the nurse said.

Adele patted Luke's arm. "Rest easy, Son. They'll be here shortly."

"Mama?" he mumbled.

She smiled. "Yes, honey. It's Mama," she answered, and took him by the hand. He squeezed her fingers so hard that it actually hurt. "Easy, Son," Adele said.

"I went," he mumbled.

She frowned. "Went where?"

"...bother the bitch."

The skin crawled on the back of Adele's neck. "What do you mean?" she asked.

"You said...bother. I went."

And then it hit her! The road where they had the wreck—it was the road where Laurel still lived. Even after Beverly told her what Laurel had said, Adele told her boys to keep bothering her, that Paynes got revenge for their own.

"What did you do?" she asked.

"Dead dog...yard."

Her heart began to pound, and she broke out in a sick sweat. "No, no, no." She moaned and dropped back into the chair with a thump.

She covered her face with her hands and began rocking back and forth. She started to pray and then stopped. What exactly should she pray for first? Forgiveness for harassing her daughter-in-law, or forgiveness for sending her son on a mission that ended in such tragedy? If she hadn't been so self-righteous, Luke would not be crippled, Melanie would not be dead, and the driver of the other car would not be facing life in a wheelchair.

"Is this it, Lord? Is this my punishment for what we did to my Adam's wife?" Adele whispered.

She held her breath, waiting for the iron fist of God to strike her dead, but she kept breathing. At that point, she began to reassess what she knew against what she would be able to live with and, slowly, convinced herself that God didn't have any hand in this, so it must have been the Devil. That was something she *could* live with. There was the very thing she needed to live with herself.

None of this was her fault after all. By the time the nurse came in with pain meds to inject into Luke's IV, Adele was back to her self-righteous self.

Bonnie held court from the backseat of Jake's truck, talking all the way to Blessings. Laurel had dressed her in gray knit pants and a red sweater that she'd picked up at a yard sale. Bonnie had insisted on adding her "diamond necklace" and bringing Brave Bear, so she and the bear shared the backseat. Laurel took comfort in the distraction of her daughter to keep from focusing on the fact that Jake Lorde smelled almost as good as he looked.

It had been so long since she'd cared what she looked like that she'd been a nervous wreck trying to find something to put on. One of the nicest things she had was a navy-blue pantsuit, and so she'd worn it with a white turtleneck sweater. The makeup she was wearing seemed overdone, although it was nothing but mascara and lipstick. She'd left her hair down without thought, unaware that it was driving Jake to distraction. And all the while she was worrying about how she looked, and Jake was thinking about tunneling his fingers through her hair.

Bonnie continued to inform. "…and then I told him he couldn't get in front of me. It's a rule, right, Mommy? If the teacher puts you in line, you have to stay where she put you, right?"

"Right," Laurel answered, and then glanced at Jake, relieved that he was smiling. "Yes, this is normal, and no, she never stops."

Jake laughed. "Truthfully, this is the best medicine for what ails me."

Laurel relaxed. "I know what you mean. I can have the worst day, and then this one comes home, and my troubles are gone. My ear gets a little tired, but it's so much better than being hassled."

Jake frowned. "Who hassles you?"

She shrugged and lowered her voice. "Adam's family."

His frown deepened. "Really? Why? How do they hassle you?"

She glanced over her shoulder. Bonnie was still talking, but to Brave Bear.

"His mother is crazy. The day he died, she called me

screaming, saying it was my fault. Reason is not her strong suit."

"Good lord," he muttered. "Does this still happen?"

"Not the phone calls, but periodically, one of the boys dumps something dead in my driveway or in the front yard. I guess they think it will remind me of Adam, as if I could ever get that memory out of my head. I found a dead dog in the yard again this morning. I guess it was there when I came home last night and I just didn't see it."

Jake thought of the wreck and the road on which it had happened. "Do they live nearby?" he asked.

"Oh, no, they live several miles north of Blessings."

Jake glanced in the rearview mirror to make sure Bonnie was still occupied and then lowered his voice. "I drove up on that wreck last night."

Her heart skipped. "When we heard about it at the gym, I worried it might be you."

That was an admission he had not expected. "Well, thank you for caring. No, it wasn't me, but Luke Payne and his wife, Melanie, were in one of the cars."

Laurel gasped. "No! You aren't serious?"

"Yes. The man who hit them was just a stranger who'd gotten lost."

"Were they hurt bad?"

Jake shrugged. "Bad enough. We'll probably hear all about it at Granny's whether we want to or not."

Laurel leaned back in the seat. Her mind was spinning in a dozen directions, but all she kept thinking was if they hadn't been trying to hurt her, none of that would have happened.

Jake reached across the seat and took her hand. "Are you okay?"

Without thinking, she held on to him, drawing strength from just his presence. "Yes, yes, I'm okay. There was no love lost between us anymore. I guess I was just thinking about karma. You know…sometimes fate deals its own brand of payback."

"Mommy, Brave Bear probably needs to go to the bathroom soon."

Jake chuckled. "And back to reality."

Laurel grinned. "Can Brave Bear wait? We're almost there. See, there's Ralph's station up head. We'll be at Granny's restaurant in just a couple of minutes."

"Yep, he can wait."

"Good news," Laurel said.

Chapter 12

JAKE AND HIS GUESTS WERE ALREADY SEATED AND HAD ordered their food when the after-church crowd began to arrive. Jake was oblivious, but Laurel saw the double takes and knew the Blessings gossip chain would have them dating by nightfall. It didn't really matter that they were both free to do as they wished. Laurel had been Adam Payne's wife, and then Adam Payne's widow, all of her adult life. This would take getting used to.

Bonnie was so excited to be dining out that she was actually quiet. They never had money for luxuries like this, and their only other place to visit was Granny and Gramps Joyner's house.

She was watching every move Laurel made, using the right fork, buttering her bread with the knife, taking small bites, and chewing with her mouth closed, just like Mommy. When a small bite of lettuce fell off her fork and into the napkin in her lap, she gasped.

"You're fine," Jake said. "That's what a napkin is for. See, mine already has stuff on it too."

Laurel patted Bonnie's leg reassuringly. "Relax honey. This is supposed to be fun. Are you having fun?"

"Yes, fun," Bonnie said, as she picked the lettuce out of her lap and put it in her mouth.

A few minutes later, a family came in and was seated at a table just across the aisle. Bonnie immediately acknowledged a little girl from her class with a giggle and wave.

The other little girl waved, and then before her mother could stop her, she was out of her chair and leaning on the end of the booth, watching them eat.

"Hi, Bonnie!"

"Hi, Judy. I'm having a fried chicken leg."

The little blonde eyed Laurel and then stared at Jake.

"Is this your daddy?"

Laurel didn't have time to react before Bonnie straightened her out.

"No, silly. My daddy's dead. This is my friend, Jake. He shot a sick possum this morning before it could hurt Lavonne!"

Laurel glanced at Jake, hoping this wasn't embarrassing him too much and was relieved that he seemed intrigued by little-girl talk.

But Judy's father, Trent Samuels, knew Jake, and when he heard the possum story, he asked Jake outright. "Hey, Jake, how sick was it? Is it what I'm thinking?"

"It was sick alright, but it was a big boar coon, not a possum."

"I called the vet," Laurel said. "He sent someone to pick it up. They're going to run a test to confirm."

Trent frowned and then shook his head. "I hate to hear that. Once rabies gets started in an area, it can spread fast. If it tests out, I'd appreciate a call so I can safeguard some of my animals."

"If it is, I believe the veterinarian is required to report it to the health department. The *Tribune* will put a notice in the paper."

"Okay then," Trent said, and pointed a finger at his daughter, Judy. "You. Back in your chair, and stay there, please."

Judy waved to Bonnie, and then frowned at her father as she sat back down.

Harold and Willa Dean Miller were sitting in the booth behind Laurel and had been unashamedly listening in on the conversation and quickly turned around to offer Laurel condolences. "Laurel, I'm so sorry for your loss," she said.

Laurel frowned. "I don't know what you mean."

Willa Dean flushed, certain she'd just committed a horrible faux pas. "Oh my. I'm sorry. I thought since you were part of the Payne family, you would have heard."

"They no longer consider me family," Laurel said. "So what are the condolences about?"

"Are you talking about the wreck last night?" Jake asked.

Harold piped up. "I heard it was terrible. Bodies were everywhere. They announced her demise at church this morning."

Jake's heart dropped. There was only one female there—the one he thought had not been seriously injured. "I was the first one on the scene. There were three people involved. You said, *she*? Are you saying Melanie Payne died?"

Willa Dean nodded. "From a brain injury."

He thought about the woman who'd been standing in the road last night—the only one mobile and the first one dead. Injuries were unpredictable, like war. Nothing was what it seemed. An ordinary road going through a desert becomes a minefield of IEDs. A car ride at night turns into a death knell for a family.

Jake frowned. Poor Melanie. Poor Luke. Their world just blew up.

Laurel felt sorry for the family, and most especially, the three children who'd just lost a mother. "I knew about the wreck through Jake, but I didn't know that anyone had passed. That's so very sad."

Before anything else was shared, the waitress arrived with their food and then gave Harold and Willa Dean their tab. Another waitress was at the Samuels' table taking orders, and the afternoon progressed.

Bonnie had her fried chicken leg along with mashed potatoes and gravy, but Laurel and Jake had settled for fried catfish dinners. The food was good, but it was the companionship that mattered most. Laurel found herself relaxing more by the minute. Yes, their presence raised a few eyebrows, but for the most part, people just waved and went about their business.

Peanut Butterman came in just as they were paying and getting ready to leave. He took keen notice of the couple and smiled to himself. There were two lonely people who needed somebody to love. It would be great if this dinner together were the first of many.

It didn't bother him that he was in the same boat as Jake. Peanut had his eye on a certain woman and had for some years. He was just waiting for her to see him as more than a customer. It would happen in its time. Until then, he was fine.

"Did you save me any fried chicken?" Peanut asked, as they passed by his booth.

"I only ate one piece," Bonnie said.

Peanut grinned. "Then there should be plenty for me, right?"

She shrugged. "I only asked the cook for one piece. If that chicken is all gone, it wasn't me," she said, and slid most of herself behind Laurel's leg.

Jake laughed. "Yeah, cut her some slack, Peanut. She's a little kid. She only ate one little piece, right, honey?"

She giggled as Peanut wiggled his eyebrows at her. She hid her face.

"Enjoy your meal," Jake said. "I better get these two home."

Bonnie fell asleep before they were out of Blessings.

Laurel glanced at Jake as he drove, thinking how normal he'd made this seem. Bonnie's childhood chatter didn't seem to bother Jake, and she hadn't felt nearly as uncomfortable as she'd expected.

"Hey, Jake?"

"Yeah?"

"This was wonderful. It was a really special time for Bonnie and I. Thank you so much."

Once again, he reached for her hand. "Honestly, it was my pleasure. I haven't felt this much at ease in years. Maybe when I get back, we can do it again?"

She heard the question, but it wasn't a question for her. "Yes, we can definitely do this again."

"Thank you."

"For what?" she asked.

He couldn't go into details for fear his voice would break. "Just thank you, that's all."

"Then you're welcome."

———∞———

Truman woke up Sunday morning with a smile on his face. This house was a far cry from a palace, but it beat a jail cell all to hell. He'd been released with the news that Nester refused to file charges, and May said as long as he never came back, she'd let him off the hook too.

He threw back the covers and walked naked to the bathroom, scratching as he went. He was in such a good mood that he decided to wash some clothes, starting with his sheets. They still had a lot of squirrel hair and nest material stuck in the cloth. He'd sleep better tonight if he didn't smell squirrel every time he turned over in bed.

So while Truman was turning over a new leaf, Adele and her family had gathered in Luke's hospital room to give him the news about his wife's death. Luke was sleeping when they came in, but woke when he heard the sound of so many footsteps.

Adele went straight to his bedside, claiming her right as the mother to break the news. David and Beverly followed, moving to the opposite side of the bed.

Luke saw their faces. He felt the tension. Something was wrong. When Adele patted his cheek and began to weep, his heartbeat accelerated to near-panic mode. "What's going on?" he asked.

"Oh, Luke! As your mother, it has fallen upon me to deliver news that will be a crushing blow to your life."

Beverly rolled her eyes at her brother and then glared at Adele. "Mama! Really?"

Luke grabbed Adele's hand and yanked it away from his face. "Save your preaching and say what you came to say."

Adele wiped her eyes and blew her nose, then delivered the news in a weird, penitent tone. "The hour after you came out of surgery, your beloved wife, Melanie, passed from this earth."

Luke gasped like he'd just been hit in the belly. "No," he said, and looked frantically at his siblings, waiting for one of them to tell him that she had lied. "It's not true! It can't be true." He grabbed Beverly's hand. "Sister, tell me that she lies."

"I'm so sorry, Luke, but she's gone."

Luke's gaze moved to his brother. "David?"

David nodded. "She fell into a coma soon after you were both brought in. She had a brain bleed they couldn't stop. I'm so sorry. Just know that Beverly and I are taking care of your boys. We had to tell them about their mama because of the funeral arrangements."

The sound Luke first began to make sounded like humming, but it kept getting louder. All of a sudden, he grabbed the plastic water pitcher by his bed and flung it at the wall.

The lid popped off on contact, and water went all over Adele's hair, her face, and her clothes. She was gasping and bawling and screaming at him that he'd gone and lost his mind when Beverly grabbed her mother and slapped her hand over her mouth.

"Be quiet! Do you hear me? There are sick people in these rooms. You can't scream at us in here like you do at home!" Adele was pushing, trying to get out of her daughter's grasp. "I'm not letting you go until you promise you'll keep your mouth shut!" Beverly hissed.

Adele's shoulders went limp. Water was dripping from her hair into her eyes. Her mascara was running, and her lipstick was smeared all over her chin. She stared at Luke as if she'd never seen him before.

"Why did you do that?" she whispered.

"If it hadn't been for you wanting revenge,

Melanie and I would not have been on that road. I take responsibility for letting you rule my family like they were your own, but you're gonna have to live with the fact that Melanie is dead because of what you wanted done."

Beverly gasped and then stared at her mother in disbelief. "What is he talking about? What did you do?"

David was shaking. He knew. He'd been standing beside Luke when she gave them the orders. "Mama told us to keep bothering Laurel," David said.

Beverly stared at her brothers as if she'd never seen them before. "What do you mean, keep *bothering* her? What have you been doing?"

Luke leaned back in the bed and closed his eyes, too weak and sick at heart to face his sister.

David sighed. "Ever since Adam's death, we've been throwing dead animals in her yard or leaving them in her drive."

"You haven't! Please say you haven't been doing this!" Beverly cried.

"She told us to, so we did it," David said. "And don't get so high and mighty all of a sudden. We all harassed her because Mama told us to."

Adele took a hand towel from the sink and began drying off her hair and face. Her clothes were going to be wet until they dried, and there was nothing she could do about that.

"She killed your brother! She doesn't deserve to live in peace."

David pointed a finger at her from the other side of the bed. "Shut up, Mama. Just stop talking. Adam killed himself. I'm sure Laurel has suffered enough, and

Luke's right. Melanie wouldn't be dead if you hadn't kept at us. Luke, get well. We'll figure the rest of it out after you get to go home."

"I'll help, too," Beverly said. "We'll figure it all out together."

"What about me?" Adele cried. "I can take care of my own grandsons just fine if need be."

"You won't take care of my kids," Luke said.

"Or mine," David said.

"Or mine," Beverly added. "I think you are about to find out what it's like to be Moses wandering in the wilderness, Mama."

Adele's expression said it all. She picked up her purse and walked out of the room without looking back.

Beverly turned to her brothers. "What do you think she's going to do?"

David shrugged. "Whatever it is, she'll do it alone."

Luke was crying. "Have you all set a day for the funeral? Do you think they'll let me go?"

"Today's Sunday. We told the funeral home Wednesday afternoon. If the doctor will let you leave for a bit, we can take you in a wheelchair," David said.

"I want to see my kids," Luke said. "I need to make sure they know I'm gonna be fine, and that I'll be there for them."

"I'll bring them tomorrow. We're keeping them out of school this coming week."

"I agree," Luke said, and then swiped the tears off his cheeks. "Mama's not the only one who'll have to live with this. I took her with me. She wanted to go, but I should have insisted she stay home with the kids. If I had, she would still be with me." Then he started crying again in earnest. "God in heaven, how am I gonna get through life without her?"

Beverly hugged him. "One day at a time, Luke."

Because Jake's plane left Savannah so early in the morning on Tuesday, he drove into the city on Monday and got a room at one of the airport hotels. He thought about all that he was leaving behind and then had to trust everything and everyone would be safe until he returned. He walked around the city for a while, but the constant movement of people and traffic was stressful, and he finally went back to the hotel, ate an early supper, and went to bed.

DeSosa was sitting on the fender of a transport truck, sharpening his knife.

"Better be careful you don't cut yourself," Jake said.

DeSosa was grinning as he looked up. "Don't be silly, Georgia boy. I cleaned my fingernails with one bigger than this back home."

A fire truck drove past the hotel with sirens screaming.

Jake rolled over and sat up, remembered where he was, then laid back down and closed his eyes.

Jake was hunkered down in a shallow ditch with his rifle trained on the horizon less than two hundred yards ahead. His ghillie suit was the same color as the sand. They knew a sniper was somewhere on the ridge, and they'd sent Jake in under cover of night almost eight hours earlier. He had slithered down into the hole and pulled a sand-colored tarp in over him. Once he'd located the sniper's position with the scope on his rife, he had been lying in wait ever since.

He could still hear faint radio chatter in his earpiece and was intently focused on the faint glint of sunlight that had suddenly caught in the scope on the sniper's rifle when he heard someone on the radio yell, "Sandstorm."

He couldn't move without giving himself away, but then neither could the man on the ridge. In less than two minutes, he would be engulfed. He could pull the tarp in around him and ride it out, but it was going to be hell on his eyes and lungs.

He could hear the roar now as the storm rolled closer.

"Move, damn it, move," he muttered, unwilling to waste the past eight hours for nothing.

The air between them was no longer as clear as it had been. What he could see of the sky was getting dark. The wind was beginning to whip at his ghillie suit, and the tarp was coming loose behind him.

All of a sudden the sniper broke. With less cover than Jake, his life was in danger. He raised up less than two inches, probably to assess his best way out, and Jake pulled the trigger.

Jake saw blood spray into the air, and then the man and the blood disappeared as the storm rolled over the hill. Jake had less than five seconds to do what he had to do. He grabbed the tarp and rolled himself in it, pulling the end down over his head and face. He was facedown with less than a six-inch span of space between him and the tarp when the blast hit. The last thing he felt was the weight of the sand and then nothing.

The next thing he heard was the faint sound of cursing. The radio was still active on his earpiece, and he recognized DeSosa's voice.

"Dig faster. That Georgia boy comes from the mountains. He won't live long under that sand. Dig, damn it, dig."

Jake woke with tears on his face. He rolled over and sat on the side of the bed, his lungs burning and his heart pounding, like they had the day they'd found him.

"Damn it, DeSosa, you kept saving me. Why couldn't you save yourself?"

He closed his eyes, and when he did, he could hear DeSosa laughing.

When your time is up, Georgia boy, it doesn't matter if you are ready or not. You'll be gone.

He got up and dressed, then grabbed a cab and headed for the airport. He'd rather wait two hours in the terminal than hang around that room another second.

Laurel looked toward Jake's house as she passed by on the way to work. After seeing the red truck in the carport for all these weeks, it seemed lonely now with it gone.

But she had one more task to do this morning before she went to work. She was going by Harper's Funeral home and sign the visitation book for Melanie Payne. It wasn't so much that she was heartbroken by what happened, as it was the human thing to do. She'd belonged to that family, and even though they'd rejected her, she wanted to do the right thing. By coming this early in the morning, Laurel was betting there wouldn't be any family on-site, because if they were, this idea ended here and now. However, when she pulled up in the parking lot, the only car there was the old black Cadillac that belonged to Evelyn Harper, the owner.

She grabbed her purse and headed inside. The door sounded a faint buzzer, and moments later, Evelyn entered the lobby.

"Laurel, good morning, my dear, and my deepest sympathies to you and your family."

"I just came to sign the visitation book," Laurel said.

"Certainly, this way," Evelyn said, and led her to a room down the hall. "I'll leave you here. If there's anything you need, I'll be in the office up front."

"Yes, ma'am," Laurel said, and hesitated a moment, then walked into the room.

Floral sprays hung from hooks on the walls. Potted plants and larges vases of flowers sat on the floor around the casket or on tables at both ends.

She felt a little sick and a little sad for what Melanie's children were facing. She and Bonnie were already living it. When she glanced into the casket, it appeared as if Melanie were just sleeping.

"God bless," she whispered, then signed the book and quickly left the building.

Today she worked at the Blessings Bed-and-Breakfast until 2:00 p.m. It would be a full and busy day, which she liked. It made time go faster.

It was fifteen minutes to nine when she parked at the B and B. Jake would be boarding about now. "Safe flight, Jacob Lorde."

She grabbed her purse, locked her truck, and hurried inside to go to work.

Yesterday, Truman Slade's one day of industry had petered out before noon. His sheets were clean, one load of clothes was washed and still in the dryer, waiting to be put up. The floor was still as dirty as before, and Truman's thoughts were jumbled.

He'd tried calling Nester, but didn't get an answer. He left a message that wasn't returned. By the time he figured out that Nester was most likely still mad, it made him angry, too.

Hell, if two buddies couldn't get drunk together and have a little scuffle without getting all bent out of joint, then they were done. He didn't need all that drama.

After eating the last of his cereal and milk, he decided to run into Blessings and stop at the Piggly Wiggly for a few things. And before he went, he just might drive out toward the Lorde property and see what the hotshot war hero was doing.

He started out the door and then stopped and went back inside to get a coat. The sky was gray, and the day was cold. No time to be casual about what he was wearing.

He drove off with a dozen ideas turning in his head until he drove by the Lorde place and saw that the truck was gone. He drove on down the road to the trailer where Laurel Payne lived, but her old truck was gone, too.

This gave him the perfect time to check out the back side of both properties. Truman believed in being prepared, and one day, he and Jake would have a come-to-Jesus meeting. When it happened, Truman needed to know where the shortest escape routes would be.

Adele Payne had spent the night on her knees, praying to God for forgiveness, then trying to figure out how to get back into her children's good graces.

She thought about having a little accident of some kind, nothing serious, but something that would require tending to. They wouldn't let her suffer alone. They surely wouldn't let her be ill on her own.

But there was always the possibility that a plan like that could backfire. She could wind up really hurt and in a hospital alone. And she didn't have money to spend on a scenario like that. So she went out onto her back porch and sat down in her rocker with a pipe of tobacco. Not a lot of women smoked a pipe anymore, but her Mammy had smoked and her Granny had smoked, and so she had the habit. She pulled the blanket close around her shoulders as she rocked, while the smoke from her pipe encircled her head before drifting upward.

It was quiet on the mountain, reminding her of the early years when it was just her and her man, before Luke was even born. After that, it seemed the babies came yearly. Beverly was next, then David, then Adam, her baby.

She rocked a little slower and was taking fewer puffs from the pipe. Her eyelids were drooping, and the sun felt hot on her chest. At least she thought it was the sun until she looked up at and saw the gray, overcast sky.

The heat in her chest was spreading and her arm was getting numb. She put out her pipe and laid it down beside her foot, then leaned back and closed her eyes. All she needed was a rest.

Beverly was trying to figure out where to put her neph-
ew's clothes until Luke was ready to go home when her
phone began to ring. She glanced at caller ID before she
answered, unwilling to get into another argument with her
mother, then saw it was one of their neighbors, probably
just hearing about Melanie's passing.

"Hello," she said, and then realized the caller was crying.

"Beverly, this is Esther Wilson. I heard about Melanie
and drove up to your mama's house to pay my respects
and… Oh lord, oh lord, I don't know how to say this.
Honey, I found your mama in the rocker on her back
porch. She's gone, honey. I guess the grief done took
her home."

Beverly felt the blood rush and thought she was going
to faint, then quickly sat down on the side of her son's
bed. "Are you telling me that Mama is dead?"

Esther let out a wail. "Yes, lord, she is. I haven't ever
found a dead body before. I haven't called anyone. All I
could think was to call you."

Beverly's head was spinning. *Sweet Mother of God.*

"Look, Esther, you would be doing me a great favor if
you would just stay at the house with my mama's body
until I can get there. You can go sit in your car if that
makes you uneasy. It won't take me ten minutes, okay?"

"Yes, I will do that," Esther said, and then sat down
on the back steps while Beverly was making frantic
phone calls to David at his work and Trisha at her home.

Tears were still running down Esther's face, but she
was feeling calmer now that she'd given the burden of
this discovery away. She looked out at the trees and the
clearing in which Adele Payne's little house had been
built, and then started rocking back and forth, shattered

by what this day had given her.

Before long she was singing, her thin, wavery voice echoing out upon the mountain. "Swing low, sweet chariot," she sang, drawing out the syllables in a slow, mournful refrain.

She could hear a car engine straining as it started up this hill, and yet she kept singing, although part of the verses were drowned out now by the sounds of more than one vehicle speeding up the drive, but she persisted to the end.

"...to carry me home."

Chapter 13

JAKE LANDED IN L.A. WITHOUT PROBLEMS, grabbed his carry-on and garment bag, and tried to find his way out of the terminal. It was the constant burst of voices over the intercom announcing incoming flights, delays on others, and reporting lost items left at the gates that made his skin crawl.

He stood a head taller than most and could see from one end of the long corridor to the other. The scuffle of thousands of feet and the underlying mumble of voices all around him was overwhelming. He didn't like the crowds, and he didn't like feeling out of control.

By the time he exited the terminal and reached the taxi stand, he was just another traveler in line, getting ready to go somewhere else. When he finally got in a taxi, the relative silence within the vehicle was welcome. He gave the driver the address of his hotel and then leaned back and closed his eyes. He didn't need to see palm trees or tourist landmarks and wasn't interested in anything but getting to the hotel. As soon as he was settled, he would call Sophia DeSosa, and if it was convenient, go to the house to pay his respects.

It took forty minutes to get to his hotel. It was somewhat off the beaten path, but the area seemed okay, and spending two nights here was far safer than bivouacked anywhere in Afghanistan.

He asked for a room on the ground floor next to an

exit. The clerk gave him a curious look, but didn't comment other than to ask for a credit card and ID. "Will you need more than one key?" the desk clerk asked.

"No. One is plenty," Jake said.

"Do you need help with your luggage?" the clerk asked.

Jake shook his head, picked up his bags, and followed the directions to his room.

The room was stuffy, but once he regulated the thermostat to a cooler temperature, it didn't take long before he began to feel the cold air. He hung up his uniform, put his shaving kit in the bathroom, and then sat down on the side of the bed to collect his wits. It was 5:00 p.m. here, but 8:00 p.m. back home. He wanted to lie down and sleep, but it was time to call DeSosa's wife.

It rang four times before someone answered, and the noise in the background was obviously making it difficult for the person to hear what Jake was saying. Finally, Jake raised his voice. "I said—this is Jake Lorde. May I speak to Sophia?"

All of a sudden, the young man shouted out, "Everyone! Be quiet! Sophia! It is Joaquin's friend. It is Jake."

Jake didn't know how to react to being a known entity to people he'd never met. Yes, he knew of DeSosa's wife. He'd seen pictures. He'd heard stories of their life together, but she belonged to a part of the man he'd never known.

Then there was a soft voice in his ear, and the image of her face slid through his mind. Now he knew what she sounded like. "Hello, this is Sophia. Is this you, Jacob Lorde?"

"Yes, I'm here in L.A. Just got to the hotel a few minutes ago."

"You are coming here, are you not?" she asked.

"Yes, ma'am, if it's okay."

There was a slight catch in her voice and then a soft laugh. "You also sound like the Georgia boy. Tell me what hotel, and I will send family to pick you up."

"No, ma'am, there's no need for that. I chose one close to your address. I'll take a cab to your house. If you want, someone can bring me back then."

"As you wish," Sophia said. "You will eat with us. You will laugh with us, and if you wish, you can also cry with us. It is what we do. We will see you soon, Jake Lorde."

There were tears in Jake's eyes when he hung up. He called the desk about a cab, then made sure he had all of the addresses he needed. After washing up, he decided to change shirts and was absently eyeing his scars as he stripped off the dirty one. They didn't define him, but the simple act of bathing or changing clothes was a constant reminder that they were there.

After getting to the lobby, he waited an extra ten minutes for the cab to arrive, and then it took another ten minutes to get to the right address. The farther he rode, the more anxious he became.

And then they were there.

He got out, pausing momentarily on the sidewalk as the cab sped away. The Spanish architecture of the house was evident by the tiles on the roof as well as the arched doorway and windows of the beige stucco house. The landscaping was cactus plants and palm trees—about as far removed from Blessings, Georgia, as a man could get.

And then the front door opened, and a dark-haired

woman in her midthirties came out and met him on the sidewalk halfway to the house.

Her hair matched the color of her eyes, and the smile on her face was welcoming. "I am Sophia. Welcome to my home, and thank you for coming."

"Thank you for the plane ticket and the invitation."

There was one small moment of uncomfortable silence, and then she threw her arms around his waist, and the moment she did, he gathered her to him in a quiet embrace. He felt her shaking and knew that she was crying.

It was the saddest day of his life.

For Jake, the next few hours passed in a haze. It was healing and exhausting, and by the time he was ready to leave, he had turned loose of the guilt of being alive when Joaquin was not. The DeSosa family accepted Joaquin's death as a result of his choice to serve his country, and they were proud of what he'd done.

Finally, it was Joaquin's brother-in-law Miguel, who took him back to the hotel. They said little on the ride over until Jake was about to get out.

Then Miguel spoke. "Thank you for coming. It meant everything to Sophia."

Jake struggled with the words until he finally said what was in his heart. "I owed your brother so much, but I came because I loved him. He was the brother I never had. He saved my life, so I am taking the job of living it well very seriously. I would never want it to be said that I did not appreciate the gift."

Miguel reached for Jake's hand and shook it. "Joaquin was always a good judge of character. You have proven that already. We will see you tomorrow. Someone will be by to pick you up at eleven thirty in the morning. You will eat with us again, and then we will all go to the service together."

"Thank you for the ride," Jake said.

Miguel smiled then. "Joaquin had a saying."

Jake interrupted. "I know that one. 'Life is the ride.'"

Miguel chuckled. "Sleep well, my friend."

"And you," Jake said, and then got out and went inside as Miguel drove away.

He nodded at the night clerk as he strode past the desk and walked all the way to the end of the hall to his room. Once inside, he checked his belongings to make sure they had not been disturbed and then locked himself in for the night.

He was tired but he needed to unwind. It was midnight at home. Too late to call Laurel. So he sat down and sent her a text. She would read it the next morning. Maybe she would call. He wouldn't mind being awakened in a few hours, just to hear her voice.

Spent the evening with my friend's family. His service is tomorrow at two. I'm tired. I'm sad. I will be glad when this is over. Hope you and giggle girl are good.

He hit Send and then began getting undressed. In less than five minutes, he'd set the alarm and was ready for bed, praying with everything in him that there wouldn't be dreams. After adjusting the thermostat for sleeping, he crawled between the covers and was reaching to turn off the night-light when his phone signaled a text. His pulse kicked as he picked it up.

It *was* from Laurel.

> Giggle girl and I are fine. Adam's mother, Adele Payne, was found dead in a chair on her back porch. I feel brave enough to say this, since you cannot see my face. I miss your presence in our lives. As Bonnie would say, I am sorry for your sad.

Jake sat reading the message countless times until all he saw was: *I miss you.* Without thinking, he sent back one last text.

> I miss you, too.

—⁓—

Laurel had awakened instantly when she'd heard her phone signal a text. Reading Jake's message made her sad for him and, at the same time, elated that he'd reached out in a time of despair. Her heart was pounding as she sent her text, and then the moment she'd hit Send, was wishing she could take it back. She shouldn't have said that, about missing him. She threw herself backward onto the bed with a flop.

"Way to go, lady. You are such a dumbass. He will never want to see your face again."

She was still bemoaning her mistake when her phone dinged. Her heart skipped a beat as she sat back up and reached for the phone and read the text.

"He misses me, too?" She giggled. "He misses me, too!" It took a few moments for all of the implications to sink in. "He misses me," she whispered, and then put herself back to bed with the phone in her hands, because his words were all she had of him to hold.

―――ᴍ―――

The next day for Jake started out as the last one had ended—back with the family. There was more food, more stories, more laughing, and more weeping. By the time they left for the cathedral, he was emotionally exhausted. He'd been told what to expect, but the ornate countenance of the old Catholic church was far grander than anything he'd ever worshiped in, and the ceremony was lost in his wish that it was over.

The family had spoken with the priest and requested certain aspects of the service be given to any of his friends who wanted to speak of how they knew him, and so they came, one by one to the front of the church, and were handed a microphone to speak. Some were sad. Some brought laughter. Even the priest told a story of Joaquin's years as an altar boy and getting caught tasting the wine. It was the laughter that Jake held on to, because he knew his time would come when there was little to laugh at.

And then Sophia reached out and patted his arm, and he stood. By his uniform, he was marked as someone from the place where Joaquin's life had ended. But it was with respect and not anger that his presence was received.

"My name is Jacob Lorde. Joaquin called me 'Georgia boy,' because that's where I'm from. I have no words to explain what he meant to me other than he was the brother I never had. He saved my life. Twice. I would have given anything to return the favor. I didn't know what had happened to him until right before Sophia sent me a package. In it, her letter said she had promised Joaquin that if anything ever happened to him that she was to send me a bottle of tequila, a plane ticket to his funeral, and to remind me that I owed him five dollars."

The congregation was in tears, and then they laughed. When Jake took a folded-up five-dollar bill from his pocket and laid it on the altar, they were crying all over again. "Here you go, DeSosa. Now all I owe you is my life."

Jake was shaking as he walked back to where he'd been sitting. He had no memory of the end of the service or of going back to the hotel. He sat in the hotel bar alone later in the evening and ordered a shot of tequila, then looked at his reflection in the mirror behind the bar, and lifted the shot glass in a toast.

"To you, my brother. You are loved. You will be missed."

He downed the drink and went straight to his room and packed, set the alarm, and sent Laurel a text. Home tomorrow. Today was hard.

Her text came back quickly, as if she'd been waiting to hear from him. Tomorrow will be better. We will be waiting.

He exhaled as if he'd been holding his breath and then lay down on the top of the bed, fully dressed in what he intended to wear home tomorrow. He was wasting no time.

Daylight couldn't come soon enough.

Laurel got up the next morning with a feeling of anticipation and, at the same time, one of dread. She had a pie in the oven before daylight, and as soon as she got Bonnie off to school, she loaded up the warm pie and headed north.

She drove through Blessings with a knot in her stomach and kept driving until she took the turn that would take her back to her past. When she reached the road where all of the Payne family lived, she started to shake. Twice she almost turned around and went home, but each time she reminded herself that life wasn't about doing what was easy. Life was about doing what had to be done.

She knew the turnoff to Beverly's home by heart, and when she got there, saw the yard was packed with cars. Dogs began to bark when she drove up and parked, and children who'd been playing out in the yard stopped to see who was arriving. She recognized her nieces and nephews and was shocked by how much they'd grown in the past two years.

Dreading the next few minutes with all her heart, she picked up her pie and slid out of the car. The air was sharp, and the sun wasn't shining. The only thing positive was that the warm pie felt good in cold hands.

She couldn't bring herself to look at the men standing around beneath the bare-limbed trees, as if they were still in need of shade. She was scared half out of her mind at how she would be received, but she kept telling herself this was the right thing to do.

She had just reached the porch when the front door suddenly opened. Beverly came out wearing an apron over what Laurel knew was one of the dresses that she probably wore to church. A half dozen women came out behind her. Laurel recognized every one of them.

The look on Beverly's face was one of shock, but Laurel came up the steps until they met on the porch. For a few strained moments, she looked at each without speaking.

And then Laurel stated the obvious. "I brought a pie. I am so sorry for what's happened to your family."

Beverly burst into tears, took the pie out of Laurel's hands, handed it off to one of the others, and threw her arms around Laurel's neck. They cried together for all they'd lost—for the family and for the years of rancor between them—until they couldn't cry any more.

"Will you come in?" Beverly asked.

Laurel wiped her eyes and shook her head. "No. I have two houses to clean before Bonnie gets home."

Beverly saw how thin Laurel was compared to before. But that determined look was still in her eyes, and she wouldn't say more. "I understand. Thank you for coming. This means the world to me...to all of us."

"And to me," Laurel said, but when she turned around to walk back down the steps, David was standing between her and her car.

She glanced back nervously at Beverly. "It's okay," Beverly said. "We've all had our come-to-Jesus meeting this week."

Laurel went down the steps with her head up, but instead of trading angry words, David hugged her. "I'm sorry," he said. "Please forgive me."

Laurel was struggling with what to say when she began seeing pieces of Adam in her brother-in-law's face. "You should be," she whispered, and then hugged him back. "What on earth were you thinking?"

David was struggling not to cry, but he managed a

wry grimace. "You already know the answer to that. None of us had a thought in our heads unless Mama put it there. Just know that I will regret what we did for the rest of my life."

"Beverly came to my house the other day. Bonnie didn't know who she was. Is that how it's going to be?"

David looked horrified. "No, no!" Then he shook his head in disbelief. "She didn't know her?"

"She won't remember any of you. She was four when Adam died. Two years of absence in a toddler's life is a lifetime, so if you want a future relationship with your niece, you will have to rebuild it."

"For sure," David said. "Luke and I will make this right."

"He's going to be okay?" Laurel asked.

David's shoulders slumped. "His body will heal long before his heart does. I'm sure you know that better than most."

"Yes, I suppose I do. So, I need to leave now. Work is always waiting."

"Let us know if we can help."

A twinge of anger shot through her that she was finally hearing this so long after the fact, and then she let it go. "We're okay, Bonnie and I. My mom and dad are getting up in years, but they're still a lot of help." And then she thought of Jake and decided they might as well know now that her life was her own. "And Mr. Lorde's son moved home. He's nearby and has been unexpected, but much appreciated help."

"Luke told me that he was the first one on the scene at the wreck. He said Jake saved his life by putting a tourniquet on his leg. It kept him from bleeding to death."

"Jake told me that it was bad. He has some issues with PTSD, and so all of that was like taking a step back into the war for him."

David's eyes widened. "I didn't know. I will make a point to thank him for that next time I see him."

"I better go," Laurel said.

David reached out and momentarily grasped her wrist. "Be happy, Laurel. Adam would want that."

"I know."

And then she was gone, but her presence there on the mountain had served the purpose for which she'd gone. The ill will was over—dead with Adele. It was past time for joy to come home.

Truman was in the bushes behind Laurel's trailer when he saw her drive away. Since she was gone and Jake Lorde was gone, he figured he could pilfer anything his heart desired without fear of being caught.

He slipped through the trees to the first building and saw one chicken in the little lot, scratching in the dirt. He saw the name painted on the threshold above the door to the coop and grinned. "So your name is Lavonne! I once screwed a girl named Lavonne," he said, and then laughed as if he'd said the funniest thing.

But the chicken meant nothing, and he didn't want to cook, so he paused, trying to decide what to do next. He saw the trailer. It was an older one. He could break into the back door easily without being seen from the road, but he knew the bitch was poor. Probably wasn't worth the trouble. It would be easier to move on up the road to the Lorde property. There was plenty there to be had.

He just had to make sure what he took couldn't be traced back to Jake. Not only was he scared of going back to prison, but he was also scared of Jake Lorde. After all, the dude had gone to war and came back crazy. He did not want a piece of that.

He noticed a shed that had seen its better days. There might be something in there he could haul off for good money, so he headed that way. He noticed, as he drew closer, that there was some kind of paper tacked to the door. When he finally got to it, he had to squint and get closer to read what it said.

It appeared to be a note from the local vet to Laurel Payne that he'd removed the carcass and was taking it back to the lab for testing. If it turned out to be rabid as suspected, they would let everyone know an animal in the area had been diagnosed with rabies.

It was the word *rabies* that finally got his attention.

"Holy shit!" he yelped, and yanked away from the doorknob he'd been holding on to and wiped that hand on his pants.

He pivoted in a panic and began looking at every bush and tree, imagining some loco animal coming after him. All of a sudden, the thought of pilfering anything on this property took a dive.

Once he realized he had a clear shot to the path leading back to the creek, he took it. He ran through the trees and bushes, scrambling down the creek bank, splashing through the water and then scrambling back up the other side, and didn't stop running until he reached his truck. His hands were shaking as he fumbled with his keys, and then finally, they were in the ignition, and he was gone.

He kept telling himself that it wasn't like he was giving up on ruining Jake Lorde's life, but he had plenty of time to enact revenge. He'd just wait until this rabies scare died down.

Jake wouldn't let himself sleep on the plane home for fear he'd have a dream and freak out the passengers. He changed planes in Tulsa, Oklahoma, and then had a nonstop flight from there to Savannah, Georgia.

The last leg of the flight was like the first. He'd bought a book in the Tulsa airport and then felt like a dinosaur reading the paperback when nearly all of the other passengers were using technology. But the truth was, he didn't mind. He'd never much cared what anyone else thought about him, and he liked the feel of holding a book. Turning the page was part of the experience, like walking through another door in a house you've never seen, wondering what was in it—what happened next—and holding the book left him in control.

Later, landing in Savannah was a huge relief to Jake. He was this much closer to home. He got his luggage, retrieved his truck from airport parking, and started home.

The day was chilly, and the sky was gray. When it began to rain, he didn't even care. He'd take rain any day over a damn sandstorm. He knew the way home, and the windshield wipers had his six.

Chapter 14

LAUREL KEPT AN EYE ON THE TIME AS SHE STOPPED AT THE LAUREL KEPT AN EYE ON THE TIME AS SHE STOPPED AT THE Piggly Wiggly for groceries. She had just dropped her last item in the basket when she heard a familiar voice.

"Laurel! Hey, honey."

She turned, smiling, and gave her mother a big hug. "Mama! You look good. Are you feeling better?"

Pansy Joyner patted Laurel's cheek. "Yes, I'm finally better. That flu bug took a big bite of me, for sure. How's my other girl? I haven't seen her since just after she got her stitches out."

Laurel grinned. "Bonnie Carol is fine, and her scar is now a badge of honor. You and Dad need to come over some night and eat supper with us."

"That sounds great. You name the night, and we're there," Pansy said.

"Well, today is Thursday. I work late tomorrow, so why don't we say Saturday around six? I'm home all day. That will give me time to make something good."

"Okay with me," Pansy said, and then took her daughter by the hand and gave it a little tug. "So, do you have anything you want to tell me?"

Laurel frowned. "Tell you? Are you talking about the feud finally ending between me and Adam's family?"

Pansy gasped. "No, I didn't know about that. Thank goodness. You'll have to tell me all about it Saturday. I was talking about the date you had over the weekend."

Laurel rolled her eyes. "Mama, having a meal with our next-door neighbor is hardly a date."

"Well, he's obviously around you enough that you're comfortable going out with him, and we didn't know anything about it."

Laurel wasn't surprised this conversation was happening, but she wasn't happy about it either. "Let's see, Mama. Let me think. Oh, he loaned me his truck the day Laurel cut her chin because mine went flat in front of his house. He's returned some of my mail that wound up in his box, and… Oh yes…this is the real kicker. He shot a rabid raccoon at my house Sunday."

"Rabies?"

"We think so. It was acting really strange. Bonnie was outside when she saw it. It's a miracle she wasn't bitten."

Pansy shivered. "Oh my, I'm so glad she wasn't."

"Me too. I know I could have called Dad, but I was afraid the animal would run off before anyone could kill it, and then we'd all have to be worried about some rabid animal on the loose. I took a chance and called Jake because he was closest, and he came."

Pansy listened, but she knew her daughter. "So, do you like him?"

Laurel shrugged. "What's not to like, Mama? He's kind to both of us."

"He was a soldier, too," Pansy said. "What if he—"

Laurel frowned. "Stop right there, Mama. You're better than that. Daddy fought in the Vietnam War. Are you going to tell me he didn't have bad times after he came back?"

Pansy flushed.

"Look," Laurel said. "I'll see if Jake will come to

dinner Saturday night. But you both need to keep in mind, he's not a stranger. He's older than me, but he belongs to Blessings just like the rest of us. Now, I have to hurry. I have to be home before Bonnie gets off the bus. I love you, but you have to remember, I've been married, birthed a baby, and I have seen the devil and survived my own kind of hell. You have no say in how I live my life because I am an honorable woman. It is just your job to love me, understand?"

Pansy took a deep breath. "You're right. I'll bring dessert," she said.

"Good. I like your cooking better than mine anyway," Laurel said, then kissed her mother on the cheek and hurried to check out.

Pansy Joyner saw the bounce in her daughter's step. She hadn't seen that in years. Laurel liked Jake Lorde, whether she knew it or not.

———

It started raining while Laurel was in the grocery, and now she was getting soaked putting groceries in the backseat. By the time she got in the truck, she was shivering and started the engine so she could turn on the heater.

She thought about the route Bonnie's school bus would take and then glanced at the time. If she hadn't stopped to talk to her mother, she would have had been able to pick Bonnie up from school, but now, it was too late. She would just have to hope the roads didn't get too slick before the driver could get the kids home. Even though their road was blacktopped, half of the route it took was on dirt back roads. It wouldn't be the first time they'd been stuck.

She drove out of town with a knot in her stomach and knew part of it had to do with her mother. The questions had made her uncomfortable. She didn't like being forced to justify her actions to anyone. She would do what she felt was right, and if she wanted to see Jake Lorde anytime he was in the mood for company, then that's what she would do.

She drove home in a snit, and when she passed Jake's house couldn't help but look for his red truck under the carport, even though she knew it was too early for him to get home. Still, she felt a surge of excitement just knowing he was going to be back within reach.

She got to the trailer and unlocked the door, then left it ajar as she ran back for the sacks. Both hands were full as she ran to the house, tracking mud and water as she went. She kicked off her shoes as she shut the front door and then headed to the kitchen to put up groceries. She stripped in the utility room and then ran naked to her bedroom for dry clothes, turning up the thermostat as she went.

Later, Laurel drove the pickup up the long drive to the road to get Bonnie off the bus. The rain was still heavy, and her driveway was mud. She had already fed Lavonne, gathered her egg, and then shut her up for the night. There was soup thawing on the stove and a load of clothes in the washer. Everything was in order. After surviving what Adam had done to their lives, she needed order to be able to function.

Sitting in the truck and listening to the rain hammer on the roof was making her sleepy, so when the bus finally appeared, she was glad. She jumped out, comfortably waterproof this time in rubber boots and a raincoat. And she had an umbrella to keep Bonnie dry until she got her in the truck.

Boyd Fisher, the bus driver, pulled to a stop and waved as she darted across the road.

"Thanks, Boyd," Laurel said.

Boyd waved. "Bye, Bonnie," he said.

"Bye, Mr. Fisher," Bonnie cried, and leaped into Laurel's outstretched arms, locked her legs around her mother's waist, and then held on to the umbrella for both of them as Laurel carried her back to the truck and put her inside.

Laurel dripped rain as she got in, and as soon as the bus drove away, she pulled out onto the blacktop to turn around and headed back to the trailer with her little girl high and dry.

"You got all wet, Mommy," Bonnie said.

"Just on the outside, honey. Did you have a good day at school?"

"Yes. Did you feed Lavonne?"

"Yes, I did, and I put her up. You'll just have to wave at the coop from the window tonight. Lavonne is warm and dry, and I want to keep you the same way."

"Did she lay an egg today?" Bonnie asked.

Laurel smiled. "Yes, she did. A very pretty one."

Bonnie wiggled with delight, and when they reached the house, she let Laurel carry her to the porch. Within moments they were both inside, and so the evening settled.

The trailer was warm. The vegetable soup Laurel had taken out of the freezer was thawed and reheating on the back burner, and Bonnie was sitting on her bed talking to Brave Bear. Laurel could hear part of the chatter

as she moved about the house. After making sure nothing was wrong and Bonnie was just filling him in on the
day, she let her play.

It was already dark, but not quite five o'clock. She
thought of Jake. Was he home, or was he still driving
in this mess?

No sooner had she thought that when her phone signaled
a text. She ran to look and was grinning when she saw who
had sent it. I am in Blessings getting gas. Home soon.

And just like that, all the tension of her day was gone.
Soup is done here. Come if you want. No RSVP needed
if you'd rather go home. She hit Send.

She laid the phone down and told herself she wouldn't
stand there and stare, but when it suddenly dinged, she
jumped. Soup please.

She sent a happy face and set the table for one more.

The moment Jake got that invitation for soup, he began
to relax and the tension in his body eased until all he was
thinking about was being in her presence. God help him,
but Laurel Payne had become his touchstone to peace,
an irony that would not have escaped her had she known
how he felt.

Jake was so focused on getting to her house that he
didn't notice he was getting close to his own driveway
until he saw his mailbox. On impulse, he took the turn
and stopped at his house long enough to turn on some
lights and turn up the thermostat. Moments later, he
was back on the road, watching for that certain hill and
knowing when he topped it, he would see her house.

And just as he'd expected, when he came over the hill

and saw the trailer all lit up like a church on Christmas Eve, the last of his tension was gone. Despite the rain and the muddy drive, it looked like a piece of heaven, right down to the light on the porch marking the way.

He parked behind her truck and got out on the run. The front door flew inward as he was coming up the steps, and then she was laughing as he leaped over the threshold and out of the rain.

"Welcome home," she said.

He grinned. "If I wasn't so wet, I would hug you. I am so glad to be back."

"Don't let a little water stop you," she said.

He shed the coat where he stood and then wrapped his arms around her. "Oh my lord, you even smell good," he said, as he buried his face in the crown of her hair.

"It's either lemon furniture oil or vegetable soup," she said, while trying not to make a fool of herself in his arms.

Jake chuckled. "You are the first pretty woman I ever knew who was willing to make fun of herself," he said as he let her go.

"Extra soup for that compliment," she said, and pointed to the old bath mat she'd shoved off to the side. "You can wipe your shoes on that rug to dry them off, and the food will warm you up."

"You have no idea how happy I am to be here," he said.

She couldn't have wiped the smile from her face if she'd had to. "I am happy you're here, too. Hand me your jacket, and I'll hang it up in the utility room to dry. I'm doing laundry, and it's warm in there."

Jake handed her the jacket and followed her to the kitchen. "My lord, it smells good in here, too," he said.

She hung up the jacket and then flashed a quick smile as she headed to the stove.

"There's fresh coffee on the counter if you want some. I made sandwiches to go with the soup. They're in the fridge on a plate. I'm going to get Bonnie washed up to eat. She did not know you were coming, so prepare yourself."

"I'll put the sandwiches on the table for you. What does she drink?"

"Her milk is in a carton in the door of the refrigerator. Her cups are in the cabinet. They're the plastic ones with handles. Pour about a half a cup for her."

"Will do," Jake said, and was suddenly at ease.

The calm in this house was the solace he needed, but it didn't last long. He heard Bonnie squeal and then doors banging, and laughed to himself. Who would have ever predicted he would become a rock star to a six-year-old?

Bonnie came into the kitchen carrying Brave Bear and talking.

"Hi, Jake. We're having soup. I have to blow on mine so it won't burn the hair off my tongue. Brave Bear is going to sit with us, but he won't eat. Bears don't like soup."

"And hello to you, too, Bonnie Bee. You buzz around like a little bee," Jake said.

She giggled, delighted with her new nickname, and then went straight to the table, seated the bear, and Laurel lifted her into a chair that had a booster seat.

"I'm sitting on a rooster seat for now, but I'm growing. One day I won't have to sit here anymore."

Jake laughed. "Rooster seat, huh?"

Bonnie nodded.

Laurel motioned toward the table. "Please. Have a seat."

"I've been sitting all day," he said. "It feels good to stand. What else can I do to help?"

"You can help do dishes afterward," she said.

"Deal," he said, and slid into a seat across the table from Bonnie, leaving the chair at the head of the table for Laurel.

And so the meal began.

Soup was salted, and soup was cooled with a small piece of ice, and Jake looked on with delight as Bonnie's quirks were duly noted.

"Mama, don't forget. I like baby samwishes."

"I never forget that," Laura said, and cut a half sandwich into thirds, and put them on Bonnie's plate.

"I don't need my samwishes cut," Jake said.

Laurel laughed.

Bonnie giggled, but she wasn't sure why. It was just very exciting to have company at night.

Bonnie glanced down at her soup, then back up at her mama. "Mama, is my soup cool enough to eat?"

"Probably," Laurel said.

Bonnie eyed the bowl again, and then instead of picking up her spoon to take a bite, she stuck her finger in it instead…a kind of six-year-old version of testing the waters. "Yep, it's fine," Bonnie said, licked the soup off her finger, and picked up her spoon.

Laurel started to correct her then let it slide. All that mattered was that she could hear Jake chuckling, which meant her daughter didn't rattle him.

Jake ate without much comment, taking in the back and forth chatter happening between mother and child. Laurel intrigued him. She delighted him. One day he would lay her down beneath him and love her like it was the last day of his life. He knew that in his soul, and they had yet to even kiss.

Laurel was antsy. Jake's presence at the table was distracting enough, but she knew he was watching her, and she didn't know how to take that. Was he thinking to himself that she was too engaged in her daughter, or that she was too ordinary to consider her anything more than a friend?

She glanced at him and caught him staring, but instead of looking away, Jake met her gaze. Then she forgot to breathe.

Everything she'd ever wanted in life from a man, she saw promised in his eyes. She glanced at Bonnie, then back at him, and his gaze hadn't wavered. The steadfast look said it all. He understood they came as a package deal.

"Did I mention how glad I am to be here?" Jake asked.

"Maybe, but I don't mind hearing it again," she answered.

Left to her own devices, Bonnie snuck the cheese out of a sandwich still on the plate and was happily biting into it when Laurel realized what she'd done. "Bonnie! What on earth made you do something like that? What if Jake had wanted that sandwich?"

Bonnie pointed. "Jake can still have it. I only ate the cheese."

Laurel heard a soft snort and glared at Jake. "Don't you dare laugh at her," she whispered.

"Thank you, Bonnie Bee. I believe I will have it," he said, and picked it up.

Laurel was still trying to make a point. "Bonnie, would you do this if your Granny and Gramps were here?"

"No."

"They why did you do it now?"

"Cause your mean faces don't scare me. Granny makes scary faces when she's mad."

Laurel thought about it a minute and then looked at Jake and shrugged. "She's right. Mom does make scary faces when she's mad."

Jake chuckled. "So did mine. I was always afraid to let her down."

"Speaking of parents," Laurel said. "Mom and Dad are coming here for dinner Saturday evening about six. I would love for you to come, if you want, but I'll totally understand if—"

"I'd love to," he said.

Laurel exhaled slowly and gave him a quick smile. She'd set the wheels in motion. Now all she had to do was pray everything went okay.

"Yay!" Bonnie cried. "Are we having fried chicken leg? Mama only fries chicken when company comes."

Laurel sighed. "She's already keyed in on my routines."

"Is there anything I can bring for the meal?" he asked.

"Mama said she would bring the dessert. I think all you need to bring is yourself."

"I can do that, and with thanks."

He finished off the last two bites of the sandwich as Laurel got up to help Bonnie down.

"You can go play for a little bit. I'll be back soon to help you with your bath and to get ready for bed."

"Okay, Mommy," Bonnie said, and grabbed Brave Bear. "If it's already bedtime, is Jake going to have a sleepover?"

Laurel gasped, and for once Jake was silent. "No, he's not, now scram."

"Bye, Jake."

"Bye, Bonnie Bee," Jake said.

Laurel's face was flushed as she turned around.

"I'm sorry. Kids do say the most embarrassing things and at the worst times."

"I wasn't embarrassed at all. It was an interesting thought," Jake said, and began gathering the dirty dishes and carrying them to the sink.

Laurel blushed.

Interesting thought? My knees are shaking at that interesting thought.

There wasn't soup left to put up and only a few dishes to load into the dishwasher. The kitchen was clean in minutes, and then there was nothing between them but a few feet and an uncomfortable silence.

"So, I better let you go get your girl in bed. One more day of school this week. Do you have to work tomorrow?"

"Yes, I'm back at the bed-and-breakfast tomorrow."

Jake took a step forward and, with one finger, lifted a stray lock of hair away from her forehead, then hesitated. "May I?" he asked.

Her pulse began to race, and her mouth was suddenly dry. "May you what?"

"Your hair… I just want to…"

She sighed. "Yes," she said, and turned around to give him free rein, and thought she heard him take a deep breath.

Then his fingers were combing gently through the length, smoothing it, bunching it then letting it fall free. When he began gathering it up, she wondered what he was going to do, and then draped it over her right shoulder.

"Ahhh. I thought I'd seen something. I knew you were hiding a secret," he whispered.

Laurel frowned. "Secret, there's no—"

His mouth was on the back of her neck, and he was kissing it. The sensation was unexpected and so sensual she reached for the back of the kitchen chair to keep from going to her knees.

Then he moved from the back of her neck to the curve of her ear. "I won't tell," he whispered in her ear.

She stifled a moan. "Tell what?"

"What you're hiding beneath all that hair."

"I don't—"

Jake pulled her hair back in place and turned her around. "I'm going home now. You two and the soup were my lifesavers tonight."

He ducked into the utility room to retrieve his jacket and walked past her with nothing more than a parting look to get his shoes. She was still standing where he'd left her when she heard his truck start up and drive away.

"Mommy! I'm ready for my bath!" Bonnie yelled.

"Coming!" Laurel said, and then ran her hand beneath her hair to feel the back of her neck. She frowned. There was nothing there. What was he talking—?

Oh!

She ran to the bathroom and grabbed the big mirror, then pulled her hair aside and angled the mirror so that she could see the back of her neck. The heart-shaped birthmark.

"Mommy, what are you doing?" Bonnie asked, as she came in carrying her nightgown.

"Just checking stuff," she said, and grabbed a band and pulled her hair up in a ponytail, then looked at herself in the mirror.

He kissed you.

She shivered, sighed, and then turned around.

Bonnie was naked, rubbing her little belly, and poking her fingers at the tiny nubbins on her chest that would one day become breasts.

Laurel grinned. "Move aside so I can run your bathwater."

Bonnie moved, but she dropped to her knees beside the tub and ducked her head under Laurel's arm to watch the water gushing out of the faucet, and then giggled as the bubbles began to appear from the capful of bubble bath Laurel poured in.

"Maybe two tonight?" Bonnie said.

Laurel looked down at her daughter and smiled. "Maybe two tonight."

Bonnie wiggled with joy at the idea of even more bubbles.

Finally, the water was ready, and the bubbles were bubbling as Laurel lifted Bonnie into the tub. Immediately, her daughter scooped up two big handfuls of soapsuds and plopped them directly onto her chest.

"Look, Mommy, I have boobies."

Laurel laughed. "I see that you do. Now I'm watching the time. You have ten minutes to play in the soap, and then you have to get out."

"Okay! Will you stay and watch me?" Bonnie asked.

"Of course, Mommy always stays when you are in the tub," Laurel said, then sat on the closed lid of the commode and watched her daughter making magic with the bubbles.

She had bubble rings on each finger, a big bubble nose. She made fuzzy bubble eyebrows and lots of big bubble boobies—sometimes one, sometimes three—until finally time was up, and the bubbles were quickly dissipating.

"Time's up," Laurel said. "Open the stopper in the tub so the water can drain out."

Bonnie did as she was told, then Laurel lifted her out and began drying her off on the bathmat between them, while Bonnie continued to talk.

"Will you read me a story tonight, Mommy?"

"Yes, I will. What story do you want to hear tonight?"

"*The Velveteen Rabbit*, please," Bonnie said.

Laurel groaned. "But, honey, you cry every time we read it."

Bonnie shrugged. "Tonight I want to cry."

Laurel frowned and then wiped a string of bubbles from Bonnie's chin. "Why, baby? Why do you want to cry?"

"Someone told me at school today that my grandma died. It made me sad."

Laurel gasped. "Oh, honey! Not Granny Joyner! She didn't die. She's coming to eat supper with us Saturday, remember?"

"I know. It's another granny, right?"

Laurel wrapped Bonnie in the towel and sat her in her lap. "Yes, it's another granny. Your daddy's mother."

"Do I know her?" Bonnie asked.

"You used to."

"Did I love her like I love Granny Joyner?"

"You used to."

Bonnie's eyes rounded, mirroring her confusion. "I don't remember," she said.

"It's not your fault," Laurel said. "They uh…they sort of moved away from us, and you just forgot her. That happens when people don't stay in touch."

Bonnie leaned back against Laurel's chest and slipped her head beneath her mother's chin. "Will you read *The Velveteen Rabbit*?"

"Yes, I will," Laurel said.

"And then I will cry. Can we say God bless to my dead grandma tonight?"

It was all Laurel could do to keep from crying. "Yes, we will add her to your prayers."

———※———

Jake unpacked his luggage as he went through his regular bedtime routine. He even put a load of towels into the washer. It wouldn't hurt if they stayed in it overnight. He'd put them in the dryer tomorrow.

He paused in the kitchen to acknowledge the bottle of tequila.

"You have good people, Joaquin. Thank you for the trip. It was almost like seeing you again."

He got a cold pop from the refrigerator and took it with him to the living room to watch some TV. After spending this evening with Laurel, there was no way he would ever get to sleep this early.

He sat down in his father's chair and, not for the first

time, thought how it still smelled like him. The pipe he occasionally smoked—the aftershave that he had worn. He sighed. It was almost like being cradled in his arms.

He turned on the TV, took a drink, and then kicked back in the recliner. A few minutes later the pop was gone, the TV was on mute, and he was asleep.

Laurel was undressing in a darkened room. She didn't know he was there. He watched from the shadows as the clothing came away one piece at a time until she was bare.

He saw her reaching for a hairbrush, and then she began brushing her hair. In the dream, sparks flew like fireflies, and the more she brushed, the higher the sparks went until they turned into lightning arcing all around her.

"Turn around and see me," he whispered, so she turned and held out her hand.

He took a step, and then another, and the closer he moved, the higher the flames grew around her. She was danger. And she was love. He chose love and embraced her—then burned up in her fire.

Chapter 15

THE RAIN TURNED TO SNOW SOMETIME DURING the night. It was sticking on the grass and bushes, on the roof and on Laurel's car, but it wasn't sticking on the ground.

She bundled Bonnie up against the cold and was congratulating herself for grabbing the little UGG boots Bonnie was wearing at the all-city yard sale in August. They were a tiny bit too large, but with thicker socks, they were perfect.

Bonnie was happy about her fuzzy boots, as she called them, and so ecstatic it was snowing that Laurel knew she hadn't heard a word she was saying. "Do you remember I'm going to pick you up from school today?" Laurel asked.

"Yes, Mommy. What about a snowman?"

"The snowman is for later, and only if it snows enough to stick. We are talking about *now*. Listen carefully, okay? Don't forget to give the note to your teacher so she'll know to keep you off the bus."

"I won't forget," Bonnie said. "Can we build a girl snowman?"

Laurel chuckled. "Then it would be a snow girl."

Bonnie frowned. "But how will people know it's a girl?"

Laurel poked her daughter in the chest. "We'll put boobies on her. How about that?"

Bonnie giggled. "Yes! Snow boobies!"

Laurel buttoned up Bonnie's coat and then helped her into her backpack. "It's time to go to the bus stop, honey. Let me get my coat."

"Can we walk, Mommy? I wanna walk in the snow."

"The driveway is still soft and muddy. Maybe we can walk on the grass, okay?"

"Yes, yes!" And out the door they went.

They were almost at the stop when they saw the big yellow bus appearing as it rounded the curve. "There it comes!" Bonnie cried.

"He sees us," Laurel said. "See, he's waving. He'll wait for you."

She got Bonnie on the bus and then jogged back to the house. She needed to hurry or she was going to be late for work.

Within a few minutes, she was driving past Jake's house with an ache in her stomach. She wanted him. There was no denying the feelings. Where their relationship went was yet to be determined, but she'd made up her mind last night that if he asked, she would not say no.

~

They laid Adele Payne to rest in the family cemetery behind her house as the snow fell on the mourners, muffling the sounds of their grief and most of the preacher's prayer.

When it was over, friends and family gathered back at Beverly's home, where they'd been ever since they'd learned of her death. Beverly was glad to get home out of the cold and was so ready for this time of mourning to be over. She wanted her home back. She wanted to be done with sadness, but their family had been shattered. It would take time for the tragedy of what happened to fade.

She stood in the warmth of her home, happy with the life she and her husband had made for themselves and their boys. They didn't have grandeur, but they had comfort, and they had enough. It still hurt her heart that they'd let Laurel suffer. She had a lot of prayers ahead of her before she would ever feel right with God.

⸻

Truman was cold. The propane tank was empty. A slight oversight on his part. Not only did he not have heat, but it also meant he couldn't warm up anything to eat. He was sitting in the living room with a blanket wrapped around him when the lights suddenly flickered, then went out.

He cursed, then got up and went to the kitchen to look through the pile of unpaid bills. And there was the electric bill—another oversight. Great. He'd spent most of his money getting his truck out of impound, and now he was broke until his monthly check arrived. He needed a lot of money to get all of this up and going.

He thought about places to heist, but not in Blessings. Not anymore. Even animals knew not to shit where they slept. He thought about the last time he'd been in Savannah, and that liquor store down by the river on the outskirts of the city. It seemed a good a place as any to heist.

He got his pistol and ammo and then wasted time digging around for his gloves before he remembered they were under the seat of his truck, and out the door he went. He didn't even bother locking up the house. There wasn't anything to steal, no lights to see by, and too damn cold to linger.

He drove away with his head in the clouds, already spending the money he had yet to steal.

When Jake woke up, he was still in the recliner, and the TV was still on mute. He was a bit stiff as he stood, but he had slept through the night. He glanced back at the recliner.

"Thanks for the good night's sleep, Dad."

He was on his way to the bathroom when he glanced out the window and saw the snow. Unlike Bonnie, he was not enamored of the falling white stuff or the fact that he'd be spending the day inside.

Once he was dressed and had a cup of coffee at hand, he sat down to go through email and messages. There was one from Sophia thanking him again for coming. He sent a response back and went through the rest, pausing to linger on one from yet another buddy in his old unit. Myron Fitz, who they'd all called Ron, was back at his advertising company and still after Jake to reconsider the offer he'd made when they were both in hospital rehab.

To Jake's surprise and Ron's delight, Jake had a knack for writing hooks—the tag line that advertisers use to sell products and grow the reputation of companies, large and small. Even though Ron had been bed-bound, he could still do ad work on his laptop, and because of their proximity, one day while they were both hospitalized he challenged Jake to come up with a hook for one of their new campaigns. Once Jake understood the concept and what they were going for, his idea astounded Ron. Ron ran it by his men at the next meeting, and it was accepted.

Jake thought it was funny.

Ron was delighted.

And after numerous other incidents during their recovery when Jake continued to repeat his success, Ron actually offered Jake a job. Jake laughed again and turned him down cold. He wanted nothing to do with big cities. He was going home.

But, according to Ron's latest email, he had a job offer he wanted Jake to consider. If Jake could work from home, would he reconsider the job offer?

Now Jake was curious.

He sent back a long message asking detailed questions, what the pay and benefits would be, and would regular traveling be involved, or could all of their face time be dealt with by Skype? As he hit Send, he thought of Laurel and couldn't help but wonder if this would play into a job that would comfortably support him—and a family—if he should happen to ever have one.

The fact that Laurel and Bonnie always came to mind when he thought of a future was a risky emotion to play with. He had no notion whether she would be receptive, but like the job offer, it was something to think about.

Truman was only a few miles from Blessings when he slid off the main road into a ditch. He tried driving himself out, but the mud was deep, and he only got stuck worse. Now he needed a tow to get out, but there were problems regarding his predicament.

A: He was a convicted felon with a firearm and ammunition in his vehicle.

B: The only friend he had who might pull him out was Nester, but since Truman had broken his nose, the friend part was iffy. Still, he had to give it a try.

But then things got worse. As he was making the call, his truck, which had been leaning precariously, just went ahead and laid over on its side.

"What the hell!" Truman yelled, and dropped the phone to grab on to the steering wheel, which was actually just a reflex, because holding the wheel meant nothing to the fallen truck without tires on the ground. "Crap on a stick!" Truman yelled, as he slid all the way across the seat, coming to rest against the passenger side door on his back. And he couldn't see his phone.

He paused to get his bearings and glanced out through the windshield at the still-falling snow. Then he looked straight up at the driver's side door, which was now on the high side of the truck. Getting out would be like climbing to the second floor of a house—without the stairs.

Frustrated, still hungry and still freezing, and still packing the gun that could get him sent back to prison, he took a deep breath and then got down on the door on his hands and knees and began looking for his phone. He finally saw it wedged between the seat and the passenger side door. But that door was wedged against the bank of the ditch. He could see it, but he couldn't reach it. After skinning the hide off his knuckles and promising God he wouldn't rob a soul if He'd just help him get out of the ditch, he thought of taking off his belt to try and reach the phone. The buckle was heavy—maybe he could drag it out.

So off came the belt. His pants slipped a little, but he didn't have time to pull anything up. Now he was on both knees trying to thread the buckle down to the phone. Finally, he got it in position right behind the phone and slowly began to pull. The buckle was heavy enough that it caught on the phone and pulled it out, too.

"Gotcha, you little bastard!" Truman crowed, then heard a knock.

He looked up. There was a highway patrolman looking down at him.

"Sir! Are you okay?" the patrolman yelled.

"Yes, yes, I dropped my phone." He held it up. "I was just about to call a friend for a tow!" Truman yelled.

"I'll call a tow truck," the patrolman said.

"I don't have any money to pay him!" Truman yelled.

"You can't pull *this* truck upright and then out of a ditch with a log chain, buddy."

"If you call him, you have to pay him," Truman yelled, but the patrolman was gone, the gun and the ammunition were in the glove box, and Truman was pretty much up shit creek.

In a panic, he pulled back the floor mats, felt around underneath the dash, and then made a rash decision and jammed the gun between the seats and shoved the ammunition in beside it. Then he grabbed a handful of greasy rags and stuffed them in on top. He started to say a prayer about the weapon, and then stopped, thinking God wouldn't give a shit if he got caught with that, so the praying ended.

An hour passed while Truman contemplated the terrible condition of his fingernails. Then he noticed one of his boots was missing a heel, at which time he got back on his knees and found the heel caught beneath the floor mat. He put the heel in his pocket and sat back on the door. He was just about to have himself a fit when the tow truck arrived and things started happening.

The patrolman came back to the window and knocked. "Do you want to get out before they pull out your truck?"

"I'll stay here," Truman yelled.

"Then hang on," the patrolman said, and disappeared again.

Truman reached for the steering wheel, but he should have grabbed his pants because his belt was still in the floor. He made a quick transition from one end of the cab seat to the other as the truck began to move into an upright position. In no time the truck was out of the ditch and back on the highway. He looked up in his rearview mirror and sighed. Here came that cop again.

Truman rolled down his window. "Thank you."

The patrolman nodded.

"The tow truck driver has agreed to bill you. I need your driver's license. If you'll get out of the truck while we write up all the paperwork, you can soon be on your way."

"Yeah, sure," Truman said.

He opened the door and stepped out onto the blacktop as his pants dropped to his ankles.

The driver of the tow truck laughed.

The patrolman grinned. "I only need to see your driver's license, sir."

Jake pulled up his pants and then grabbed his belt out of the truck.

"I was using it to get my phone," he muttered as he threaded it through the belt loops, then handed his license to the cop.

The tow truck driver took a picture of the license with his phone then sent it to the office for the boss to okay.

The patrolman had already run the tag, knew the truck belonged to a convicted felon, but he had no outstanding wants or warrants, and it wasn't against the law to slide into a ditch on a slick road. And now he saw that the driver's license matched the owner of the vehicle and that Truman did not appear incapacitated in any way other than the fact that he had no butt to hold up his pants. His job here was done.

Truman was stunned when both the driver and the cop drove away. His original plan had been to rob that store, but he made that promise to God about not robbing anybody if He'd just help him get out of that ditch.

His shoulders slumped.

It was hard being honest.

He sat there a few minutes, running scenarios through his head, and then remembered his Aunt Sugar. He didn't know if she was still alive, but she might let him stay with her a bit until he could get his monthly disability check.

Satisfied with the new plan, he very carefully turned the truck around. He had to go back through Blessings to get there, but he was going to pay Aunt Sugar a visit.

—∼—

Sugar Thomas had spent most of her adult life living down the fact that her sister Candy had married Baker Slade, the most worthless man to ever walk their side of the mountain. She tithed at church, didn't gossip, and liked her privacy, which was why she and her man had built their little house up so high. She told people it was because she felt closer to God, but the truth was, few people bothered to drive that far, which suited her just fine.

She was in her kitchen putting on the kettle to make some elderberry tea when she thought she heard a car coming up the road. She turned off the fire under the kettle and went to the window to look out and saw a pickup truck approaching.

"Who on earth might this be?" she wondered, and went to the hall closet to get her rifle.

Now that she was a widow, the burden of taking care of business fell on her shoulders, and this was no exception. She checked to make sure the gun was loaded and then stepped out onto the porch with it cradled in her arms.

Her eyes weren't what they used to be, but when she saw the man who got out of that truck, she didn't have to look twice. It was Candy's youngest offspring, an unfortunate happening that occurred during her tenth year of married life.

She pulled herself up to her full height of six feet and swung the gun around so that it was aimed in the vicinity of his feet.

Truman panicked. He'd left the truck running

in case he might need to make a fast break, and it appeared his instincts had been right. It appeared he was going to have to sweet talk her some. "Aunt Sugar! It's me, Truman."

"I know who it is. That's why I have aimed at your feet. If you wasn't kin, I would have already shot the hat off your head as a reminder that I don't like company, don't want company, not having any, either."

Truman sighed.

So much for mooching a place to stay. Still, he might be able to get her to come up with some cash. "I will be honest, Aunt Sugar. I have had a run of bad luck and—"

"Do you have a job?" she asked.

"Uh, not at the moment, which—"

"Did you get fired?"

"No, ma'am, I—"

"So, if you weren't fired, and you don't have a job, that tells me you're living on welfare. Have you even held a job since you got out of prison?"

He shrugged. "No one wants to hire me."

"Funny how that happens when you went to jail for robbing honest, hardworking people. I guess word gets around."

Truman felt the ground falling out from under plan B.

"It's cold, and it's dark in my house, Aunt Sugar. I need to buy propane and pay my electric bill. I was wondering if—"

She pulled the trigger.

Dirt flew up on his shoes and his pant legs, but he was already running. He swung into the seat, shoved the truck into reverse, and backed out of her sight before he slowed down enough to dare turning around.

Now he was mad, and it was all Jake Lorde's damn fault. If he'd kept his mouth shut back in the day, Truman would never have gone to jail, and he wouldn't be in this mess.

He stomped the accelerator as he headed down the mountain. This time he was calling Nester and wasn't taking no for an answer.

⁓⁓⁓

The snow lasted long enough that Bonnie got to make her snow girl before she went to bed that night. Laurel spent the evening poring over recipes, and then in the end, opted for meat loaf because it was her daddy's favorite.

Jake had read Ron's offer, sent emails back and forth regarding how they would furnish the client's info, what the focus of the new ad would entail, and if someone else would be responsible for the artwork that goes with the campaigns.

By the time the day had ended, he'd had three phone calls from Ron, and Skyped once with the head of the art department. They almost had him sold.

He went to bed thinking about the offer, and then woke up on Saturday thinking about supper with Laurel and Bonnie. It was going to be a good day.

⁓⁓⁓

The last time Laurel had looked at the clock it was just after 4:00 p.m., and now it was close to six. Her parents were sticklers for punctuality. They would be here anytime.

Her phone dinged with a text. She glanced down and smiled. It was from Jake. She wiped her hands and read it. Do you need anything before I head your way?

She smiled. Just you and your appetite.

She hit Send and then ran down the hall to make sure Bonnie was still clean. Just as she went to open the door, she heard Bonnie talking.

"Don't lick your fingers. Don't talk with your mouth full. Use your fork, not your spoon, and sit up straight. You are slumping in your chair."

She sighed. Those words never came out of her mouth. They sounded like what she'd heard growing up. It appeared Bonnie was in need of getting Granny's approval, too. She opened the door.

Bonnie's blue jeans were still clean and so was her yellow sweater. The ribbon was still in her hair, and she had added her ruby necklace to the ensemble. Laurel could only imagine the conversation that would ensue once her mother saw that, but she didn't care. Her mother had never really approved of Adam, and now Laurel knew Pansy would be setting herself up to disapprove of Jake. Her mama needed a hobby.

She sat down on the bed beside Bonnie.

"Hey, honey. Granny and Gramps will be here anytime. Why don't you go to the bathroom real quick and then come to the kitchen. You can help me finish setting the table."

"Okay, Mommy," Bonnie said, and set Brave Bear aside before running out of the room.

Laurel was on her way back to the kitchen when she saw car lights through the living room curtains. She turned on the porch light and moments later heard one set of footsteps coming up the step.

It was Jake.

She stood at the door, holding on to the doorknob

until he knocked, and then yanked it open so fast it made him blink. He grinned.

"Uh, I saw your headlights," she said.

The storm door was still shut between them, and so he was still standing beneath the porch light when it dawned on her that he still couldn't get in.

"Oh. Sorry," she said, and unlocked the door.

He walked in, shut it behind him, and then gave her a big hug. "Ummmm, once again, you do smell good."

Laurel patted his chest. "You just like my cooking," she said.

He stopped her then. "I like the cook, too."

And once again her heart was doing double-time. Before she could comment, Bonnie came running into the room.

"Yay!" she said.

Jake picked her up on the run and gave her a quick hug. "Bonnie Bee, you are looking very charming."

"I'm wearing my ruby necklace," she said, patting her chest.

"I see that, and I like the bow in your hair."

Laurel sighed. He not only lifted her spirits, but he was giving Bonnie the most positive feedback she'd had with a man since before her father's death.

Jake put Bonnie down and was taking off his coat when more car lights appeared through the curtains. "And that would be Mom and Dad," Laurel said.

Jake heard the tremor in her voice. He got that this was a big deal for her.

"I will be on my very best behavior, I promise," Jake said.

"You're fine. It will all be fine," she said, but her

hands were shaking a little as she opened the door to let them in.

Pansy handed Laurel the dessert she'd promised, a coconut cream pie, and then went into search mode when she saw Jake, giving him the serious once-over. Benny was more gracious.

"Mom, Dad, you both remember Charles Lorde's son, Jake."

"Sure do," Benny said, and shook his hand. "I hear you're ready to put roots back down on your home place?"

"Yes, sir, and glad to be back," he said, and then smiled at Laurel's mother. "Mrs. Joyner, it's nice to see you again. I think the last time I remember seeing you, you were manning the microphone at the Peachy Keen Queen contest."

Pansy actually smiled. "Why, my goodness! That was a good eight or nine years ago."

"Yes, ma'am, that sounds about right."

"Mom, you and Dad can put your coats on my bed."

"I'll take them," Jake offered. "I need to leave mine as well."

Pansy's eyes narrowed immediately. "So you already know where my daughter's bedroom is located?"

Laurel gasped. "Mama! I can't believe you would—"

Jake took the coats out of their hands, ignoring the tone in Pansy's voice. "Actually, I know where Bonnie Bee's bedroom is, because I carried her from the truck into the house after she came back from ER, and since there is a door directly across from her room, I'm guessing it's Laurel's. Am I right?"

"I'll show you," Bonnie said, and led the way with Jake right behind her.

Laurel turned, glaring at her mother until Pansy had the grace to flush.

Benny never knew what to do with the women in his life, so he patted Laurel's shoulder and took his wife by the hand.

"Supper is about ready," Laurel said. "Come into the kitchen. We can continue the inquisition there."

Pansy sighed. "I'm sorry."

"You should be," Laurel muttered, and led the way, with Jake and Bonnie right behind them. She set the dessert aside for later and began dishing up the food and carrying it to the table.

Bonnie was basking in being the center of her grandparents' attention.

Jake was being quietly helpful, and Laurel was still seething.

Finally, it was ready. Laurel set the last dish of food on the table and put Bonnie's booster seat in the chair closest to her.

"Okay everyone, please take a seat. Mom, you and Dad like to sit together, and I'm riding herd on Bonnie, so she's sitting by me. Jake, since you don't need your meat cut, I'm trusting you'll be fine on your own at the end of the table."

Jake laughed. "I'll mind my manners."

Pansy sniffed at the comments, but she was taking notice of the comfortable manner with which they talked to each other. He was definitely not a stranger to this house. She sat down beside Benny while eyeing Jake's seat at the table.

Laurel caught the look and stifled a groan. At the time, seating Jake there seemed logical, but she could tell her mother had just read this as the "head of the table."

Laurel wanted to shake her. "Dad, would you please say the blessing?"

"I can say a blessing," Bonnie said.

"No, Bonnie. Gramps is going to say it."

"That's okay," Benny said. "I'd like to hear Bonnie Carol's blessing."

Bonnie beamed as Laurel gave Jake a frantic look. He winked.

"Bow your heads," Bonnie announced. "Good bread. Good meat. Get your fork. Let's eat."

Benny chuckled.

Pansy was still blinking.

Jake was entranced. "Good job, Bonnie Bee. Where did you learn that one?" he asked.

"At school. I know another one."

"No, thank you," Laurel said. "One was enough. Dad, help yourself and pass it down."

"Meat loaf!" Benny cried. "That's my favorite."

"And that's why I made it," Laurel said.

When the meat loaf reached Jake, he served himself a piece, and then set it back down on the table and gave it a gentle push toward Laurel. "Didn't want to pass a hot dish over Bonnie's head," he said.

"Thank you, Jake. I appreciate that," Laurel said.

And so it went until all of the food had been passed and the meal began.

Bonnie took one bite of the meat loaf and then held up her fork as if she were at school holding up her hand for permission to speak.

Laurel rolled her eyes. Since when had she ever asked permission to speak in this house?

"What is it, honey?" Laurel said.

"What's that on Jake's 'tatos?"

"It's black pepper," Jake said.

"I want some, too," Bonnie said.

Laurel was about to argue, and Pansy was already setting her jaw to disapprove, when Jake defused the whole situation. "How old are you?" Jake asked.

"I'm six."

"Oh, I'm sorry. You have to be eight to have this."

"Really?" Bonnie asked.

He nodded.

"Why?" Bonnie asked.

Laurel put down her fork and gave him one of Bonnie's wide-eyed looks. "Yes, why Jake?"

"Remember how you put ice in your soup so it won't burn the hair off your tongue?"

Bonnie nodded.

"So, you can't cool black pepper with ice. It just makes it hotter. You have to be eight before your tongue says, okay, now I can have black pepper if I want because it won't burn me anymore."

"My tongue will say that?" Bonnie asked.

He nodded. "It will let you know when it's ready for this stuff."

"Okay," she said.

Benny gave Jake a wink, and Pansy was trying not to smile.

"Thank you for that perfect explanation," Laurel said.

"My pleasure," Jake said, and scooped up a bite of his potatoes, while Bonnie began feeling her tongue to see if she could feel it growing older.

Laurel leaned back in her chair, absently watching the people around her table, trying to picture this

happening over and over in the future, then caught Jake
looking at her.

He smiled, and her heart melted.

She smiled back. Yes, she *could* picture this.

Chapter 16

THE SUPPER DISHES WERE CLEARED OFF THE TABLE, AND fresh coffee was hot and ready to be served with dessert. Pansy's homemade coconut cream pie had been cut and plated.

Laurel kept thinking the evening was actually working out and started to relax. She glanced at her dad and Jake every so often, unaware her mother was watching her just as closely.

———————

Jake and Benny were sitting at the table talking about Ralph Sinclair's gas station and how they missed Ralph's presence in the community.

Jake's plan to put in an offer had changed after Ron Fitz's offer to go to work for him, but he was still considering both options.

"Someone's sure to buy it," Benny said. "Ralph had a good business."

"I agree," Jake said. "Someone will snap it up as soon as Mrs. Sinclair puts it up for sale."

Pansy carried two pieces of pie to the table and set them in front of each man.

"Coconut cream pie is my absolute favorite," Jake said.

"I hope you like it," Pansy said.

"I know I will," Jake said.

Laurel carried the other two plates to the table. "Sit down, Mama."

Pansy looked around and frowned. "Where's Bonnie? Isn't she going to have dessert?"

"She's playing. I kept a piece back for her."

As soon as the women were seated, both men dug into the pie.

"Oh man," Jake said. "I haven't had coconut pie this good since Mom died. It's delicious."

Pansy beamed.

Benny winked at her. "Good stuff, Pansy. Just like you always make."

Bonnie entered the kitchen carrying her overnight bag, her coat, and Brave Bear. "Mommy, I think I should stay all night with Granny and Gramps."

Laurel groaned. "Bonnie, we discussed this already. This is not—"

Pansy patted her daughter's arm. "No, don't fuss at her. We'd love to have her. She is always a delight."

"Please, Mommy. Brave Bear wants to go too."

Pansy saw the stuffed toy, and then she saw the medal. "Well, I'll say, Benny, would you look at that?"

"That's quite a bear, Bonnie Carol. Do you mind if I take a look at him?"

Bonnie handed him the stuffed toy and then leaned across her grandfather's arm as he began to examine it. He looked the medal over carefully and looked up at her. "Where did you get this, girl?"

Bonnie pointed at Jake. "Jake gave me Brave Bear 'cause I was having bad dreams."

"What kind of bad dreams?" Pansy asked.

"We'll talk about it later, Mama," Laurel said.

Pansy pointed to the medal. "Is that real, Jake Lorde?"

He shrugged. "Everybody gets hurt in war in one way or another. I didn't do anything to earn it, and she needed it."

Benny shook his head. "Never quite thought of it as a toy."

Laurel shoved her pie aside without having taken a bite. "Bonnie, go play in your room awhile and make sure you packed your toothbrush and jammies."

"Okay, Mommy."

As soon as Bonnie was gone, Laurel turned to Jake. "I invited you to a meal, not a judgment hearing. I am sorry for this."

Jake shook his head. "Hey, it's okay. Questions are fair."

Laurel's dad was still stuck on the fact that he'd given the medal away, and Jake saw it.

"They gave me a medal for getting blown to kingdom come," Jake said, and his voice was shaking. "I'm alive, and the man who saved my life that day now is dead. I wish I could wipe every moment of those years at war from my heart. Bonnie was having bad dreams...dreams of hiding from her daddy because she can't remember what he looks like anymore, and she was afraid he'd be mad."

"Oh dear," Pansy muttered. "Laurel, you didn't tell—"

"I didn't know either, Mama. Bonnie told Jake, not me. He gave my daughter a way to cope. Because Brave Bear has a medal, to her it means he is a hero. And she needed a hero. Jake sacrificed his own feelings to help her."

"And to help you," Jake said. "You are a kick-ass

woman who's been dealt a bad hand this early in life, and I admire you. Now, Mr. and Mrs. Joyner, I think it's time I headed home." He reached for Laurel's hand and gave it a quick squeeze. "Thank you for supper; it was wonderful. Mrs. Joyner, your pie was delicious. Mr. Joyner, good to see you again."

Laurel's heart was breaking. She saw the shadows in his eyes. She felt his disappointment.

He got up from the table, but his gaze was on Laurel. She was hurt, and she was angry. But he was only making it worse.

"I'll get my coat and see myself out," Jake said.

"No, I'll get your coat. You are still my guest," Laurel muttered, and stormed out of the kitchen.

Jake was waiting at the door, and when she handed him the coat, he wrapped her up in his arms. "It's okay," he said.

"No, it's not," she said. "I'm sorry. None of that is their business. Lord, I've dealt with this my whole life. Mama is a meddler."

He gave her a last hug and then put on his coat and dug the car keys out of his jacket pocket. "I'll call you," he said.

"Thank God. I was afraid you'd never want to talk to me again."

"You are so silly," he said softly. "I want to kiss you, but not here with this acrimony hanging between us."

She sighed. "Rain check?"

"You know it," he said, and then he was gone.

Laurel watched him driving away and then headed for the kitchen.

Her mother was washing up pie plates and chattering

as if nothing had happened, and it made Laurel furious. "Mama, Daddy, I am so angry with the both of you right now that I can't even talk. Get Bonnie and go home."

Pansy looked stunned. "But, honey, we didn't—"

"Oh, yes, you did. You know it. You meant it. This is my home. He was my guest. You were rude. Both of you."

Benny sighed. "I'm sorry. It just took me aback to see something as special as the Purple Heart on a toy."

Laurel threw up her arms in disbelief. "You weren't even listening to him, were you? You were already wrapped up in your opinion! He told you why. He does not hold himself up as a hero. The medal makes him feel like an imposter. He's struggling. With everything. And you, Dad, who came home from Vietnam to such hate, should have more empathy. Go home now and think about yourselves, and do not ever do this again. Not to me. Not to him."

There were tears in Pansy's eyes, but she didn't argue. "I'll get Bonnie."

"I'll warm up the car," Benny said.

"Don't forget your pie," Laurel said.

Benny picked it up on the way out.

Bonnie came bouncing up in front of Pansy and threw her arms around Laurel. "Love you, Mommy. I'll be good."

"You're always good," Laurel said, and hugged her close.

"We'll bring her home tomorrow evening before dark," Pansy said.

"Fine," Laurel said. "Call if she needs me."

"Of course," Pansy said.

Laurel opened the door, smiled at her daughter, and then looked at her mother as if she'd never seen her before.

Pansy was trying to think of what to say, but Laurel ushered them out too fast. Now she was worried. Her daughter had never been this angry with them. Ever.

She got Bonnie in the car and buckled up, and then they drove away without talking. With Bonnie in the backseat, they couldn't discuss what had happened.

"Well now," Benny said.

Pansy sighed. "Let's just get home."

Benny nodded.

Laurel watched until their taillights disappeared over the hill, then picked up a pillow from the sofa and flung it across the room. She was so angry she couldn't think beyond getting to Jake. She would not sleep this night, knowing he was hurt by something her parents had done. So she grabbed her coat and purse and headed out the door, locking it behind her.

She drove straight to Jake's house, so angry she was shaking.

When she pulled up in front of the house, the porch light came on. The door opened as she walked up the steps. Jake was standing in the doorway. She started talking.

"I am so sorry. I couldn't go to bed tonight until I made sure you were okay. I have no explanation for the fact that my parents turned into jackasses. Can you—"

"Yes, I can," Jake said, and put a hand on either side of the doorframe. "But you need to know that if

I let you into my house, I will take you to bed, so it's your choice."

Her heart was pounding, but she didn't hesitate. "I choose you."

She saw his eyes flash as he crossed the threshold. He swung her up into his arms, carried her back into the house, kicking the door shut behind him as he went. He didn't put her down until they were in his bedroom.

The light in the hall turned their embrace into a shadow dance as Jake cupped Laurel's face and lowered his head. Her lips were parted, her breathing was rapid and ragged, and that's when a quiet peace washed through him. This moment and them—he'd questioned the wisdom of this before, but not again. This was so right.

Her face was cold, but his lips were warm as they slid across her mouth, then centered. The kiss deepened, and when he heard her moan, he cupped her hips and pulled her close.

Time ceased until he paused to inhale. His lungs were burning because he'd forgotten to breathe. Her arms were around his neck, and the curves of her body were aligned against him as if she'd been made to fit. There was a knowing inside him that once they did this, despite the chaos in his life, he would never let her go.

"Sweet mercy, woman, you turn on every male instinct I have. I want you so much."

Laurel was shaking, but not from fear. "I want this to happen. I need to feel like I matter again."

"Ah, Laurel...you matter to me."

She started to undress, but he stopped her with a look. "Let me," he begged.

She took his hands and put them on her body. It was all the invitation he needed. He stripped her of her slacks, pulled the sweater over her head, and dropped her underwear at his feet before she knew what was happening.

Then he reached behind her head, pulled the band from her hair, and when it fell across her shoulders, covering her breasts and his hands, he lost his mind. He took her standing up, with her back to the wall and her legs wrapped around his waist, and then took her to bed and started all over again.

When Laurel climaxed the second time, she couldn't believe it was happening. The body-shattering rush of blood went from her belly to her brain so fast she thought she was falling, and while she was still riding the high, he took her back to that pinnacle so fast that she screamed. That was when Jake's climax finally rolled through him.

Laurel was lost. She didn't know what just happened had even been a possibility.

Jake was still, and then he raised up on both elbows. "That happened before I thought. I didn't use protection. I—"

Laurel put a finger across his mouth. "I'm on the pill. We're good."

"Oh, thank God," he said, and brushed a kiss across her lips, then kissed the hollow at the base of her throat. "I never meant to put you at risk."

She was looking at the scars now, trying to wrap her head around someone being injured like this and being alive. "Oh, Jake...these scars. I hurt for every agony you suffered."

"It's over and part of my past. Now is what matters.

This thing that's happening between us means everything to me. I know it happened so fast, but—"

She interrupted. "No. Fast does not factor into this. When a person has faced their own mortality and lived to tell about it, I think the rules of polite society fall by the wayside. You have seen how fast life can end, and waiting for what you want seems unnecessary when it's already been offered. We made magic, Jacob. I don't take that lightly."

He traced the lower edge of her lip with his thumb, then pulled her close and whispered in her ear. "So I think our first kiss has possibilities."

She wrapped her arms around his neck. "Yes. Definite possibilities."

He rolled over onto his back and took her with him, then pulled her close and closed his eyes. He didn't intend to fall asleep, but he did, and she had not intended to stay the night, but she was.

And he began to dream.

Laurel woke in a panic as Jake groaned in her ear. At first she thought she was home and someone was breaking into her house, and then she saw where she was and remembered.

Jake moaned again, and then moments later the muscles in his arms begin to twitch. He had readily admitted he suffered PTSD, and she suspected this was what was happening. He was dreaming, and there was no telling where the dream would take him. Staying where she was might be a mistake, and while she wasn't afraid of what was beginning to happen, she had the good sense to make sure she got out of the way.

Without making a sound, she slowly eased out of the bed. The house was a bit chilly, and she didn't know where to look for a blanket, so she began getting dressed instead. Then she curled up in a rocker near the window, pulled her knees up to her chin, and waited.

———~~~———

Jake's unit was on the move. They had bivouacked outside a small village the night before and Jake, along with some of the others, was standing in the strip between their camp and the village, handing out gum and candy to the little ones who were curious about the Americans bedded down in what amounted to their backyard.

Jake squatted down to get on eye level with a little boy and was handing him a piece of gum when they began hearing artillery fire.

Women in the village began screaming for their children, and the soldiers were on their feet and running for their vehicles when the first missile hit the village.

He turned to look just as the little boy he'd been talking to disappeared in falling rubble.

"Son of a bitch!" he yelled, and started back when they were ordered to move out. "Sarge, the kid—"

"Get in your truck, Lorde. They're shooting at us. We're moving out."

Jake could hear screams even as they were in motion. There was a lump in his throat and a knot in his gut. The dust was billowing up behind their transports, and they were sitting ducks.

When Jake threw up his arms, Laurel knew something bad had happened in his dream. She flew out of the chair and ran to the foot of the bed, wanting to hold him, but afraid to get too close. "Jake, wake up. You're having a bad dream. You need to wake up."

That voice.

He sat up with a jerk, his heart hammering against his rib cage, and saw Laurel dressed, standing at the foot of his bed.

"Oh my God, did I hurt you? Did I scare you? What happened?"

She crawled into bed with him and grasped both of his hands. "No, no, nothing like that. But I woke up when you started to dream, I think. I just got up and got out of the way."

He pulled her into his lap. "I'm sorry. I'm so sorry. I got selfish and let what I wanted override what I knew was best. I shouldn't have—we shouldn't—"

"Oh no. You don't make my choices for me," Laurel said. "I'm not a fool. I saw some of this with Adam. I'm not a novice at anything anymore. Trust me. I can handle this, if you can handle me."

Jake pulled her close. "It will get some better. The doctor said it *will* get better."

"Then so it will," she said. "In the meantime, can we just let this relationship do its thing without trying to force something into a place it doesn't need to go?"

"What do you mean?" Jake asked.

"I mean, if you're willing, I'm willing to do this with you. I don't want to wait until you *think* it's okay."

He gave her a quick hug of thanksgiving. "One day at a time?"

"Yes. One day at a time," she said.

"Come get back under the covers. The house seems cold."

Laurel gasped. "Oh no!"

"What?" he asked.

"I have to go home and turn the heat lamp on for Lavonne. It wasn't that cold when we fed her, but if the temperature drops, she could freeze. I'm sorry, but Bonnie would be devastated if anything happened to that chicken."

Jake got up and started pulling on clothes. "I'll follow you home."

"You don't have to do that," Laurel said.

"Our night is only half over," Jake said. "I'm down with ending it in your bed instead of mine."

"I don't have a single reason to disagree," Laurel said, and grabbed her coat and purse.

Jake sat down to put on his boots, then got his coat and car keys and paused by the window. "The wind is up. No wonder the house is getting cold. I'm going to turn up the heat before we go."

The bitter blast hit them face-first the moment they walked out of his house.

"Oh my lord," Laurel said. "Winter has come to the mountains for sure. I'll see you at the house." Then she made a run for her truck.

Jake was right behind her.

They arrived at her trailer within minutes, and instead of parking where she usually did, she drove past the house to the chicken coop and used the headlights to see by.

Her hands were shaking as she struggled with the

latch, and then suddenly, Jake was right behind her. "Let me help," he said.

As soon as he opened the gate, she ran into the little yard and then opened the door to the coop. There was just enough light for her to see the little black Australorp fluffed up in her nest.

"Poor little chickie, are you cold?" Laurel said, as she quickly plugged in the heat lamp and then put more straw into the little hen's nest, piling it high around her so that she was neatly tucked in.

Lavonne clucked a couple of times in what Laurel read as a gesture of gratitude.

"You are so welcome, little girl. Sleep warm," Laurel said, and then slipped out of the coop, locked the door behind her, and ran out.

"I've got the gate. Get in the house. You're freezing."

She stopped by her truck to kill the engine and grab her purse. She was sprinting for the back door when Jake caught up with her. They went up the steps together and then into the house as she unlocked the door.

The relief of being out of the wind was immediate. Laurel ran to turn up the heat while Jake locked up behind them. She was back in the kitchen within seconds.

"Thank you for coming with me," she said, and wrapped her arms around his waist.

He tilted her chin to meet his gaze. "Baby, there's no way I would have let you drive off in the night alone. Without rushing anything between us, I'd like to think you've dealt with your last crisis on your own."

There were tears in her eyes, but her voice was steady. "You have become my knight in shining armor. I never thought I'd feel hopeful or happy again."

SHARON SALA

252

He brushed a kiss across her lips and then let her go.

The central heat kicked on as Laurel was hanging up their coats. He was still thinking about the job offer with the ad agency when Laurel's cell phone rang.

She jumped.

"Oh no, that has to be Mama." She looked at caller ID and frowned. "And it is. I hope Bonnie's not sick." She answered quickly. "Hello, Mama, is Bonnie okay?"

"Yes, but she woke up crying. She heard the wind, I think, and won't go back to sleep until she knows Lavonne's heat lamp is on."

Laurel's panic eased. "Put her on the phone," she said. She listened, waiting for her mother to give the phone to Bonnie, and then heard the teary little voice. "Hello? Mommy?"

"Yes, honey, it's me. Granny said you were worried about Lavonne, but she's fine. I put more hay in her nest and turned on her heat lamp."

"You did?"

"I sure did, and you know what, she went 'cluck cluck' twice. I'm pretty sure she was saying thank you."

She heard Bonnie giggle softly.

"Now you go get Brave Bear and crawl back into bed. You can tell him Lavonne is fine, and you're fine, and Granny needs her sleep, okay?"

"Okay, Mommy."

"I love you," Laurel said.

"I love you, too," Bonnie said.

The connection ended.

"Is she okay?" Jake asked.

"She is now that she knows Lavonne isn't cold. Oh my gosh, I am so glad I thought of it."

"You take care of everyone and everything, including chickens, but who takes care of you?"

She looked at his face then, seeing the honesty in his expression and the dark, steady gaze in his eyes. "You did tonight. The job is open if you want it."

He leaned across the table and took her hands. "Yes, I do. Actually, it's the second job offer I've had in the past few days."

"Really? What was the first?" she asked.

"Working for an Atlanta ad agency."

She tried not to let on what she was feeling, but she was somewhat anxious now. "You're moving?"

He shook his head. "No. Never. It would be a working-from-home job. Technology will be my friend."

"Thank goodness," she said. "I'm not much of a city girl. So how on earth did you find advertising?"

He grinned. "Actually, advertising found me," and he proceeded to tell her about convalescing with a buddy from his unit and how what began as a joke turned into a talent he never knew he had.

"Oh, Jake, that's amazing," Laurel said. "Congratulations."

"I haven't accepted yet, but I'm probably going to."

The wind popped the skirting on the trailer. The sound made her shiver.

"Do you want anything warm to drink? Some coffee, some hot chocolate?"

"All I want is you," Jake said.

She held out her hand. "I know where there's a big bed just waiting for us."

"And I know how to warm it up," he said.

"Yes, you sure do," Laurel said, and led the way.

Chapter 17

NESTER WAS SPORTING TWO BLACK EYES AND A BANDAGE across the bridge of his nose. His upper lip had a couple of stitches in it, and his nose, for the time being, was still packed with gauze. The last person he wanted to see on his doorstep was Truman, and he fixed him with a pointed stare.

"What the hell do you want?"

"I need to talk to you, Nester. My heart is heavy, and I can't let these hard feelings go on between us any longer."

Nester sighed. He didn't believe a word Truman was saying. He wanted something else, he just knew it, but he looked like he'd been run over by a herd of sheep, and he didn't have the heart to turn him away.

"Well, get on in here, and get it said. I'm still not feeling so great, as you can see."

He led him into the kitchen and pointed to a chair on one side of the table.

"You sit there," he said, and then took the one on the other side so that they were sitting face to face. "Okay, you're sorry. What else brings you here?"

And Truman unloaded his woes, beginning with waking up to no heat or electricity, which morphed to the story about sliding off in a ditch and losing his pants in front of a tow truck driver and a cop, and ending with getting shot at by his aunt and admitting he needed a place to stay.

Nester wanted to tell Truman it was no more than he

deserved, but Truman had been his friend since grade school, and he didn't have it in him to be that mean.

"If I let you stay here, you have to clean up after yourself and wash dishes when you dirty them, and you have to take a bath."

Truman stifled a groan. "Every night?"

"Mostly," Nester said. "I don't live with no pigs."

"I'll be happy to do that and whatever you need me to do, buddy," Truman said. "And I'm real sorry about busting your nose. I was just shit-faced drunk. You know I don't have any sense when I get like that."

Nester blinked and then winced. "Well, I know it now," he muttered, "so get your things and bring 'em on in. You can have the bedroom at the end of the hall."

Truman shifted in his seat. "Well, I didn't actually pack a bag, so—"

Nester slapped the table with the flat of his hand. "Then go home and pack one. You aren't going to wear my clothes, use my razor, or anything else personal like that, understand?"

Truman nodded. "Yes, yes, I do. I'll head on home now and get some things. I sure appreciate this, Nester, and as soon as my monthly check comes, I'll get square with the world and be out of your hair."

"Alright then," Nester said. "Hurry on back. I'm not keeping late hours since I got out of the hospital."

"I'll be back within the hour, I promise," Truman said, and bolted out of the house before Nester could change his mind.

By night they were settled in front of the television with Pepsi-Colas and popcorn, watching an NFL game. Even though the heat was on and the curtains were drawn, they couldn't help but notice the house was getting cold.

Finally, Nester got up to check the thermostat, and when he walked into the hall, he could tell that the wind had risen. He turned up the heat and then went to the kitchen and looked out toward the security light in the backyard. Nothing was falling, but the temperature drop was drastic.

"Ooh boy, it's gonna put ice on the ponds tonight," he said, as he went back into the living room.

Truman thought about his cold house and shuddered. "I can't thank you enough for taking me in like this."

Nester shrugged. "You're welcome. Besides, it won't be forever," he added, and gave Truman a hard look, just as a reminder.

For Laurel, waking up with Jake was new and comforting. Just the thought of knowing there was someone to help when the going got tough was huge, but falling in love with him meant even more.

As for Jake, he'd been awake for almost an hour just watching her sleep and wondering what it was about her that had stolen his heart. Part of it, he knew, was her valiant spirit. She had seen more than her share of true horror and despair, and survived it without bitterness. Yes, she was wary, but she had every right to be.

And she was beautiful. Hair the color of autumn, huge, dark eyes that looked straight into his soul, a slightly turned-up nose, and curvaceous lips begging to be kissed. The added bonus with Laurel was Bonnie. The little girl had stolen his heart before he'd ever dared to love her mother. He had never intended to take this road with her, but was so damn grateful he had.

When she opened her eyes and saw him, she smiled. That was what he'd been waiting for.

She was his sunrise.

Jake had gone home sometime before 10:00 a.m., and Laurel got busy. She had to do laundry today because the following week was going to be a busy one. She ate half a sandwich around 2:00 p.m. and was putting clean sheets on Bonnie's bed when she heard a car driving up.

She glanced out, saw her parents' car, and knew they were bringing Bonnie home. She smoothed out the last wrinkle in the top sheet then headed for the door.

Both parents came in with Bonnie, which told Laurel she was either in for another grilling or they were going to apologize. Bonnie was the only one smiling when they came up the steps. Laurel let them in and gave Bonnie a big welcome-home hug.

"I'm so glad you're home," she said. "Did you have fun at Granny and Gramps's house?"

"Yes, and Granny made me biscuits with chocolate gravy for breakfast."

Laurel laughed. "Yum. She used to make that for me, too. Let me have your bag so I can wash the clothes in it. Take Brave Bear to your room, hang up your coat, and don't mess up the bed. I'm in the middle of making it, okay?"

"Okay, Mommy," Bonnie said, and skipped off down the hall.

Laurel turned to her parents. "Thank you for bringing her home."

Pansy took her daughter's hand. "Honey, we want to apologize for our behavior last night. We were out of line, and we're so sorry that we embarrassed you. I so hope we didn't hurt Jake's feelings."

"Thank you," Laurel said, and didn't elaborate on anything more.

"I saw the old truck parked out by the chicken coop," Benny said. "It didn't quit on you out there or anything, did it?"

"No. It was dark before that cold spell hit, and I needed better light than a flashlight to see by when I went out to tend to Lavonne."

"Ah…well, good deal," Benny said. "You know if it gives you trouble, just give me a call. I worked on that engine for quite a few years when we owned it. I think I still know a thing or two."

"If I need help, I'll let you know," she said.

"Well then, we'll let you get back to work," Pansy said. "Thanks again for letting Bonnie spend the night. She is a delight to us."

"You're welcome," Laurel said, and opened the front door to see them out. "Drive safe. I have a really busy week, but I'll be calling to check on the both of you. Stay inside, and stay warm."

They kissed each other good-bye, and then Pansy and Benny headed home.

"She was still pretty cool," Pansy said. "I thought she'd be in a better mood by now."

Privately, Benny thought his wife was often a meddler, but she was his meddler, and so he forgave her. However, others weren't as predisposed to be that forgiving.

"Well, honey, she wasn't in a bad mood last night.

She was angry and embarrassed and, I think, also hurt by what we'd done. So it's not that she's in a bad mood. We let her down. Getting over that is going to take time."

"I guess," Pansy said, and changed the subject.

Back in the house, Laurel finished making beds and was just about ready to sit down for a bit when she looked up at the time, realized it was getting dark and they still had to tend to Bonnie's little hen. She walked down to Bonnie's room where she was coloring with Panda Bear and Brave Bear.

"Hi, Mommy. Panda and Brave Bear are picking out my crayons for me."

"And they are doing a great job. That picture you're coloring is beautiful, but you need to put it aside for a bit. It's time to go feed Lavonne. Get your coat, and you better get your sock cap and gloves. It's very cold out."

Bonnie leaped off the bed and ran to her closet while Laurel went to get her own things. They met in the kitchen all bundled up for the cold, and out the door they went with Bonnie talking at every step.

It was too cold for one little hen to be outside, so Laurel had left the door to the coop closed all day, keeping her from being out in the pen. When they opened the door to the coop, Lavonne came running.

Bonnie squatted down and began petting the little black hen, then picked her up and carried her around as Laurel filled up the water and added new feed. She sprinkled a little oyster shell in with it, which would make the shells of her eggs stronger, then looked in Lavonne's nest and pulled out the egg.

"Good job, Lavonne!" Laurel said, as she held it up.

Bonnie beamed like a proud mother. "She's a good girl, isn't she, Mommy?"

Laurel laughed. "Yes, she is a very good girl. Now tell her good night. We're finished here, and she's probably hungry."

Bonnie put her down by the feed and then watched for a few moments as the little hen began pecking. Satisfied that all was right in the chicken world, they made sure the heat lamp was on, closed the door to the coop, and then latched the gate in the yard as well.

Bonnie ran ahead of Laurel and was already inside by the time Laurel went up the steps.

The sun was setting on a very cold day.

The next morning, Laurel was getting Bonnie ready for school when her cell phone began to ring. The first call was from Peanut Butterman. She frowned. She was supposed to be cleaning his house this morning.

"Hello?"

"Hey, Laurel, this is Peanut. Blessings is completely without power, so we'll have to cancel the cleaning today. Come any other time you can this week, okay?"

"Oh my gosh! Do you know what happened?" she asked.

"Not certain but it's looking like vandalism out at the substation or something. I heard the police department got a tip, but don't know more than that."

"Oh wow. We have power," she said.

"I think you all are on another power source. The one that Blessings is connected to is old and has been there forever."

"So there won't be school," Laurel said.

"You should be getting a message about that too, if the school has a way to notify parents without their usual power sources."

"Okay, thanks," Laurel said, and disconnected.

Moments later, she got a similar call from her other client, Myra Franklin, who owned the florist, and she also rescheduled.

About five minutes later, Laurel's phone signaled a text from the school. Obviously they'd figured out a way to notify the residents. No school today.

"Hey, Bonnie, no school today," Laurel said. "Put your old clothes back on and go play. We're both home today."

Bonnie clapped her hands and disappeared.

⁓⁓

Jake was online, checking email and writing a letter back to Ron Fitz. He'd taken risks with his life every day on active duty, so risking some time out of his life to pursue the possibility of success in an ad agency seemed plausible, even smart. And the danger of getting blown up on the job seemed infinitesimal to none.

After hitting Send to the email, he made a call back to Peanut Butterman.

Despite the lack of power, Betty Purejoy was answering the office phone from home by call forwarding. "Mr. Butterman's office."

"Hey, Betty, this is Jake Lorde. Is Peanut in?"

"Hello, Jake. No, he's not in. I'm answering his calls from my home. I don't think anything is working in town. Blessings is without power."

"The whole town?" Jake asked.

"Yes. Something at a substation. You have power where you live?"

"Yes, thank goodness. It's really cold to be without heat today."

"Tell me about it," she said. "We have a wood-burning fireplace, or I'd be in bed under a pile of covers."

"Do you want me to give Mr. Butterman a message?"

"No, it's okay. I'll talk to him later. It's nothing pressing."

"Okay, but I'm giving you fair warning. If I run out of wood and the power stays out, I might be heading your way."

"I wouldn't turn you away," Jake said.

By noon, Bonnie was bored. She wanted to go outside and play, but Laurel kept telling her it was too cold. Then she wanted to go check on Lavonne, but Laurel reminded her that opening the door in the coop would only make it cold in there again and they needed to let Lavonne stay warm.

Bonnie dragged her feet as she left the room. Laurel grinned as she watched her go. She was really learning how to milk her chances.

With extra time on her hands, Laurel got out her invoices and receipts and started catching up on book-keeping. Being self-employed with the IRS was a whole mess in itself, and she hated to get behind.

Bonnie wandered through the house again. "Mommy, can I go visit Jake?"

Laurel didn't look up. "No. I told you it's too cold. You should check and see if Brave Bear is sleepy. He might need a nap."

"Okay," Bonnie said, and dragged her feet even more as she left the room.

Laurel chuckled and kept working.

The next time she looked up it was almost 1:00 p.m. She pushed her chair back from the table and went to get Bonnie. She was probably getting hungry. But when she looked in Bonnie's room, it was empty. Brave Bear was tucked in with a blanket with Panda Bear right beside him, but no Bonnie in sight.

"Bonnie!" Laurel called. "Time to eat some lunch."

When Bonnie didn't answer, she frowned. Was she hiding? Had she fallen asleep somewhere else?

She quickly looked in her bedroom, and when Bonnie wasn't there, her pulse skipped a beat. "Bonnie! Bonnie! Where are you?" Laurel yelled, and began running through the house.

She looked in every closet, underneath both beds, and by the time she looked outside, she was praying to God Bonnie was out there in the chicken yard. She was in tears when she saw everything was still shut and latched.

She grabbed her phone and her coat, buttoning it up as she ran. She was off the back steps and running, calling Bonnie's name with every step. She searched the yard. She searched the loose skirting under the house in case Bonnie had crawled under.

Even though the gate was still latched at the chicken pen, she unlatched it and looked in the coop anyway.

Laurel's heart was hammering so loud she couldn't breathe. She stood on the leeward side of the coop out of the wind and closed her eyes, trying to remember what the last thing Bonnie asked her was about.

Jake! Of course! She'd run off to see him.

Laurel's hands were shaking as she made the call, and when Jake answered, she started to cry. "Jake, is Bonnie with you?"

He shoved his checkbook aside. "No."

"Oh my God. I can't find her," Laurel cried.

"How long has she been gone?" Jake asked.

"I don't know for sure. Maybe thirty minutes. I told her to go play. I was catching up on bookkeeping. I wasn't paying close enough attention. She's gone. I can't lose her, Jake. I can't."

"Where are you right now?" he asked.

"Outside by the coop."

"Go in the house, get a blanket and a first aid kit. I'll be there in five minutes."

Just having a plan made Laurel react. She shoved the phone in her pocket as she ran, and was still in the house when Jake drove up. She ran out with the first aid stuff in a bag and the blanket over her shoulder, straight into Jake's arms.

"We're going to find her, baby. Believe it. Now tell me, where haven't you searched?"

She thought a moment and then gasped. "The creek. When I thought she'd gone to your house, I assumed she'd gone by the creek, then when you said—"

"We still need to look," Jake said. "Let's go!"

They ran without talking, each locked into the "what ifs" of their fears. Jake thought of someone taking her and remembered the noise he'd heard of an intruder on the other side of the creek bank. Best not mention that unless it was a last resort.

Laurel was so scared she couldn't breathe. She was afraid to talk for fear she'd start screaming and never stop.

As soon as they reached the trail that Bonnie always took, Jake saw the first sign. "She was here. There's a footprint. It's too small for anyone else."

Laurel nodded and down they went.

"Call her name as we walk," Jake said, and led the way slowly along the frozen creek, watching for signs. The gravel surface on the shores made it difficult for a track to be left, and she was so small that the weight of her steps didn't leave an imprint.

"Bonnie! Bonnie! Where are you?" Laurel called, searching the brush along both sides of the banks as they walked, praying for a sign.

They hadn't gone more than a hundred yards when the creek took a turn to the right, and the moment they turned that corner, Jake's heart nearly stopped.

"There! The ice has been broken. She fell in the creek," he shouted, and started running.

Laurel was behind him, crying now because Bonnie was nowhere in sight.

Jake stopped at the site and knelt, looking closely at the tracks, and trying to figure out what she had done next.

"Where is she? Oh, Jake, where is she? Bonnie!"

The silence only added to her panic as she started turning in circles, racing from one bush to another, shoving vines aside.

Jake ran after her and grabbed her hand and then pulled her to him and quickly hugged her. "Okay, honey. Listen to me."

Laurel was shaking. Her eyes were wide with shock, and Jake needed her to focus so they could find Bonnie before it was too late. He cupped her face. He kissed her lips. She was breaking his heart.

"Now, we're going to calm down a minute and look at what we have. Come with me."

Laurel grabbed on to his hand with desperation and followed him as he pointed. "Here's where she climbed out of the creek. It's not deep you know, and here's a step, and there's another step. I think she's confused. Probably the shock of the cold water and the fall got her turned around. She's backtracking now, going back toward home, and here, I think, she stopped again. Shit. She's going in circles. Now her tracks are so mixed up, and she's back on the gravel. It's impossible to see where she went next."

"I'll search that way, and you go the other," Laurel said.

Jake hesitated and then looked at his watch. "By your count she's been missing at least an hour. And she's wet and the temperature is below freezing. We need help. Go back up where you can get a signal and call the County Sheriff and the Blessing's Police. Call anyone else you know who might be free to come help. It will start getting dark within the next three hours. We don't have much time."

Laurel heard what Jake wasn't saying. If they didn't find her before night, she would die.

"Go!" he said.

She turned on her heel and started climbing the bank while Jake started running. He ran all the way along the creek to the trail leading to his house without finding one sign, and then turned around and retraced his steps, searching the other side of the creek bank, then farther south past Laurel's trailer. He ran until he came upon thick brambles that had grown across the water and knew she would not have tried to go through them.

He was retracing his steps when he heard the first sirens. Within minutes, the bank above him was lined with searchers.

Lon Pittman slid down on the seat of his coveralls and ran to where Jake was standing.

"Any sign?" he asked.

"Nothing beyond where she fell in the creek. All you can see is where she got turned around. She was walking in circles when we lost her trail."

Lon nodded, but he was already thinking beyond a little girl getting lost. He was thinking of abduction.

Jake saw Lon looking up and had to tell him what he'd heard weeks earlier. "You need to know that a while back I was down here clearing brush and heard someone on the other side of the creek following me through the trees. I didn't see anyone, but when I challenged, they turned and ran. I heard footsteps running through the dead leaves."

"Well, hell," Lon said softly. "I sure don't want this to turn into a child abduction case."

"Neither do I, but I had to mention it," Jake said.

Lon nodded. "Okay, I'm going to put some of the searchers on both sides of the creek. How far north did you search?"

"All the way to where you'd come out at my house."

"Then I'll move some others down there, and they can search father. What about south?"

"About an eighth of a mile south of Laurel's, the passage is blocked by a lot of overgrowth and dead trees. I've already been there and back."

Lon pulled his two-way and started issuing orders, walking north as he went. Jake crossed the creek and walked with him, praying for a sign.

Chapter 18

LAUREL WAS SO SCARED SHE COULDN'T CRY. THIS WAS worse than the day Adam died. This was *her* baby, and she'd let her get lost. Laurel was given the job of staying at the command site, holding Bonnie's school picture so the searchers would know what she looked like, filling them in on what she'd been wearing.

An entire hour had passed since the searchers' arrival. She'd been so certain that they'd find her fast and still nothing. When another truck rolled up behind her, she didn't even turn to look. Then someone put a hand on her shoulder.

"Laurel?"

She turned around, saw Adam's brother, David; Beverly's husband, Garrett; and a half dozen other friends of the Payne family and burst into tears. David held her until she managed to regain some control, and then patted her on the back.

"Tell us what to do," he said.

Laurel wiped tears, told them what Bonnie was wearing and that Deputy Pittman was running the search.

"We'll find her," David said.

"It's been hours. She got wet," Laurel said.

"Just pray," David said. "We'll stay till she's found. We won't ever leave you on your own again."

Laurel watched them hurrying away, and then dropped to her knees, too overcome to stand another moment and then thought of her parents. They couldn't help search, but they needed to know. Laurel took the phone out of her pocket and punched in the numbers. It rang three times before she heard her mother's voice.

"Hello?"

"Mama, it's me, Laurel. Bonnie is missing. Searchers are everywhere. I can't lose her. I'm so scared I feel like I'm going to die. I need you."

"We're on the way. Have faith, child."

The line went dead in Laurel's ear.

—⁓—

Because of the power outage and the businesses staying closed, it took Ruby Dye a while to learn about the missing child and the ongoing search, but it didn't take her long to organize aide for the searchers. Within an hour she and Lovey were heading out of town with jugs of hot coffee and as many sandwiches as they had been able to make at Granny's Country Kitchen. Bringing up the rear were at least a half dozen cars full of women, all bringing what they had on hand.

Upon arrival, they drove right up to where all the cars were parked and started carrying folding tables, while others came with food and drink. It didn't take long for searchers to see the setup, and they stopped momentarily for a warming cup of hot coffee and took off carrying a sandwich or a cookie.

Ruby found Laurel sitting on the ground with her arms wrapped around her knees, staring off toward the line of trees above the creek. She knelt down beside her and put her arms around Laurel's shoulders. "Laurel, honey, get up. The ground is cold."

Laurel blinked, surprised by the sound of a woman's voice, and then saw Ruby Dye. "My baby is wet and cold and lost. I lost her, Ruby. If they don't find her, I will die."

"Where's your mama?" Ruby asked.

Laurel shuddered. "On the way."

"Okay then. Now listen to me. Someone's going to bring you some hot coffee. Drink it. You won't do anyone any good if you're sick when they find your baby."

"What if they don't?" Laurel asked.

Ruby frowned. "And what if they do? Think positive. Tell the universe what you want. Demand it, honey. Sometimes a woman has to shout real loud in this world to be heard."

Laurel dropped the phone back in her pocket and then pulled herself up from the ground. She kept hearing Ruby's voice.

Tell the universe what you need. Women have to shout to be heard.

For the first time, she stepped out of her panic to see what was going on around her—at the vast number of vehicles, at Ruby and her friends setting up a refreshment center, at the sound of a chopper now flying overhead. Everyone was actively doing something to find her child except her. She didn't know her parents had just driven up or that they were frantically moving through the cars, looking for her at that very moment.

Her fingers curled into fists as she turned and strode toward the trailer. Her steps were long and sure, and by the time she got up to the back steps and turned around, she was so angry she was shaking.

She lifted a fist to the sky, and the rage that came out of

her was the pent-up sorrow of two years a widow, hanging on to what she had without care for herself, working when she was sick, working when she was so tired she didn't think she could put one foot in front of the other. The fury in her voice was unmistakable—the sign of a woman who had been pushed one step too far. And when she started with a scream, the sound carried on the air and down into the creek. Every man searching within hearing distance heard it, and then stopped what they were doing—a witness to a mother who was shouting down God.

"Don't you do this to me, God! I don't know if You're listening, but this is a message to the universe. I lost my husband. I nearly lost everything we had, and I survived it. But I will not lose my last bit of joy. You cannot have my baby! Do you hear me? She is mine!"

And then she saw her parents coming toward her and collapsed on the porch as they took her in their arms. Men were standing with tears running down their faces, while others cleared their throats and looked away.

A cold chill stopped Jake when he heard her scream. If they lost Bonnie, he lost Laurel, too. He couldn't bear the thought of losing either one, but both? It wasn't to be borne.

He stopped in his tracks. It was time to rethink this.

Searchers had yet to find a single sign of any footsteps indicating that she'd been taken. There were no tire tracks and nothing to show where she might have been dragged up the bank or carried out. So if she wasn't abducted, then she's got to be here. *Think of where she could be, but in a new direction. Were there caves?* He couldn't remember any, but the overgrowth was heavy enough to hide them if there were.

He turned around and began retracing his steps, returned to the place where she'd fallen in, and then started over, this time looking for any kind of a place to hide. Then he squatted down to look at the creek from Bonnie's viewpoint. She was a very little girl. It wouldn't take much to hide her.

He went all the way up one side of the creek from his house to Laurel's, searching for access to a cave or crevice along the ground level, and then crossed the creek and began to do it again, but walking slower, looking for ledges or overgrowth hanging all the way to the ground. And then he saw the button, and his heart skipped a beat. He dropped to his knees as he picked it up and turned it over in his hand. It was a little black button. Small button. Small child. It had to be hers and not from one of the searchers.

He dropped it in his pocket and then got down on his hands and knees and began looking at the area from what would have been her perspective. Almost immediately, he saw the overhang only a few yards away.

"Please God, let this be it," he said softly, and crawled over to the hanging limbs and vines and pushed them aside.

She was in there! So far back. Lying on her side, so still.

"Bonnie! Bonnie!" he yelled.

The lack of response was sickening.

He stood, let out an ear-splitting whistle, and then shouted. "Here! I found her. She's here!"

Men nearby radioed the others, and even as he was back down on his belly and crawling into the crevice, the creek was swarming with searchers. Someone crawled in beside him. He didn't bother to look. It would take both of them to get her out without causing her harm.

"Son of a bitch," the man said. "How on earth did you find her?"

"A button. I found a button," Jake said, and then looked to see who it was. It was David Payne.

They crawled a few feet farther, and then David stopped. "I can't reach her. I'm too big to go any farther."

Jake was in the same condition. He tried calling her again. "Bonnie! It's Jake. Wake up, baby, wake up."

She didn't move, and Jake's mind was racing when the obvious hit him and he started backing out. When he got up and turned around, he was shocked to see how many men were behind them.

"She crawled back so far into a crevice that we can't reach her. It has to be someone smaller and thinner. Get her mother. Get Laurel. She's the only one small enough to do it."

Deputy Pittman didn't waste time. The moment the words came out of Jake's mouth, he was on his two-way giving the order.

Less than two minutes later, Laurel came sliding down the side of the creek, pushing her way through the crowd of searchers, and then stumbling through the water to where Jake was lying.

"You found her! Is she alive?" Laurel cried.

"I don't know, and I can't reach her," Jake said. "You can do it, Laurel. Go in on your belly. When you reach her, grab hold of her arms and yell, then hold on to her. I'll pull you both out."

Pittman was already radioing for an ambulance as men began organizing a relay. Once they got her out, they would have to get her up the steep bank.

Ignoring the freezing temperatures, Laurel took off her coat, shedding anything bulky that could slow her down, and then dropped to the ground and quickly crawled out of sight.

There were no words to describe the shock of seeing Bonnie's lifeless body, but she kept on crawling. "Bonnie! It's Mommy. Can you hear me, baby?" she said, while still inching toward her baby's body.

Twice her head banged on the rocks above her head, and both times she knew she was bleeding, but she didn't stop. And then the horror set in. She was as far as she could go and still just a few inches shy of being able to reach her. For a few panicked moments she thought that she'd failed, and then again, she heard Ruby's voice.

Women have to shout to be heard.

"She's mine," Laurel said loudly, and pushed forward, taking skin off her chin from the gravel on which she was crawling, while the rocks above her dug into the flesh on her back.

She didn't feel a thing.

Shock swept through her as her hands finally closed around Bonnie's wrists. Bonnie was so cold, and the fabric of her coat was utterly frozen. Then she felt a faint pulse beneath her fingertips and let out a scream.

"I've got her, and she's alive. Pull, Jacob, pull!"

Jake could just reach her ankles, and he began to pull her while inching them both backward. He went slow, knowing Laurel would have to ease Bonnie onto her back before they could safely get her out. He pulled until his entire body was back out into the open, and then he got to his feet and pulled her even farther, pulling until he saw the ripped shirt and the blood on Laurel's back, and nearly fainted.

No, damn you, no. Don't do this. It's not about you anymore. They are your life. You are their future. Shake it off.

It was only a couple seconds of hesitation, but it felt like an eternity to Jake before he got himself together and pulled them the rest of the way out.

The moment the searchers saw her, their admiration for the young widow grew in leaps and bounds. They could see the evidence for themselves. She'd sacrificed her body to get her baby, and in that moment, Laurel Payne became a hero in their eyes.

Then they saw Bonnie. Blue and lifeless. Jake reached for her wrist. There was a pulse.

In an instant, Lon Pittman was beside them, wrapping Bonnie in heavy blankets and issuing orders. Laurel was frantic. Her reluctance to give over her baby was obvious, and then Jake took her by the shoulders and turned her toward him.

There was a brief moment in which a look passed between them that no words could have ever explained, and then he was putting her coat back on her, sending her up the bank with her baby. "Laurel's hurt, too," he yelled, as the men began pulling her up. "Make sure they take her with them."

Searchers began climbing out of the creek by the dozens. David Payne stopped long enough to shake Jake's hand. "This is the second time you have saved a member of our family. You are one hell of a man, Jacob Lorde."

Jake watched him go up the creek bank and then had to wipe his eyes before he could climb out because there were too many tears to see where he was going.

Laurel's parents were waiting as they pulled her up. Once they realized she was injured, they sent her on her way with a promise to follow them to the hospital.

The EMTs were already loading Bonnie into the ambulance when another deputy stopped them and loaded Laurel in as well. "She has multiple head and back contusions," he told them, then slammed the door and sent them on their way.

Searchers who'd been out in the cold for more than three hours were elated when they saw Ruby Dye's coffee station and headed for it. The hot coffee began warming them from the inside out, and although there was relief that the little girl had been found alive, her condition was still too critical to rejoice.

It was then the talk around the coffee station turned to Laurel Payne. The ones who'd seen the ripped shirt and the bloody gouges in her back told the story, and those who heard it retold it yet again, until what Laurel Payne had done seemed far beyond a mother's sacrifice to save a child. It had turned into a story of heroic proportions.

Laurel knew none of it nor cared. She just needed to hear a doctor tell her that Bonnie Carol was going to live.

Jake climbed out of the creek and ran toward his truck, his heart heavy with dread. He needed to get to the hospital, but he was afraid of the verdict.

Ruby Dye saw Jake, and she saw the fear on his face. She could only imagine what he was thinking. She handed him a cup of hot coffee as he passed their table.

"Drink it. It's hot. You're cold. God is good, Jake. It has to be okay."

He paused as she handed him the cup and hugged her.

Ruby wasn't expecting that, but she wasn't one to turn down a hug.

"Thank you," Jake said, then took a sip of the coffee as he continued toward Laurel's house.

It was unlocked. Laurel would not have her purse or the keys, and she needed a clean shirt. The one she was wearing was in shreds.

He entered and went straight to her room and dug through her drawers until he found a sweatshirt. It would be soft against the bandages that would be on her back, and it would be warm. It took him a couple more minutes to find her purse and keys, and then he darted across the hall to Bonnie's room to get Brave Bear, and then he was off, locking her house up behind him.

He drove to Blessings with a knot in his stomach and praying for mercy. Bonnie had to be okay. She just had to. Then just before he reached the city-limit sign, he remembered the power outage and wondered if the power was back on, then let it go. The hospital would have backup generators. No matter what shape Blessings was in, his girls would be cared for. That's all that mattered.

It was obvious by the number of cars in the ER parking lot that many of the searchers had followed the ambulance to get an update. Until they knew there was going to be a positive outcome, there would be no celebration.

He grabbed Laurel's things and walked into ER and was immediately enveloped within the milling crowd. People wanted to ask how he'd found her, what he'd seen, how she looked, or talk about what Laurel had done, but he didn't stop to talk. He just nodded and kept moving until he heard Laurel's voice. He parted the curtains and walked in.

Her parents were standing on one side of an examining table, while nurses were cleaning the wounds on her back, washing the bloody gouges with antiseptic solutions, and all the while Laurel was begging them to let her see Bonnie.

When she saw Jake, she just held out her arms. He handed her things to her parents and bent down and kissed her.

Laurel had his hand in a death grip and couldn't stop talking. The panic in her voice was as raw as the wounds on her back. "You saved her life, Jake. The doctor said another thirty minutes, and she would have been gone. Oh my God, how did you ever find her in there?"

Jake reached in his pocket, pulled out the button, and dropped it in her hand. "I found this."

Laurel gasped. "It's from her coat!" She began crying all over again. "They won't let me see her. I need to know what's happening. Please go check for me. I have to know."

"Where is she?" Jake asked.

"Two bays down, I think. I keep waiting to hear her cry. I've never wanted to hear her cry in my life, but I need to hear it now."

"I'll be back," Jake said, and left without speaking to her parents.

They had yet to apologize to him, and he wasn't looking forward to another session. He had no idea that they'd already apologized to Laurel.

A nurse walked into the bay just ahead of him, and when the curtains parted, he saw Bonnie. She wasn't moving, which scared the hell out of him. He pushed the curtain aside and walked in.

Dr. Quick recognized Jake, and he'd already heard enough to know he was the one who'd found her. At first, Jake didn't speak. He stood to one side, out of the way, and listened, garnering enough information to know she was still alive, but not out of the woods.

When Dr. Quick finally stopped and stepped back, Jake spoke. "I'm here for Laurel," Jake said. "She's frantic. What can you tell me?"

Dr. Quick pointed to the warming blankets they were putting on Bonnie's body. "Her core body temp is low. Those are warming blankets. It's a bit touch and go right now as to how she's going to respond. She had no injuries or broken bones. X-rays have determined that. We're just working to offset the hypothermia. Prayers will help, and time will tell."

"Has she regained consciousness at all?" Jake asked.

"No, but it's early, and at this point, I'm not real concerned."

"Would you consider her condition serious or critical?"

"Right now, I'd say serious, but if she doesn't improve, that could change."

"Are you going to move her now?" Jake asked.

"Yes, she's going to the ICU."

"Will you let Laurel see her in there as soon as they get her bandaged up, even if it's not visiting hours?"

The doctor's eyes narrowed thoughtfully. "You are quite the advocate in her mother's absence. Yes, you can tell her that I'll waive the visiting restrictions so that her mother can briefly see her."

"Thank you," Jake said, and then gave Bonnie's leg a brief pat. "You need to wake up soon, little girl. Who's gonna take care of Lavonne?"

"Who's Lavonne?" Dr. Quick asked.

"Her pet chicken," Jake said.

Dr. Quick looked back down at the child on his examining table. "What a cool kid—a chicken for a pet. I have a good feeling about this. She feels like a fighter to me."

"She is a special little girl," Jake said, and went to give Laurel the news.

Chapter 19

BY THE TIME JAKE GOT BACK TO LAUREL, HER BACK had been treated and bandaged and she was wearing the clean sweatshirt he brought. Some of the Payne family was there also, and looked about as uncomfortable around Benny and Pansy as he felt.

Laurel was still sitting up on the exam table, her legs dangling off the side. There weren't any bandages on her head, which meant no stitches, but he could see a couple of places that appeared to have had the hair clipped back and, when he got closer, saw little butterfly patches on the wounds.

"Jake! What did they say?" Laurel asked, and pulled him down beside her.

"Dr. Quick said her condition is serious, not critical, but if she doesn't improve in the next few hours that could change." He took Laurel's hand. "They X-rayed her. She has no physical injuries at all. All of her problems are related to the hypothermia."

Laurel moaned. "Can I see her? I want to see her now."

"They are moving her to the ICU, but Dr. Quick said he'll make an exception for you about visiting hours so that once you leave here they will get you into the ICU to see her, regardless of the time. They have warming blankets on her. I saw an IV in her arm. He said pray. The rest of it is wait and see."

Laurel kept looking at his face, searching the now

familiar landscape of his features and thinking what a gift his presence was in their lives. "Forever, Jake Lorde. That's how long I'll love you for what you've done."

The emotion that bubbled up in Jake was so sudden he couldn't speak. He had to take a deep breath, and even then barely managed a wobbly smile. "That's pretty public, honey. I have a whole lot of witnesses who are going to help me hold you to that."

Pansy slipped up beside them and wrapped her arms around his neck. "I'm sorry, and so is Benny."

Happy the hard feelings had passed, he gave her a quick hug. "Thank you."

Laurel slid off the exam table, holding on to Jake to steady her legs. "I don't know what's taking them so long, but I'm going to see my girl."

"Wait, I'll go with you," Jake said, which set the exodus from ER into motion.

The Payne and the Joyner families walked out of the ER with them to an elevator, then up to the critical care unit.

Laurel's back felt like it was on fire, but she didn't say a word. It had hurt like hell giving birth to Bonnie. A little more pain along the way was nothing compared to the joy of still having her daughter in her life.

When they got to the ICU waiting room, everyone else took a seat, while Jake took Laurel up to the desk. As soon as she identified herself, the nurse walked her inside.

Jake went back to the waiting room and sat in the first empty chair, leaned back, and closed his eyes. He couldn't remember how this day had started, but he would never forget how it was coming to an end. God willing, every day forward would be better than the last.

The power came back on in town just as the sun was setting, and it was just after midnight when they learned Bonnie was waking up. At that point the whole waiting room erupted in a cheer.

The Paynes left their blessings and went home.

Benny and Pansy were exhausted by the whole ordeal, but so grateful to be back in their daughter's good graces and forgiven by Jake that they deemed their discomfort had all been worthwhile.

Laurel came out of ICU with happy tears and fell into Jake's outstretched arms. The worst was finally over.

The next five days were a steady mix of ups and downs, of chaos and calm, but on the fifth day, Laurel took her baby home. She was so glad to be leaving that hospital she could hardly think. She hadn't spent a night in her own bed since it had happened. She'd missed a whole week's worth of work and even more weight she could not afford to lose.

There was so much catching up to do and not a lot of money to do it with, but none of that mattered because Bonnie was okay. Today was Saturday. If everything went as planned, Bonnie would be back in school on Monday, and their world would get back to normal.

Now she and Bonnie were in the backseat of Jake's truck, trusting him to get them home. She looked down at her sleeping daughter, at the dark eyelashes shadowing babyish cheeks, still unable to get past the horror Bonnie must have gone through.

When questioned, Bonnie couldn't remember anything of what had happened. She didn't even remember running away or falling through the ice into the water or being lost.

Laurel was glad Bonnie didn't remember it, but she would never forget. What had Bonnie been thinking when she'd crawled into that crevice? How scared had she been? Had she called out for her mommy and wondered why she never came? The whole thing broke her heart, and if not for Jake, the ending would have been fatal.

She looked up from her daughter's face to the man in the driver's seat. She had a partial view of his profile and a good view of the back of his head. There were no words to describe how dear he had become to all of them or how he'd picked up the slack over and over during the past five days, doing everything from taking care of Bonnie's little black hen to bringing in Laurel's mail. There were so many things she'd been concerned with, and each time he'd made the worry go away. He made falling in love so easy.

As they took a turn in the road to leave Blessings, sunlight was suddenly in her eyes. She turned her head against the glare and quietly fell asleep.

Jake was driving, happy that Laurel was in the backseat with Bonnie in her lap and Brave Bear tucked beneath Bonnie's chin. Getting to take them home was like writing *The End* to a horrible tale.

He was almost out of town when he realized it had become noticeably quiet. When he looked up in the rearview mirror and saw that they were both asleep, he smiled. The last vestige of the nightmare fell away.

They slept until he reached her house. It was the sudden silence that woke them both.

"Mommy, are we home?" Bonnie asked.

"Yes, ma'am. We sure are," Laurel said.

"I want to see Lavonne," Bonnie begged.

"As soon as we get our stuff in the house, we'll both go see Lavonne," Laurel said.

"She'll be glad to see the both of you," Jake said. "I am definitely too big for that coop. I kept getting in her way, and she didn't like that a bit."

"How do you know she didn't like it?" she asked.

Jake reached over the seat and lightly tweaked her nose. "Because she kept pecking my boots with her little beak."

Bonnie giggled, which made him smile. He was falling in love with that sound and with her.

He unlocked the doors to the trailer as Laurel and Bonnie got out. Bonnie was so ready to run, and Laurel was afraid to let her go.

"Let's take it easy for a bit," Laurel said, as Bonnie walked into the house with Brave Bear under her arm.

"Good luck with that," Jake said, and set the suitcase with all their stuff down.

Laurel took the moment to hug him. "Don't think I haven't missed you and snuggling with you and all that other stuff," she whispered.

He kissed her. "About that other stuff...I miss it, too."

"Soon," Laurel said.

"It's okay," Jake said. "I'm not keeping score. The fact that we're not going anywhere is good enough for me. Now, do you need anything before I head for home?"

"You already stocked my refrigerator, so we're

good to go on food, and the rest of it can wait. I'm just glad to be home."

"I'm glad you're home, too," Jake said, and then when she would have moved away, he held her for a moment more. "There's something I want to tell you."

She smiled. "I'm listening."

"First thing I want to say is that I'm so in love with you I can't think straight."

Laurel sighed. "Oh, Jake, I love you so much."

He slid his hands on either side of her face. "I don't know how you feel about yourself, but I think you rock. You went in after Bonnie at your peril and suffered greatly without comment. I don't know many women who are that courageous, and I am so proud that you are mine to love."

"It's not courage that leads us to such things. It's love. At those points, there are no other decisions to be made."

He hugged her again, still careful about not hurting her back. "Promise you'll call if you need me?"

"I will," she said.

"And don't worry about cooking tomorrow. I'm bringing Sunday dinner from Granny's."

"Thank you again," Laurel said.

"Sleep when she sleeps," he said. "I love you, and I'll see you tomorrow."

⁓

Truman and Nester were hanging out in the cereal aisle at the Piggly Wiggly, arguing the merits of two different choices of cereal, when they both keyed in on the conversation in the next aisle.

"I heard the little Payne girl went home yesterday," one woman said.

"Yes, they did. I saw Jake Lorde driving them home. What a nightmare they've all endured."

"Yes, and isn't Jake Lorde just the handsomest thing ever? He's such a nice man, and now a true hero to Laurel Payne and her girl. I heard the little girl was minutes away from dying when he found her."

"I know. Just like in the movies, right? What a hero!"

They kept talking as they moved out of hearing distance, but as soon as they were gone, Nester eyed Truman. He knew there was no love lost between them and guessed anything that made Jake Lorde a hero was bound to piss Truman off, and he was right.

"That just makes me sick," Truman said. "He got my ass thrown in jail, got hisself nearly blown up in the war and comes home a hero, and then turns himself into a hero all over again. Someone needs to take him and his ego down."

Nester frowned. "Technically, he didn't do anything to get your ass thrown in jail. He just happened to witness you doing that to yourself. If you hadn't committed a robbery, you wouldn't have gone to prison."

"Shut up," Truman muttered. "I got my own outlook on stuff, and in my world, he fucked me up."

Nester frowned again. "Sssh, dang it, Truman. We're not in some bar. We're in the grocery store. There's women and kids all over the place. You can't go talking rough like that around here."

Truman glared. If he hadn't needed a place to stay so bad, he would have parted company with Nester on the spot.

"Fine. He's a damn hero. Are we gonna get sugar-coated Bunny Pops or cinnamon-coated Apple-O's?"

"The Bunny Pops," Nester said. "Cinnamon gives me heartburn."

They tossed the cereal in their basket and headed up the aisle toward checkout. But Truman had plans, and they didn't involve eating kiddy cereal. He wasn't going to be satisfied until he found a way to hurt that man.

By a week later, life had settled back into a regular rhythm, and Thanksgiving was approaching.

Jake had contacted Peanut Butterman and told him he was no longer interested in purchasing Ralph's station, then explained that he was starting work with the Atlanta ad agency on the first of December and would be working from home. Peanut made note of the decision, congratulated him on the new job, and went to The Curl Up and Dye to get his bimonthly trim. It wasn't so much that he liked his hair consistently neat as it was that he liked watching Ruby Dye cut it. She was, in his opinion, one fine woman, even if she did change her hair color with the seasons.

That evening, Laurel was talking on the phone with Jake, and she brought up Thanksgiving. "I'm making Thanksgiving dinner. You are, of course, officially invited to sit at the head of the table, to be the carver of fine turkeys and all-around good-looking host."

Jake beamed. It was nothing short of a fantasy life. "If I'm to garner all of those positions, why don't we have the dinner at my place? There's more room, and it will be family and friends introduction to *us*."

Laurel sighed. "We are an *us*, aren't we?"

"We are in my world," Jake said. "I was counting on you and Bonnie being on the same planet."

She laughed. "Okay then. At your place, but I will clean the house ahead of time for you and do the cooking."

"And if you will make a shopping list, I will buy the groceries."

Laurel was so elated about the way their future was going that she had to remind herself it was real. Being in his house making meals felt like playing house. She was so ready for their life together to officially begin.

—⁓—

So as they'd planned, on the weekend before Thanksgiving, she and Bonnie went to Jake's house with her cleaning gear on, and she did to his home what she did to all of her customers' places. She'd not only cleaned it from top to bottom, but also, as her daddy would say, put a spit-shine on the floors to boot.

Bonnie was outside playing around the barn where Jake was working when he ran out of nails and called a temporary halt. "You need to stay in the house with Mommy while I go get some more supplies, and then we'll get busy again, okay?"

"Okay," Bonnie said, and grabbed on to his hand as they walked toward the house, chattering with every step that they took.

Laurel was on the back porch shaking out throw rugs when she saw them coming toward the house. It was such a sweet sight to see Bonnie clinging to Jake's hand. There was a moment when she regretted Bonnie would never remember her father, and then she decided to let it go. Better Bonnie forget everything than remember what he'd turned into before he died.

Jake saw her watching, saw the thoughtful expression on her face, and guessed she was having a momentary struggle with her past. He didn't begrudge her a minute of it, because his own past was a daily struggle in itself.

"Are you finished?" she asked, as Bonnie bounced toward the back steps.

Jake shook his head. "No. I just ran out of supplies. I'm going into Blessings. Be back shortly. I brought Bonnie to the house because I didn't want her playing out there by herself. There are still too many things needing to be fixed before I'll call it safe. Do you need anything?"

"No, but thank you for asking. If I finish before you get back, we'll go home."

"Then I better have a good-bye kiss from both of you, just in case," Jake said.

Bonnie threw herself into his arms and smacked him soundly on the cheek. He returned the favor and sent her on her way, then turned to Laurel and put his arms around her. Their kiss was slow and measured enough to ensure he was leaving the lady with more than a fluttering heart.

"Love you," he said softly.

Laurel sighed. "Love you more."

"Impossible. Both of you be careful. I'll call when I get back," Jake said.

She watched until he was gone and then went back inside, unaware that Truman Slade had not only witnessed their lingering good-bye, but that he was about to set that barn ablaze.

Truman had thought long and hard about what he could do to make Jake's life miserable. He'd spent the past few days watching Jake fixing things and making improvements to the property and thought the surest way to upset Jake's world was to destroy part of it. He already had it all planned out. Set fires to both sides of the barn at once. He couldn't hang around long enough to watch it burn, but since Jake had just left the property, even if the woman spied the smoke early on, there was no way she could put out both fires.

He began gathering up the rags and the gasoline he'd brought with him and slipped out from the trees into the barn.

—៸៸៸—

Bonnie was about to take off her coat when she let out a groan.

"Oh no, Mommy! I left Brave Bear in the granary. Can I go get him? I'll run fast."

"Want me to go with you?" Laurel asked.

"No, Mommy, I can do it."

"Okay," Laurel said, "but come right back, or I will worry."

"I know. I will hurry so fast you won't believe it," Bonnie said, and ran out the back door and headed toward the barn as fast as her little legs could carry her.

Truman didn't hear the kid coming until she was already in the barn. He watched her grab a toy from the doorway of a grain bin and then just when he thought she was going to leave without seeing him, he backed into a rake leaning up against the wall and groaned. He'd been made.

―⁓―

Bonnie heard the sound and turned to look, then saw a man standing in the shadows. His face was all frowns, and his smile looked mean. She was scared. It was a stranger, and Mommy told her over and over not to talk to strangers, but he was in Jake's barn. She pulled Brave Bear close against her chest.

"What are you doing?" she asked, staring at the rags and a red plastic can at his feet.

Truman growled beneath his breath, and when she started to dart toward the exit, he grabbed her.

"Don't you scream!" he said. "I'll kill that pet chicken of yours, and I might kill your mama."

Bonnie's mind went blank. The threat he'd made was too horrifying to consider.

"Do you hear me?" Truman growled.

She nodded.

"I mean it. You tell and they're dead."

He turned her loose and shoved her toward the doorway, then grabbed the gas can and made a run for the creek, unwilling to trust the kid to keep her mouth shut. He ran all the way back to his truck, cursing his luck all the way home, and told himself there would be another day.

―⁓―

Bonnie ran into the house with Brave Bear clutched beneath her chin, then ran into the living room and crawled up into Jake's big chair and closed her eyes.

Laurel didn't see her come in, and by the time she was finished and deemed the house fit for a holiday party, she thought nothing of the fact that Bonnie was quiet as they started home.

They drove all the way without talking, and again, Laurel was so wrapped up in plans for Thanksgiving that she didn't key in on Bonnie's silence. It wasn't until they were going into the house that she realized Bonnie was trembling.

"Honey, is something wrong?"

Bonnie shook her head and ran into her room.

Laurel frowned, dumped her stuff on the sofa, and followed her, but then couldn't find her after she got to Bonnie's bedroom. "Bonnie? Where are you, honey?"

She heard sounds over in the corner and found her hiding between her bed and the wall. "What on earth, Bonnie Carol?"

But Bonnie wasn't talking, not even when Laurel got her off the floor and then cuddled her in the rocker. "Did you hurt yourself?" she asked.

Bonnie shook her head.

Laurel kept rocking and patting, trying to find a way to ask a question without making her clam up even more. "Did somebody hurt you?" she asked, and, the moment she did, felt Bonnie tense. "Who hurt you?"

Bonnie hid her face against her mother's breasts and wouldn't talk.

Laurel's heart began to pound. The only person who'd been around her all day was Jake. There was a second when she let herself doubt him, and because it was her daughter, she had to ask. "Did Jake hurt you?"

She shook her head no, but she wouldn't look up and wouldn't turn loose of the bear.

"Honey, Mommy can't help you if you don't tell me what is wrong."

Bonnie started to cry. Now Laurel was scared.

She grabbed her phone and called Jake.

Jake was already on his way home with the nails when he got Laurel's call. "Hey, baby, did you remember you needed something after all?"

"No, but there's something wrong with Bonnie. The moment we got home she ran into her room and was hiding behind her bed. I've got her in my lap, but she won't talk. Did she hurt herself when she was in the barn with you?"

Jake heard the doubt in Laurel's voice, and it nearly broke him. "No. I'm nearly home. I'll be at your house in five minutes."

Laurel groaned. She'd hurt his feelings, but she couldn't help it. Her first line of defense began with her child.

She was still in the room with Bonnie when Jake came inside, and she could tell by the length of his stride he was upset. He burst in, saw Bonnie rolled up in a ball in her mother's arms, took a deep breath, then sat down on Bonnie's bed.

He glanced at Laurel, but his focus was on Bonnie. "Hey, Bonnie Bee, will you come sit in my lap?"

Bonnie bailed out of her mother's lap so fast it startled the both of them. "What in the world?" Laurel muttered.

Jake shook his head as he pulled her close, then held her without talking until he felt her breathing level out. "What did you and Mommy do after I went to town?" he asked.

"Nothing," Bonnie said.

Laurel frowned. "No, that's not exactly true. You went back to the barn, remember?"

Bonnie hid her face in Brave Bear's chest.

"Oh my God," Laurel whispered. "Was someone at the barn? Bonnie, did someone scare you? Did someone touch you?"

Bonnie wouldn't answer and wouldn't look at her mother.

Jake's heart was pounding now. He felt it coming, even before Bonnie confirmed what he feared. "Was there a man at the barn?" Jake asked, thinking of that intruder from so many weeks ago.

She dropped her bear and covered her face with both hands.

"Shit," Jake said softly, and then tricked her into an answer. "Do you know him?"

She shook her head, confirming for both that an intruder had been inside that barn.

Laurel put her hands over her mouth to keep from screaming. She couldn't panic. Not yet.

"So, what was he doing when you saw him?" Jake asked.

"Standing by the wall."

Jake swallowed past the lump in his throat and hugged her a little tighter. "Tell me what he was doing?"

"He had rags and a red can like Gramps's."

Laurel frowned. "A red can like Gramps's?"

Again, Jake came at the question from another angle. "What does your Gramps keep in his red can?"

"Gasoline for the lawn mower."

Jake reeled. Someone had been going to set the barn afire. For all Jake knew, it could be smoldering right now. "Did he set a fire?"

"No."

"Did he touch you?" Jake asked.

Bonnie burst into tears.

Jake felt like he was smothering. He was so scared to ask the next question that he could hardly speak. "Where did he touch you?"

"He pinched my shoulders hard," Bonnie said, sobbing with every breath.

"Son of a bitch," Jake whispered, and started rocking her where they sat. "Talk to me, baby. Tell me what he said so I can find him."

"He said he would kill Lavonne. He said he might kill Mommy if I told, then pushed me away. I ran to the house, and I heard him running, too, but he didn't catch me."

"He was running away too," Jake said. "And you promise he didn't touch you anywhere but your shoulders?"

Bonnie nodded. "They hurt right here," she said, patting them.

Laurel slipped the long-sleeved T-shirt up enough to look, and they saw the bruises already forming on her baby-white skin.

"Thank you for being so brave," Jake said, and then glanced at Laurel. "Do you have a gun here?"

"No, and you can imagine why not."

He thought of what Adam had done to himself and nodded.

"Right. So, put your coats on and come with me. I'm going to stop by the barn and make sure it's okay; then I'm calling the police. We are all going to stay together until the bad man is gone, okay?"

Laurel couldn't help but breathe a sigh of relief.

Bonnie clung to Brave Bear as Jake carried her to his truck; then he sat her in Laurel's lap. The moments Laurel had of distrust seemed fair to Jake. Her first allegiance had to be for her child. He leaned in and kissed Laurel.

"It's okay," he said. "You were well within your rights to ask whatever you needed to ask."

Chapter 20

JAKE DROVE UP TO HIS BARN AND PARKED. WHEN HE GOT out, he paused to look at the loose dirt at the entrance to the barn and saw the tracks of a man's tennis shoes superimposed over his own boot tracks. He saw where Bonnie had gone in and where she'd come running out, and then he sidestepped the prints and walked into the barn.

It didn't take but a few moments to find the pile of oily rags, and it was easy to see where the gas can had been sitting. Whoever it was had intended to burn him out, and Bonnie caught him in the act. He shuddered, thinking but for the grace of God what could have happened to her.

He left the rags where they were for the law to see and then went back outside and trailed the prints of the tennis shoes until they disappeared down the creek bank. He didn't go any farther. Since the man had let Bonnie go, it stood to reason he decided to run and take the risk of her not being able to identify him.

He kept trying to think of who would want to do this to him. Surely not any of the Payne family resenting his relationship with Laurel, because they had been on the outs with her for too long to care about anything she did.

He called Lon Pittman at the Blessings PD. This crime was out of his territory, but he knew Lon could get the county law in here faster than any phone call that he might make.

Avery, the dispatcher, was on duty when Jake's call came in. "Blessings PD."

"Avery, this is Jake Lorde. Is Lon around?"

"He's out on patrol. Give me a minute and I'll patch your phone call through to him."

A few moments later, Jake heard Lon's voice. "Jake? This is Lon. What's up?"

Jake quickly explained what had happened, and the moment he did, Lon remembered the call Peanut Butterman had made about Ruby Dye overhearing Truman Slade threatening to pay Jake back for putting him in jail.

"So, the little girl saw him?" Lon said.

"She has the bruises on her shoulders where he grabbed her to prove it."

"I have something you need to see," Lon said. "I'll be right there."

"We're down at my barn. I'll wait for you here."

Then he got in the truck, and as soon as he shut the door, Laurel grabbed his arm. "What did you see?"

"A pile of oily rags and footsteps where he ran away," Jake said, and then ruffled the top of Bonnie's hair. "Deputy Pittman is coming out here right now. I'm going to show him the stuff and talk to him some more. Do you two want to go in my house, or are you okay to sit here?"

"I wanna stay with Jake," Bonnie said.

"I wanna stay with Jake, too," Laurel said, and laid a hand against his cheek.

He turned it palm upward and kissed it, then eyed the way she was sitting against his seat. "Are you okay, baby?" he asked.

"Yes."

"Your back isn't hurting sitting like this, is it?" he asked.

"No. It's nearly well. I mostly forget it was ever sore."

"About what happened to Bonnie—if this has anything to do with me, I am so sorry," Jake said.

Laurel frowned. "That doesn't even make sense. We have no way of knowing what's going on in other people's minds and can't be responsible if we become random victims, okay?"

"Tell her that and make it alright," Jake said, looking at the shadows still in Bonnie's eyes.

Jake felt sick. Someone had threatened the safety of people she loved. She would never be the same naive little girl she'd been before that happened.

"We'll figure it out," Laurel said. "As long as we're together, we can conquer anything."

"I would like to believe that," Jake said.

"You have to, Jake. I need you to be as positive our lives together are going to work as I am."

Jake leaned over and kissed the top of Bonnie's head and then Laurel's lips. "You two mean the world to me."

"Okay then," Laurel said. "The end."

He grinned. "The end?"

"Of your momentary lack of faith," she said.

He laughed. "God, I love you."

Bonnie looked up. "I love you, too, Mommy."

Jake grinned. "See, it's unanimous. The end again."

By the time Lon Pittman arrived, the mood had lightened some, but once they began repeating what had happened, the horror of what Bonnie had narrowly escaped was back.

Lon took pictures of the tracks, of the rags, and recorded Bonnie's statement. He and Jake were standing outside Jake's truck when Lon brought up what Ruby Dye had overheard.

"I need to show you something," Lon said. "I can't say it has a thing to do with what happened here today, but I can't say it doesn't. Right after you came home, Ruby Dye overheard two men in the hardware store talking about wanting to get to you for some payback. It had to do with something that happened between the two of you years back."

Jake frowned. "Something between me and another man?"

Lon nodded. "Ruby had the presence of mind to take their pictures when they weren't looking. You're going to know one of them."

Jake saw Truman's face and took a deep breath. "Son of a bitch."

Lon tapped the phone to make Truman's face larger and handed it to Jake. "Show this to Bonnie."

Jake opened the door to his truck and leaned inside. "Hey, Bonnie, do you know who this is?" he asked, and flipped the phone around.

Bonnie screamed and covered her face.

The skin crawled on Jake's back. "Is this the man who scared you?"

"Yes, make him go away!" she cried.

"I am going to kill him," Jake muttered.

Laurel frowned. "You know who this is?"

"Truman Slade. I'm the one who testified against him and put him in prison. I was seventeen years old when I witnessed him committing a robbery. Lon said Ruby Dye overheard him wanting to pay me back. She reported what she heard then."

"Then why didn't they do something?" Laurel asked.

"Because it's not against the law to brag about what you might do. You only get in trouble after you do it," Lon said.

Jake patted Bonnie's leg. "Don't you worry, Bonnie Bee. This man is never going to hurt you again."

Laurel was beginning to get scared. "Please don't do anything that will get you thrown in jail."

Lon grimaced. "I echo her sentiments. Don't be crazy, Jake."

"I'm not crazy. I'm mad, and I'm going to make Truman Slade sorry he was ever born. Call your mama, honey. Ask her and your daddy to come get you. You two go stay with them until I can get back."

"Wait, Jake," Laurel said. "Lon, can't you just arrest him?"

Lon shrugged. "Oh, we could, but there's not enough evidence to hold him, and Bonnie would have to testify in court as to what happened. Ruby Dye would have to tell what she overheard, and then the consequences wouldn't amount to anything except to make him madder. Do you want that?"

"No," Laurel said.

Jake took her by the hand. "Then trust me."

"I'll call Mama," she said.

Jake shut the door and gave Lon's phone back to him. "If you arrested him just for the bruises on Bonnie's shoulders, what could you charge him with that might stick?"

"Trespassing on your property. The rest of it a good lawyer could explain away. They'd have to prove those were his rags, and he could easily claim they were already in the barn. He took the gas can with him."

"What about the bruises on Bonnie's arms?"

"He could claim she was falling, and he caught her to keep her from being hurt. It won't matter what she says. She's only six. They will take her apart."

"Then we've covered all the legal bases. I'll be taking care of this on my own," Jake said.

Lon frowned. "I don't want to have to arrest you."

"I'll be fine, and Truman will be leaving this state of his own volition."

"Then don't tell me anything more, and don't tell me what you did."

"Deal," Jake said.

Lon drove away, and Jake took the girls back to her house.

"Dad and Mama are on the way," Laurel said. "They're going to take us home with them. Do you know where they live?"

"Yes. As long as you two are safe, I'll be fine," Jake said.

He let them out, waited until they were inside, and then headed for town. He didn't know where to find the sorry bastard, but he wasn't going home until he did.

―♏―

Truman was a little bit antsy about getting caught. He didn't think there was any way that kid could identify him, but he felt like it wasn't wise to take chances and staying in town with Nester seemed like pushing his luck.

Nester's truck was not in the driveway when Truman returned, and he took it as the opening he needed. He got in through a back window that wasn't locked, packed up his things, and then rummaged through Nester's house looking for the stash of money he knew he kept. He went through Nester's bedroom with no luck and finally found it in the kitchen in an empty cereal box at the back of the pantry. It was a big roll of cash, but too many one- and five-dollar bills to suit Truman. It didn't total up to as much as he'd hoped, but it was enough to get him out of town.

He went right back out the same window he'd gone in, dumped his things in the back of his truck, and headed out of town, unaware that he was already under the gun. Jacob Lorde had finally found him.

Truman was thinking about leaving the area for the winter, and while bunking with Aunt Sugar was out of the question, there were other places he could go. He was trying to decide if he should just winter in a warmer climate on his own, so focused he didn't see the red truck behind him until he reached his house and got out.

Jake had spied Truman just about the time he parked at Nester's house. He watched as Truman crawled in a back window, watched him come out with a bag and a satisfied smirk, and wanted to take him down right there. But they were both in Blessings, and he didn't need any witnesses. So he followed Truman's exit out of Blessings all the way to a run-down property a couple of miles out of town. When he saw Truman get out, he accelerated, parked right behind him, and got out on the run.

He had his hands around Truman's neck and shoved him up against the truck before Truman knew what was happening. Jake threw the first punch, popping Truman square in the face.

"You are one sorry piece of shit," he said, and even as blood was spurting, Jake punched him again.

"What? Stop! What's the matter with you?" Truman yelled, and spit blood and teeth off to the side of his foot.

"You have two choices," Jake said. "You can stand here while I beat the breath from your body, or you can get your crap out of that house and leave Blessings and never come back. If I see you here again, I will kill you on sight. You scared a little girl within an inch of her life today. You have no idea how tempted I am to just kill you anyway and throw your sorry ass in the swamps."

Truman began to freak. "I don't know what you're talking about. You've made a mistake. I didn't—"

"She identified your picture. A picture a concerned citizen of Blessings took after overhearing you and your buddy trying to figure out how to pay me back for testifying against you. You threatened that little girl with murder."

"I did not. I only said I would kill her damn chicken, that's not—" The moment Truman said it, he groaned. He'd just admitted his guilt. "Uh, I—"

Jake doubled up his fist and hit him again. "You lie. You told her you would kill her mother."

He hit him again, then again, and then again, until Truman was so bruised and bloody he could barely see. "Don't hit me again. I'll leave, I swear it," Truman cried.

Jake's pulse was ragged and the rage to destroy was almost overwhelming. "You have twenty minutes to get everything you want out of that house, or I'm dragging your body to the swamp."

Truman turned and ran into the house, crying for mercy with Jake right behind him. He grabbed a pillowcase and gathered up his meager assortment of pans and dishes from the kitchen, and then began stuffing his clothes in a suitcase and took it to his truck. Then he began carrying stuff out in his arms until everything he owned in the world was in the back, blowing in the wind. And then he remembered.

"My TV," Truman cried.

"You have three minutes," Jake said.

Truman rushed into the house and came out staggering under the weight of the old-style set. It was all he could do to get it into the pickup and then close the tailgate. The only good thing about its weight was that now the loose clothing wasn't so likely to blow out.

"Time's up, and you're still here," Jake said, and started toward him.

"I'm leaving now. I'm driving away," Truman screamed. "You have to move. It's your fault I can't leave."

Jake pointed in Truman's face. "I have lived through the Devil's own war. I have been blown into pieces, and I didn't die. You can't kill me, you sorry bastard. God doesn't want me dead, so you better run. You run and you don't stop and you don't look back. If I ever catch you again, one of us will die, and you know it won't be me."

Truman was crying and screaming as Jake got in his truck and backed up, giving Truman just enough room to get away. As soon as he had the space, Truman shot out of the yard as fast as his old truck would take him, heading back to the main road. He didn't know Jake

Lorde was still behind him until he looked in the rear-view mirror and saw sunshine reflecting off the hood of that big, red truck.

"No, no, no." Truman sobbed. "He said he would let me go. What's happening? What's he doing? Oh my God, he lied! He's still gonna kill me."

Truman stomped the accelerator and hit his top speed of sixty-five, driving for hours with only one stop for gas, all the way to the Florida-Georgia line with that red truck right behind him all the way.

It was almost sundown when he crossed into Florida. He looked up just as the red truck pulled over on the other side of the border and stopped.

Truman started crying. Jake Lorde had kept his word. He'd let him leave in one piece. He looked down the highway at the cars speeding along beside him and kept driving. The farther he got from Georgia and Jacob Lorde, the safer he would be.

The next time he glanced in the rearview mirror, it was dark, and all he saw were headlights. In a weird kind of way, it was comforting to know they were all going the same way.

———⁂———

It was almost midnight when Jake pulled into the driveway at Benny Joyner's farm and killed the engine. Lights were on all over the house, and before he could get out of the truck, the front door opened and Laurel was running out to meet him.

A sweet feeling of belonging swept over him as he got out. A few more steps, and she was in his arms. "Are you alright? I was so worried. Why didn't you call?"

"I'm fine. It's all good. I didn't think about it," he said. "All I wanted was to get home to you."

"Come inside out of the cold."

Jake walked in with her. He just wanted to get his girls and go home, but he would tell the story now, so he wouldn't have to repeat it again.

"Jake, good to see you're okay," Benny said, and shook Jake's hand as he led him to the sofa in the living room.

Laurel quickly sat down beside him, leaving her parents to their matching recliners.

"What happened? Did you find Truman Slade? Did he admit—?"

"Yes, I found him. Yes, he admitted it, after some persuasion on my part, and I gave him a choice. I could drop his sorry ass, excuse my language, Mrs. Joyner, in the Georgia swamps, or he could get out of Georgia and never come back."

Laurel saw the bloody knuckles on Jake's hands. "Oh, Jake, your poor hands."

"I was so mad that I didn't feel a thing," he said. "They'll heal."

"So what took you so long?" Laurel asked.

"I followed him to the Florida-Georgia state line."

Benny's eyes widened, and then he started to grin. "I'll bet he drove puckered up all the way, knowing you were right behind him."

Jake shrugged. "It will be a while, if ever, before he sleeps sound again."

Pansy kept eyeing her daughter's new man with a mixture of concern and respect. He had a way about him of seeming scary without saying much. Then she let it go. Maybe she was just used to Benny. She'd pretty much ruled the roost under this roof their whole married life. Maybe Jacob Lorde was what most men were like who tended to their own. Maybe Laurel had done fine by choosing this man after all. Lord knows her girl deserved a long and happy life.

"Well then," Pansy said. "I hear we're having Thanksgiving at your place."

"Won't be called *my* place much longer," Jake said, and gave Laurel's hands a quick squeeze. "The girls and I are working on an *us*."

Benny leaned back in his recliner, absently rubbing his round belly. "Considering the short time you've been home in Blessings, you sure didn't waste any time settling in," Benny said.

Jake heard a tiny hint of criticism and ended it before it went any further. "I guess I was ready for some loving. I had a lot of years of fighting to put behind me," Jake said.

Then they heard the sound of running footsteps as Bonnie dashed into the room with Brave Bear under her arm. "You're back!" she said, and ran straight for Jake.

He sat her in his lap, at which point she settled against the breadth of his chest as if she'd been doing it all her life, and then noticed the bloody bruising on Jake's hands.

"Are you ready to go home, Bonnie Bee?" Jake asked.

She was running a fingertip close to the scrapes without touching them. "Are we going to my home or your home?"

"Wherever Mommy says," he answered.

"We're going back to our house tonight, honey. We

have stuff to do, and we need to be up early. Only a couple more days of school, and then you're out for Thanksgiving."

Bonnie sat up and shifted so she was looked straight at Jake's face. "Did you find the bad man?"

He nodded.

"Did you fight with him?"

Jake frowned. "Why do you ask?"

"You got hurt here," she said, pointing to his hands.

"They're okay. I'm okay," Jake said.

Bonnie looked at her mother. "He was brave for us, wasn't he, Mommy?"

Laurel sighed. Bonnie obviously knew more about what had been going on than she'd thought. "Yes, he was very brave for us."

"And he got hurt doing it," Bonnie said, pointing to Jake's hands.

Laurel nodded. "Yes, he did hurt himself."

Bonnie looked down at Brave Bear and then up at Jake, then back down at the little bear with the Purple Heart medal pinned upon his chest. "Mommy, I need you to take this off for me," Bonnie said, pointing to the medal.

"But why?" Laurel asked. "If you take it off, you could lose it, and—"

"I think we should pin it on Jake's coat. He was brave for us, so he should be wearing it now."

Tears came to Jake so fast they startled him. His heart was beginning a stutter-step that made it hard to catch his breath.

Laurel unfastened the medal with shaking hands and then turned and pinned it onto Jake's coat.

Bonnie smiled, then reached out and patted it, as if to settle it into place. "Look, everyone. Jake is a hero."

Jake wrapped his arms around Bonnie and buried his face against her hair.

Laurel heard her mother blow her nose and her daddy start muttering beneath his breath. He was counting to twenty, which is what he always did when he didn't want to lose his cool.

She wrapped her arms around her baby and her man and hugged them so tight that she made Bonnie squeal. "You're a'squeezin' my breaf," Bonnie cried.

"You're a'squeezin' my breaf, too," Jake said, and wiped his eyes and kissed his girls. "Go gather up your stuff. I have a hankering for a warm bed and a quiet night."

"Don't we all," Benny said.

A few minutes later, they were in the truck and heading home. Bonnie fell asleep in the backseat with Brave Bear tucked beneath her chin.

Laurel rode up front with Jake, and every time she glanced at him, she saw lights from the dashboard reflecting off the medal on his coat. He seemed so at peace with it now. That was good. She kept thinking— God knows he'd earned it the first time, but it was always how a man feels about himself that makes it right.

Jake had saved Bonnie, and tonight Bonnie saved Jake.

Her granny used to say, "Everything in life always comes full circle, because that was how life worked—life without end, Amen."

Epilogue

THANKSGIVING CAME AND WENT, AND IT WAS A rousing success.

The turkey was cooked to perfection. Jake showed Bonnie how to make a wish on the big wishbone and proposed to Laurel and Bonnie in front of her parents.

Laurel got an engagement ring.

Bonnie got another necklace. This time it was a tiny little diamond in a tiny little heart.

Jake was officially engaged to his girls.

He began his new job on the first day of December and scored his first kudos from Ron Fitz for creating a marketing catchphrase for a client who manufactured lingerie.

When they signed the client, a large box of Silky brand lingerie promptly arrived in Laurel's size, compliments of Fitz Advertising, Inc. Inside was an embossed card with Jake's phrase: *Wearing a Silky Bra? Indulgent foreplay for the man who wants you to take it off.*

Jake and Laurel were married at 2:00 p.m. on Christmas Eve at the First Baptist Church in Blessings. Bonnie Carol was the flower girl and flung flowers about with such wild abandon that they weren't just in the aisle, but in everyone's hair and in the laps of those closest to the aisle. She was a hit.

Laurel's sister-in-law, Beverly, was her matron of honor.

Jake asked David Payne to be his best man, and

when the wedding was over and the bride and groom cut the cake and then toasted each other, they were drinking Joaquin DeSosa's bottle of tequila instead of champagne.

The marriage healed hearts, ended a feud, and sealed the past and the present in vows of holy matrimony. It was the wedding of the year.

The next morning, while Jake and Laurel were settling into their new lives and opening presents, and Bonnie Carol was standing at the kitchen window admiring the fancy new chicken coop Jake had built for Lavonne, Ruby Dye found a fancy-wrapped gift at her front door.

It had *To Ruby* on the card, but not who it was from.

While she was standing in the doorway trying to figure out who her secret admirer might be, she began hearing what sounded like a motorcycle running at high speed.

She walked all the way to the steps of her front porch to see it coming down her street, when all of a sudden it shot out of the alley just to the left of her house and went straight up the alley across the street and disappeared. She only had a glimpse of the rider—black leather, long legs, and a swath of hair flying out from under that silver helmet like a cape, before she began hearing sirens.

Either that rider had crashed and it was an ambulance, or he was going fast because he was being chased. In a fit of good cheer and because it *was* Christmas Day, Ruby shouted aloud, "Ride safe and ride fast, whoever you are. God is in His heaven and the Devil's on your tail."

Then she clutched her present against her robe and hurried inside out of the cold.

She'd surely find out what was going on before the day was over. That's how things went when you lived in Blessings. Nothing stayed a secret for long.

About the Author

New York Times and *USA Today* bestselling author Sharon Sala is a member of RWA as well as OKRWA. She has more than ninety-five books in print, published in five genres: romance, young adult, Western, general fiction, and women's fiction. First published in 1991, she is an eight-time RITA finalist, winner of the Janet Dailey Award, four-time Career Achievement winner from *RT Magazine*, five-time winner of the National Reader's Choice Award, five-time winner of the Colorado Romance Writers Award of Excellence, and winner of the Heart of Excellence, as well as the Booksellers Best Award. Writing changed her life, her world, and her fate. She lives in Oklahoma, the state where she was born.

The Blessings, Georgia series

Touching, funny stories that will break your heart on one page and heal it on the next.

by Sharon Sala

New York Times and *USA Today* Bestselling Author

—◆◆◆—

Mercy Dane has trouble fitting in when she moves to Blessings to get reacquainted with her long-lost sister. Her hard-knock life has made her tough and a little wild. But when tragedy strikes, she learns Police Chief Lon Pittman might be the man to break through her barriers of mistrust and loneliness.

Watch for the next book in the series:

A Piece of My Heart

Coming soon from Sourcebooks Casablanca